I0760448

CHEZ USHER

For readers captivated by the lush prose and psychological intricacies of *The Great Gatsby* and *The Secret History*, *Chez Usher* is an irresistible invitation to Key West's shadowed heart — a place where decadence, desperation, and decay converge.

When architect August Dupin is lured to the crumbling mansion of his former lover Roderick Usher, he finds himself drawn into a world where secrets lurk behind every velvet curtain and nothing is quite as it seems.

Roderick and his enigmatic twin sister, Madeline, are as glamorous as they are doomed — vivid, unforgettable characters who navigate their fates with a dark grace reminiscent of Fitzgerald's tragic heroes and Tartt's magnetic misfits.

Hendricks' prose is atmospheric and evocative, painting Key West's tropical beauty with a noir edge, weaving a tale of tragic beauty, forbidden desires, and the haunting legacy of family ties.

With its exploration of human frailty, obsession, and the inexorable pull of the past, *Chez Usher* is more than a thriller — it's a meditation on the price of passion and the fragility of identity.

Prepare to lose yourself in a world of dazzling decadence and haunting mystery.

This edition first published 2024 by Fahrenheit Press.

ISBN: 978-1-914475-82-5

10 9 8 7 6 5 4 3 2 1

www.Fahrenheit-Press.com

F 4 E

Chez Usher

By

Vicki Hendricks

Fahrenheit Press

"*Chez Usher* marks the darkly glorious return of one of the best to ever do it: Vicki Hendricks. A richly gothic, camp-tinged riff on Edgar Allan Poe, *Chez Usher* offers a uniquely dark spin on sex, drugs and bad behavior in Key West, with a cast of desperate characters skilled in canny manipulation. Not to be missed."

— Megan Abbott, New York Times best-selling author of *Beware the Woman*

"Vicki Hendricks is back! It's a good thing, too, because this twisted and extremely sexy reworking of "*The Fall of the House of Usher*" is a tale only she could have told. True love, offhand sex, languid heat, tropical foliage, and a malevolent mansion combine here for a book I couldn't put down. Pick it up; you'll miss something wonderful and unique if you don't."

— SJ Rozan, best-selling author of *The Murder of Mr. Ma*

"The gothic chills of Edgar Allan Poe meet the gonzo debauched mayhem of Florida Man in Vicki Hendricks' superb *Chez Usher.* I loved this book — sexy, dark, depraved, and spooky, this is gothic noir at its finest. A rock n' roll Poe retelling that fits the madness of the 21st century."

— Halley Sutton, USA Today best-selling author of *The Hurricane Blonde*

"An ethereal, evocative, and unputdownable homage to Edgar Allen Poe. What Vicki Hendricks did for noir in Miami Purity, she does for the haunted house story in *Chez Usher.* Don't miss this one"

— Sara Gran, best-selling author of *The Book of the Most Precious Substance*

"When one of noir's legendary mavericks takes on Poe, you know it's going to be a funky, bizarre and nerve-jangling ride. This book oozes cool, creepy vibes as dark as the shadow *Chez Usher* casts over the neighborhood. Hendricks has triumphed!"

— A. Neil Smith, best-selling author of *Slow Bear*

"A fierce and fearless talent."

— Denis Lehane, author of *Mystic River*

Contents

To Edgar (1809-1849)

Many thanks for sharing your demons

Chapter 1

Another Fucking Day on The Rock

Madeline leans over the dining room table to get in Roderick's face. Ancient dust motes swarm behind him in the last slanted rays of a Key West sunset. "Repairs on this place won't help, Bro. You know that. It's fucking unnatural — evil."

She despises the house, years of festering rot under a bright Victorian paint job, the ancestral home she's chained to for life. She's sick of the whole island — no wonder it's called "The Rock." She pushes her fingers through her short black coif, slugs the last murky inch of her Margarita, and slaps the gold-rimmed tumbler onto the mahogany sideboard.

Roderick pales. His hand jerks to his forehead as if to steady his brains. "Please, Maddy. Lower your volume. My symptoms are terrible today. I'm having severe hyperacusis. Not to mention, my eyes will never stop hurting from the glare. There's a knife right down the middle of my head." He stands carefully and crosses the room, shielding his eyes. Disgust freezes on Madeline's face while he tugs the maroon velvet drapes closed, one by one. He dims the switch to light a glow in the crystal chandelier.

"Maybe if you cut back on your scotch."

"Pfft." Roderick won't meet her eyes. "Look who's talking."

"Rarely touch it." Madeline drags a finger from her bottom lip down her bronzed throat to the crevice at her collarbone. A habit, manufactured years ago, to look contemplative for prospective girlfriends. She drops into a chair and leans against its heavy back, grinding her newly veneered teeth. The carved devil face she's tried to ignore since childhood grins up at her from the corner table leg.

"Listen to me, Maddy. We're out of time. We've got to renovate the whole east wing before the roof caves in."

"Fuck it." She laughs. "Don't try to con me, Bro. *He's* got a mind of his own. Fuck. Now you've got *me* calling this house a *him*. Listen. Fixing this place is a waste of money — that we can't afford."

"Let me get August. He's a brilliant architect. He'll know how to implement my new plan." He opens his palms on each side. "Broke or dead? You choose."

She shakes her head. "Ah, I get it. You want him back, your old lover, those bedroom eyes and muscled flesh. Grew up in Georgia, right? That smooth drawl. Jo-ja... Jaw-ja ..."

"He's lost the accent."

"Damn. Guess you already talked to him." She tucks a wedge of hair behind her left ear. "Hey, look, there's a new crack — *quelle* fucking *surprise*." She points to it.

Roderick counts on his fingers. "August must be well over thirty by now."

"So, invite the old fart down for a fuck. Don't employ him."

"Look. We can trust him. And he's likely to be... affordable."

"Let's throw a lavish party. Invite all your tranny pals. You can seduce your heart-throb with Key West Bohemian glamour."

"*Trans* — for god's sake — Madeline. Get with the program."

"A term of endearment. Transexuals and transvestites. Are you okay with that?" Roderick closes his eyes and uses his thumbs to apply pressure under the brow ridge.

"Bro." She waits for his attention. "No amount of Vaseline is going to make this dick slide. Sooner or later, the house is a goner, and he'll take us out with him. You know that better than I do. You can tan yourself into cowhide, bleach your hair, and ignore your teeth, but you can't disconnect the twin-circuit in our brains."

"I'm getting my molar implant tomorrow. If I can stand to walk out in the sun."

"Take a parasol." She grins and puts a firm hand down on the table. "I'll plan the party. A thing of grandeur to remember us by." She stands and shoves her chair away. It topples backward, whacking the floor.

"Fuck." He rubs his thumbs behind his ears. "Mads, August is our last chance to save ourselves. Listen. If we use glass construction for the whole east wing, there won't be anything to reflect or attract the power of the house. He'll die. We'll be done with him." He looks her in the eye. "I know how to talk to August."

"Put a glass building in Old Town? Fucking ridiculous. I've had it with your babble."

"Oh? Really? Well, you'll be hearing much more. My theories about the universe are coming back into style. Darwin is fucked! Amino acid sequencing in DNA is mathematically impossible through random chance."

"Roderick, stop."

"All the cards are back on the table." He snorts. "I bet I'll be asked to give Great, Great, Great Grandad's 'Eureka' lecture again. I'll Usher in a new era. Ha!"

Madeline snorts.

"Besides that, new thermodynamic research bears out my theory regarding the house. Let me explain the genetic pattern of cause and effect underlying increased entropy and our disintegra—"

"Roderick, you're exasperating! Do whatever you want." She turns at the doorway. "Maybe you already have. I'm planning a masquerade party to rival the Fantasy Fest Ball."

She steps into the hall. Her black cat, Maddy J., slinks from the shadows and passes between her ankles, twining, rubbing her face, twining. She sweeps her hand from head to tail tip. She was never impressed with Roderick's reputation as a fucking genius. Must be the Usher magnetism... Time to start on her own plan before it's too late. In fact, August might fit right into it.

Chapter 2

The First Question

August lifts the heavy filigree lid of the mailbox, New York City classy. One of Garo's expensive online finds. He feels like a movie star just getting their mail. He shuffles the envelopes. No check from Fire Island Fever in the Pines. It's got him wondering. As usual, ads for credit cards and insurance, a check for Garapet — Garo. Modeling your pecs pays a heck of a lot better than what he earns as an architect — Garo, modeling his pecs, anyway.

He climbs the gleaming, lacquered steps to the apartment. Rays of dusk cast cheery spangles across the wall through the crystal fixture. Even after two years of living here with Garo, he can't stop gawking like a rube. The building is from the same era as the Dakota, but without fanfare, a subtle Victorian exterior, gaiety within. The full interior remodel was finished before he moved in, but the architectural parti was preserved. He wonders if the mood lighting was planned or serendipitous. He wants a chance to do something like this... to make architectural magic with his own interpretation of a classic concept.

"Reaching for the stars" got him through high school to scholarships and fellowships in college, insulation against his pop's booze-hound rages. Did Pop know he was gay? He never thought it through, but Pop's absence at graduation meant something. Mom was too fragile from chemo to attend, but even on her worst days, she glowed with pride, a bit of happiness he was able to give her. No reeking hogs to tend, no sweaty John Deere cap on the head of the golden boy. Now, eight years out of architecture school, and he's still been scrambling to get minor renovation work — until Fire Island.

It's been a hard day. He slumps against the wall, mechanically flipping through the envelopes again. God, the check from Fire Island better just be late. If the funding fell through, two months of working on plans and estimates, and he'll have zip to show for it. He should have increased his hourly by asking for a larger retainer — among other time-frame considerations.

A snatch of conversation comes back, a remark about "being generous with other people's money." He wonders if there's new resistance to his choices of top-notch "green" materials and cutting-edge environmental features. He couldn't be prouder of his layout of GaAs solar panels, ingeniously hidden in the chic minimalist modernist design. Of course, it will take longer to implement and cost more than a mediocre plan. Both partners agreed it would be an environmentally responsible work of art to be enjoyed and admired by future generations. Everything is covered in the contract. No way he'll give up his principles to save them a few bucks.

Garo is probably waiting with a special dinner. Tuesday is designated date night since both of them work long hours. He straightens up and smooths his hair on the side, recalls the luscious feeling of pleasure that awaits. What about Key West? Fuck. He's been pushing away thoughts of Roderick's offer all afternoon. Bizarre. Roderick, living down there, calling him out of the blue — or out of the depths. He's stressed and excited at the same time. It could be a life-changing project — or a narcissistic trap to cause him more pain. He won't go. He slips his key into the lock.

A rich atmosphere of browning cheese — lasagna. He crosses the foyer into the dining room. Delicate frosted stemware, holding a triple pour of Garo's everyday pinot, awaits on the Carrara marble bar, bottle and cork beside it. Garo, a romance-novel cover-model, can afford sixty-dollar bottles of wine. Augie, a Georgia cracker, always feels guilty during the first few sips.

Garo sashays into the dining room, a swish of plush white bathrobe revealing a dark-muscled thigh. He sets his glass on the sideboard and opens his arms. From Lebanon or heaven? Layers of dark curly hair frame his smooth cheeks. Dimples, full lips, dramatic jawline, the most gorgeous, sweetest guy August has ever met.

"Gars, wow, I almost mistook you for young Clark Gable." There's slight disdain. "Or Marlon Brando." His tastes are out of date. His movie-watching days were spent with Mom on classics, waiting for his father to come home, hoping he wouldn't.

Garo's eyes, Mediterranean deep, tease from under thick lashes. "Alexander Godunov has been mentioned, but I have way better hair."

It seems like a week since the last sex. August closes over him, roving from forehead to lips to throat to thick-furred chest, and down into the lowest nest of curls. The robe drops, piling itself, whipped cream, around their ankles. Garo kicks it away, and they tangle and bump their way down the hall, kissing, grabbing. August's hip glances off the door jamb without pain.

Together they tug off his pants and shirt, falling into the king-size bed. August rolls beneath Garo, breathless, gasping, straining his neck to glimpse the Adonis rising above him.

Too soon, the room comes into focus, and the usual question. How long can this dream last?

Later, naked at the dining room table, August dips a bite of bread into garlicky oil and wipes his hands on the cloth napkin covering his lap. He chases the garlic burn with the pinot and motions to his bare chest. "We should do this more often before it gets too chilly."

Garo wipes olive oil from his lips with his apron, his one article of clothing. "Whenever you want."

"Whenever *you* want. I'm you're slave." August fans his mouth. "The garlic. I love it, but — whew — this will linger."

"A willing slave?" Gars puts on his sly grin. "Would you get the dishes, Sweetie? I need to do a probiotic mask —"

"Sure! You cooked." He swirls his wine. "I have to tell you... Gars, my check didn't come. I don't know —"

"Hey — no more talk about money. It will come. Tons."

He moves his last piece of crust around the plate, wiping up every thin smear of tomato sauce, wondering if Gars truly believes that. He doesn't believe it himself anymore. With all his silly dreams of becoming a young phenomenon, bulked up early by The Design Excellence Honor Award from AIAS, he took an unchallenging apprenticeship, as brief as the law would allow. "You've been saying that since we met, and it's not looking any better."

"It's in you. Augie, you've got years! How many architects are famous at your age?"

"Fame's the last thing —"

"With fame comes fortune. It takes decades. Look at Louis Kahn — nearly sixty when his architectural creativity started to thrive."

"How do you know about Louis Kahn?"

"There's a biography out."

He tries not to look surprised. "I haven't seen you with a book."

"Huh? You think I can't read?" Here comes the grin. "I read the review in the *Times*. I could fool you, but I won't."

August chuckles. "When would you have time to read a book? With your work hours — and cooking for me — you barely have time to sleep."

"Write this down — you *will* be famous. I know how to spot em. Right now, helping you out, it's my greatest pleasure — making you happy." He blows a kiss. "That's what money is for. In twenty years, when I'm pudgy and bald, your turn."

August winces with the truth of needing help, but he's sure it wasn't a dig. "You'll turn into Richard Gere or George Clooney. You won't need me."

"In case I turn into Mickey Rourke, I'm socking it away. No worries." He puckers his lips. "I'll always need you, rich or poor."

"I want to help you sock it away. So we can... keep living the good life in forty or fifty years." He wanted to say, "get married."

"Augie. Stop. I love you. We're perfect together and nothing else matters. Subject closed."

August smiles. Garo is innocent enough to believe that. He

never saw the homestead, the secret, swampy pit that divides them. Never will. "When I get the first big check — after I'm caught up on the rent — I'm gonna buy you that Michael Armani sectional."

"Amini — easy to confuse. No way. That was wine-talk. I'm not gonna drape my sweaty balls on a $12,000 sofa."

"It *would* require undies. Okay. I love your Hemingway couch anyway." He wishes he could say *our* Hemingway couch, but he hadn't paid a cent. He owns nothing here.

"Our couch, August. You helped pick it out."

Hemingway reminds him of Key West. He stands and gathers the plates and silverware. "I got an offer from an old friend this morning." He takes a breath. "Might be a project in Key West coming up."

"Yeah? That's great. What kind of project... what kind of old friend?"

"Is there more than one kind?"

Garo shakes his head. "Not that I know of — in the male category."

"It was a short fling — seven or eight years ago." August thinks about the definition of *short* — and *fling*. Not sure if he's being as honest as he should. "An older guy. Roderick Usher. He has a twin sister, Madeline. I think I told you about him. The scientist who wrote a book?"

"I doubt it. No."

"If he's serious, the job sounds like something that might get me a start, a huge remodel requiring foundational engineering. Plus, exposure to Key West society."

"Exposure in Key West? Plenty of that." Garo snickers.

August chuckles along, but his face goes red.

"You doubt that he's serious?"

"I don't know. He's an odd guy, eccentric. From what he describes, my geotechnical specialty is something he needs. I'm going to ask for a large retainer up front. No money and I'm out of there."

"I trust you, Augie. No need to convince me. You don't have... feelings for this guy?"

He chuffs. "Hurt maybe. I was so innocent." Roderick's willing slave. He sets the plates back down and wipes his hands on his napkin. He goes around the table to Gars, arms moving out for a hug. Gars stands and takes his face in both hands. He kisses August on the forehead. They close the gap, a perfect fit. Why, for god's sake, did he bring up Key West? He should have told Roderick no to begin with. He's angry at himself. He ends the hug with a squeeze and turns to stack the bread plates.

"How long do you expect to be gone?"

"I changed my mind already."

"No." Garo takes his arm and motions him to set down the plates. "You need this." He puts his hands on August's hips, turning him. "You'll make me think you don't love me... if you can't trust yourself."

His throat tightens. "Now it's a test?"

"For Christ sakes, no. Just go, sweetheart. You think I'm worried about some old fucking queen — who hurt you, besides?"

A breath rattles in his throat. Surely, he's outgrown Roderick's charisma. "I'll see what needs to be done and come back here to make calls and do quotes."

"Don't rush it."

"Gotta get out of there before Fantasy Fest anyway. Not my idea of fun."

"From what I've heard, it sounds awesome. Unique." He clamps his lower lip with his perfect teeth. "I might be able to get a gig in Paris, and you won't feel rushed to get back."

"Paris?" August's stomach contracts. He knows it's a done deal. He wonders if Gars has been waiting for a good chance to go.

"A French film company's been after me for a commercial. I bet they can plug me into their schedule. Neither of us will be bored sitting at home alone at night."

August drops into a chair. "You never mentioned that." Visions of Garo in a French club, or a bath... his smooth, shapely back... his shining, sweaty glutes pumping atop furred, wiry French thighs... high on X... slick with semen... pumping....

Bitter lasagna leaps into his throat. He grabs his glass for the last drops of wine. They've talked about their pasts, getting each other hot — Gars, with much to say and no hint of jealousy. Less to tell for August and much jealousy to conceal. "I can finish the preliminaries in a couple of days. You'd hardly know I was gone."

"Crazy-talk, Augie. It might be your big chance. Take your time, do a good job. If it's a stupid booty call, I'll send you a ticket to join me. I think you can amuse yourself — museums, the Eiffel Tower."

"I've never been to Paris."

"You're not worried about me, are you? You know how I feel. I did it all in my youth. Everything you can think of. It was dangerous, and I was lucky. We have a real home together. That's all I want, now and forever. I love you. I'll call to remind you every night before I get into bed — alone."

Can he change his mind right now and go to Paris? "I'm sorry. I trust you. It's just..."

"I know. Listen, I look forward to practicing my French and eating a few pastries — very few." He grabs at non-existent love handles. "Don't blow your big chance for me."

"I forgot you speak French." He tries to hold his face in a neutral expression.

Garo jumps up from the chair. "If I do get a gig — we don't even know yet. Christ sakes!" He puts both arms on August's shoulders and draws him in for another hug, hard cheekbone to hard cheekbone. He pulls back and looks into his eyes. "Key West isn't exactly a hermitage. I should be the one worried."

August knows that's a joke. Garo is the irresistible one, to men, even to women, without trying. "I've read too much about steamy Paris — *Tropic of Cancer*." He fakes a chuckle, but it comes out more like a sob.

Gars gives him a look. "Yeah, way too much reading."

Chapter 3

The Beginning

Near dusk, the pink Key West taxi rounds the curve and passes the black, red, and yellow striped concrete buoy anchored on the side of the road. Southernmost Point in the U.S.A., it claims. Black limos parked end to end. Drivers lean against the hoods and vape as they gaze out at the choppy, chalky, green Atlantic. A humid wind smashes waves against the sea wall.

The taxi pulls up at a wrought iron gate. August is stunned by the classic Queen Anne Victorian structure within, the asymmetric beauty of turrets and steeply pitched roofs. Pastel pink, blue, beige. It seems unlikely those were the original colors, but the effect suits the tropics.

He assumed Roderick was a permanent resident of Manhattan when they were together for those three months. Not one word about a home in Key West, a mansion. And there's no sign of damage. When discussing the trip, Roderick implied the place was on the verge of tumbling into the ocean. Would Roderick bring him down here for a booty call on a lie that he would see through instantly? Sweat drips inside his shirt. He whips off his tie and opens the top two buttons. He considers telling the cab driver to turn around. His expense report will include the wasted hours of travel.

He pays the driver. The fare is more than expected. "Wait right here — I'll signal you if I want you to leave."

The closer he gets the more he's mesmerized. The shadow of the house spreads across the lawn and over the clouded water. The structure is solid and powerful, yet playful in personality.

Dusk bounces glints from the waves onto the arched windows, like loose particles of energy. Somebody has pulled the shades evenly, half-shut eyes, squinting against the glare. The asymmetrical facade includes a wraparound porch and a corner turret. If Roderick could possibly be telling the truth about "impending disaster," it's someone's duty to save this classic structure.

A limo lets out two towering transvestites with slim hips and quarterback shoulders, their identical, red, sequined gowns tapering to v-backs nearly in the cleft of their asses. They wobble up the path on four-inch heels, holding half-masks on sticks across their eyes, biceps bulging above black Cinderella gloves. Oddly alluring. A long-haired blond woman, broom in hand, floats past, black gauze whipping in the breeze, her shaved pubis and nipples glowing neon pink through the fabric. Two shapely men on a lawn swing, each clad in a single fig leaf, share a toast. He's heard about Key West, but this is way beyond his imaginings — and comfort level. He'd like a pizza, a Bud, and cool sheets in front of his motel TV.

Sheer willpower moves his legs. He's overheated and self-conscious carrying his travel bag and laptop. He wishes he'd stopped at the motel, instead of worrying about being late. He packed a light silk shirt to change from the wrinkled, sweat-pitted button-down, but has nothing right for this shindig. Roderick promised a costume. God knows what that might be. Not worth changing into anything for the short time he plans to spend.

He recognizes Roderick on the porch, his hair bleached and powdered into burnished gold. He appears to be naked behind a banner across the railing: USHER HOUSE ANNUAL AIDS BENEFIT. He's got to be near forty-five by now. He holds a drink, using it to gesture at the house, conversing with a young guy wearing rainbow paint. Only rainbow paint. August turns to the street to signal the taxi for five minutes more. It's gone.

Roderick moves to the top of the steps and waves. He's bare far below the navel. August smiles, trying not to grimace. With his conservative tendencies and lack of charm, he might blow his chances before he even finds out if a project exists.

Roderick swoops from the porch to engulf him in a hug and a cloud of gardenia scent.

"August! Welcome to Key West, where *gay* means ecstatically happy and wonderfully free. Welcome *chez moi*." Roderick kisses him hard on the mouth, way too long. August stiffens and holds onto the bag and briefcase. Roderick steps back and takes a sweeping look. His high cheekbones and tight chin hint at surgery, but his lids are at half-mast, eyes faded and too shiny. His chest is smooth under metallic gilding, arms toned and waist slim. Gold powdered pubic hair peeking out above coppery fake fur adheres to the bare skin from his haunches to calves. Boot tops of rough suede end in patent leather cleft hooves. August tries not to stare, but isn't that the point, to draw his attention? His instinct is to run.

Roderick lifts a long silky tail and whinnies, a musical sound. "I'm a unicorn — *was* a unicorn," he says. "The headpiece got too fucking hot."

"It's great — the fur..."

Roderick pulls out the waistband with his thumb and peers down inside. "The horn is down here."

August bends forward on reflex. He blushes.

Roderick grins up at him, teeth startling white against his tan face. "Fantastic to see you! I can't wait to see more."

August tries to smile. It's the exact conversation he hoped to avoid. "An AIDS benefit every year?"

"Actually, this is our first one. We hope to host future benefits until the entire world is AIDS-free. Then we'll find another cause."

"Uh. Well, I hope you didn't bother with a costume for me. I'm beat. I just stopped to say hi on the way to the hotel — I need to be fresh in the morning."

"You're so fresh, darling, you make everyone else look rotten." Roderick tilts his head, sending a sad, charming plea from his drowning eyes.

Familiar words. Mae West? He hesitates, remembering Roderick. A step will lead to a mile. "Uh. One drink."

"Yes! A top-notch mojito — and a nibble from the buffet. I'll be hurt if you can pass it by." He puts a palm on the small of August's back and propels him through a hall long enough to echo with their steps. August's cotton-poly blend shirt is sticky against his skin and he wonders if Roderick can feel the sweat.

They enter a large dining room with a cathedral ceiling and heavy hand-carved dining table and velvet drapes. Straight ahead are sliding doors to a pool and a romantically lit beach. Double French doors open to the left into a short breezeway with a ceiling twenty feet above. Beyond it, three more sets of French doors are open into a ballroom with loud conversation spilling out. Sparsely costumed people line up at a well-stocked bar with a precarious pyramid of limes. Farther back, a flowing chocolate fountain beckons.

Roderick turns into the breezeway and bows, gesturing to a lush buffet on the right. "Rare ahi tuna, mussels from New Zealand — and oysters Rockefeller, to die for. You hardly see those nowadays, except at Chez Usher parties. They're my faves. And here's the lobster Bianca pizza. Yum."

August swallows a mouthful of saliva. It's been a long time since the spongy bagel in the airport.

"First, your costume. Much more comfortable than these business togs."

August puts up his hand to stop him, but Roderick motions to a man in formal attire to take him upstairs. "Right now, we only employ Roget and the cook. Roget can help you with anything you need."

"Nice to meet you, Roget." August follows along through the quiet, darkened interior, letting himself be absorbed by old-style luxury, graceful, curved stairs and ornate banister, wainscoting and dark antique paintings in gilded frames. Usher ancestors? It would be easy to fall in love with the grandeur and mysterious personality of the place. A location fit for a Boris Karloff film. Can't wait to tell Garo.

They pass the second floor. Laughter mixed with passionate grunting seeps from under the closest door. Roget leads on to the third floor, where the hall runs left and right. They take a right through heavy wood fire doors, barn style. August would like to feel the wood, the heft and thickness, and see how the doors move, but Roget keeps up his pace. August follows to the far east end of the hall, to a room half the size of Garo's apartment, with a poster bed, Persian rugs, a carved desk, a sitting area. One arched window is wide open to the Atlantic horizon.

Roget leaves and August goes to the window. He breathes in salty, mildly sulfur air and looks below at the patio off the breezeway. A black transvestite singer, accompanied by a four-piece band, belts out a voice he could mistake for Nina Simone. Multi-colored lights dash across low palms from a disco ball somewhere under the eaves. Party noise drowns the low surf on the edge of it all. With the exception of the transvestites' pounds of sequined fabric, he estimates total cloth per hundred guests to be less yardage than he has in his carry-on.

His costume lies across the bed in a clear plastic bag — a slinky white robe with a belt — silk maybe. Embroidery and ruby-like stones encrust the lapels and sleeves. *Prospero* is sewn in fancy script on the breast pocket. *Prospero*? Spanish for *prosperous*? A Medieval-looking crown rests on the pillow.

He takes off his shirt and pants, slips on the robe, and ties the sash. More pale skin showing than he would like. The damn thing will slide open every time he takes a step. Why is he doing this? Lucky thing, he has on newish boxer shorts. One mojito and some oysters, and he'll make his getaway.

There's no pocket for his cell, so he slips it into his pants on the bed, noticing that it's nine o'clock. Gars should be touching down at Charles de Gaulle within the hour and taking the train. He should be able to catch him before he gets to the hotel and goes to sleep.

He sets his suitcase on the bed to keep everything together for a fast exit. He looks into the mirror and places the crown on his head. Uncomfortable and idiotic. He starts the journey to the ground floor, hoping Roderick will be too busy mingling to try to flirt him into staying. He can't wait to talk to Gars.

Roderick is at the bottom of the staircase. "Ah, Prince Prospero! You look divine. I forgot about those pretty freckles on your chest. A little pale to wear white, but we'll soon fix that. The crown jewels bring out your sparkle."

Prospero is vaguely familiar. "Who am I?"

"A literary character. I bought it online. Elegant, isn't it? I admit, I got it for myself, but then..." He shrugs. "I did this instead." He reaches for August's sash.

August grabs it.

Roderick smacks his own cheek in mock guilt. "To the mojito bar!"

Left on his own, August eats six oysters and several thick pieces of the best ahi tuna of his life. He can do that dish for Gars, black sesame and coarse salt on both sides, a quick sear, simple. As he sips his third mojito and pokes a banana slice into the hot fudge fountain, he makes eye-contact with a guy wearing a white shirt and tie, standing on the opposite side of the fountain. No. Please. He looks down at the banana.

Roderick sidles up, and the guy moves on — no pants below his long shirt.

"I'm worried that I underpriced the base on a few of the items in the auction. If the bidding stops early, can you give it a boost? Mind?"

"I was just leav..." The closest he's been to an auction is watching TV. "A fake bid? Is that legal?" Fudge drips from his banana slice onto a pyramid of kiwi and strawberry pieces. "I might accidentally buy something. I can't even pay my —" He sees the last statement sink in. Too much to drink. He has to quit thinking about the late check from Fire Island. He doesn't fit with the money here.

Roderick takes his hand, guiding the banana slice into August's mouth. He barely chews and swallows before it's followed by Roderick's fingers holding a chocolated kiwi to his lips. He has no choice but to slurp it. He snatches the napkin as Roderick starts blotting his lips.

"August, relax. These are our people. It's all donated art, for AIDS. Nothing's illegal among friends, you know?" He giggles. "If you accidentally buy something, I'll cover it."

"I guess I can help you out." He wipes the corners of his

mouth.

"You're a gem!"

Roderick turns, gives his furry butt a wiggle, and strides off. August looks around, hoping for no encounters. He aims a square of poundcake toward his mouth, and a dollop of fudge drops onto the sleeve of the robe. He ducks his head to lick it off and moves toward the stage.

"Testing, one, two, three; one, two..." Roderick's voice booms over the speakers. "Can ya'll hear me?"

Roderick is behind a podium, looking naked again, speaking into the microphone. "Friends and fiends, time for the bidding to start. Checks will be accepted — but only big ones!" He moves center stage and points to the first item on the table, a colorful street scene of Jimmy Buffet's Restaurant, Margaritaville, per the sign. "Donated by Kennedy Studios, a Key West landmark on Duval Street, from an early limited edition of 200 Giclée prints. The bidding starts at $250. So low! Do I hear a bid? Great Christmas present for your relatives up North. We're here to donate!"

The crowd is paying more attention to their plates. "Three hundred!" August yells. Organ music rises from behind heavy curtains, a haunting cord, startling. He hadn't noticed that the whole room is painted black, lit by four dim chandeliers down the middle. Spiders are illuminated by black lights in the corners. Walls painted just for the party?

Roderick is pointing to him. "Prince Prospero! Wanting to take a piece of Key West to back to Manhattan."

A huge orangutan raises his hand. "Three-fifty."

A painted skeleton in a G-string bids three-seventy-five.

"Ladies, gentlemen, and others, don't nickel and dime me. This is for AIDS. Against AIDS! Continued vaccine research, money for those who can't afford their medications. We've come far — let's keep going!"

The hidden organist slides down the black keys in a way that draws goosebumps. "One thousand!" August belts out. Roderick flinches, but the smile flips back into place fast.

"That's the way, Prospero. How about you, Ian?" He turns his eyes on the orangutan, an intimate glance. "Can you keep up the pace?" Roderick steps from behind the podium and cocks his hip, aiming his groin at the orangutan and slipping his thumb inside the low-rise fur. His fingers curl in a come-along gesture.

"Twenty-five hundred!" the orangutan shouts, raising an arm that streams orange dreadlocks like a cape.

August looks at the broad bushy back, not fake, it would seem. He gets a chill.

"Going once." Roderick waits a few seconds. "Sold! To the wildest animal in the kingdom!" He bangs the gavel on the podium, and the orangutan lets out an authentic call of ape enthusiasm. The organist blasts a home run.

August strays back to the dining room buffet, choosing a raw oyster. He's done his duty, is none the worse for it, and has satisfied Roderick. He doctors the oyster with horseradish and slurps the sharp, savory lump.

There's a loud crack and a crash. Pitch black. Screams! He pushes his way against the flow of guests into the entrance of the ballroom. An auxiliary overhead light comes on along with the black lights.

Roderick, still on stage, fumbles with the mic, blows into it. It's working. "Please, don't panic. Stay. The night is juvenal. Anyone hurt?" The crowd is silent. "Of course not! Please accept my apologies for an old house with a strong will."

The chandeliers have broken from their stems and hang by cords. Loose pieces of glass are caught in a near-invisible netting, strung across the ceiling. Unbelievable! Roderick expected this to happen.

Glowing in the black light, plaster dust clings in a lightning pattern on the black curtain in front of the organ, and there's a wide crack in the ceiling. No visible damage to the wall itself. Impossible. He looks more closely at the ceiling. Everybody needs to be cleared out. He reaches for his phone, considering a call to the police. Across the room, Roderick stumbles and almost falls off the stage. August makes his way over. "You okay?"

Roderick slips his hand into the low front of his costume.

"Perfect." He flashes a Cheshire grin and goes back to the mic.

August shakes his head and turns toward the patio. Roderick will never speak to him again if he calls the police. He decides to take a look at the outside wall and foundation.

It's near dark, so he follows the glow of solar lights, surveying the edge of the house. He stumbles into the side of a lounge chair, catching himself with one hand on the armrest, dipping toward the occupant. "Madeline! Sorry!"

She's slightly heavier than he remembers her in New York, but the high cheekbones and perfect complexion are stunning, a more delicate reflection of Roderick's features.

Her body is mostly covered by a slender blonde who continues fondling Madeline's exposed breast with long, white fingers and black nails. The blonde head turns southward, kissing bare skin toward a fringe of glittering pubic hair. Her finger probes inside Madeline's G-string.

August straightens his crown. "So sorry!"

The blonde tilts her head to give him a vicious stare.

Madeline smiles and places her hand on the woman's cheek, turning her face back to business. "August. So nice to see you. Lenore De Vere, August Dupin."

"Pleased to..." He talks to the back of Lenore's head. "I didn't mean to —"

"No problemo. She doesn't mind. Do you, Lenore?"

Lenore lets out a snarl. He steps back and looks at Madeline's face. "Did you hear that crack?"

"Crack, snapple, and pop? Sure." She straightens her legs, motioning to Lenore. "Sweetie, let's start over later."

Lenore gives him a peeved look and rolls herself to a standing position, sliding up her bikini top to partially cover her nipples. Several strands of Aladdin-style pants are stuck in her crotch, and she releases them. She bends forward to give Madeline a long kiss, and the strands of fabric separate in back, exposing two perfect, tan cheeks.

Madeline blows a kiss and turns back to August. "Sweetie, I was so excited when Rod told me you were coming. You're a doll. I hope this party poop isn't too much for you."

He loosens the robe where it's glued itself to his thighs. "You heard that loud crack? The chandeliers —"

"No injuries, right?"

"The glass was caught in the net... I'm afraid the roof will come down — there's no net to stop that."

"Brilliant! We should get one."

"Seriously. I've never heard of anything like this."

"You'll hear about it again. This house gets moody. *He's* old, in his last years. We're all falling apart. You need to fix us."

A waiter comes by with shots. August refuses. Madeline slugs one and takes a second. Guests are strolling or standing in clumps with their tall drink refills, laughing too loud. Is he the only sane person on the premises?

He tries not to sound hysterical. "Seriously? Are you heavily insured? There could be psychological damages."

"No worries." She studies the golden liquid in her glass and shoots it. She purses her lips. "Party on down, chaw-ming young August from Jaw-ja. Gimme a kiss."

He bends to kiss her cheek and she flings an arm around his neck and pulls him forward. Her lips lock onto his mouth and her alcohol-cooled tongue pushes inside. His hand goes down on the cushion, just missing her breast. She slips her fingers inside his robe.

"Christ!" He breaks her hold and steps back.

She's laughing. "Augie. No underwear awowed. Allowed."

Okay, she's drunk. He never knew her to be into men. He tightens his sash. "I'm making a short night of it."

She wags her finger. "No underwear. I wrote the invite myself." She puts the finger inside her G-string, watching his eyes, reaching for his hand, trying to pull him closer. "Loosen up, Aug."

"Maddy, I have a wonderful partner now, a gorgeous model. I told Roderick when he called."

She finds her tall glass on the patio and takes a long draw. "Bet you din... dint. Fuck. I'm so dwunk." She laughs and takes a breath. "A model, huh?" She clucks her tongue.

"I might've forgot to mention it."

She cocks her head.

No mistaking Roderick's motives now. He turns away. He hasn't gotten a look at the foundation, but does it matter? If he has any sense, he'll call to make apologies in the morning and head for the airport. He's been fooling himself all along, trying to. But he needs the job — desperately.

He's had too much to drink to be upset — or to think. And there's Paris! Damn. What time is it?

Chapter 4

The First Mistake

It's late for calling Garo, but he's going to do it as soon as he gets out of there. He changes into his pants and shirt and lays the costume on the bed. He cringes at the chocolate stain on the sleeve, hating to leave it to set. On the second floor he sees a bathroom just off the landing and runs a sink of cold water to soak the stain. Somebody will find the costume in the morning and know what to do.

He reaches the ground floor as a woman's scream comes from the open doors in back. He heads in that direction. Loud voices and running. Through the breezeway, a crowd in the ballroom is blocking his view. It's his perfect chance for a getaway without goodbyes. He can't go. It would be rotten to take off like that. He sets the suitcase behind a chair in the hall.

He works his way through the people. Madeline is out flat on the Spanish tiles, her red lipstick shocking against her bleached complexion. The lacey black cover-up is caught on one hip, revealing glitter and G-string. There's a blood smear on the floor near her head.

Roderick slides past. "Maddy!"

Lenore drops to her knees in front of Madeline. "Call 911! Somebody. Quick!" She rests Madeline's head between her thighs and moves a chunk of hair from across her left eye.

Roderick puts his hand on Lenore's shoulder. "Stop. You, go home, Lenore. She'll be fine. Not your problem." He projects his voice into the crowd. "Nobody call 911. Her doctor is here. Do not call 911. Do not. Please."

The orangutan, Ian, steps in front of August, holding a cell phone in his rubbery fist, his hairy back blocking the view. "Dr. Tarr is on his way from the patio."

Ian turns and August sees that he has removed his mask, rubber cheek pads attached to a hairy forehead. His real forehead is more bizarre, two horns implanted near the hairline and a decorative row of bumps above his eyebrows. His chin has four conical protrusions. He touches his tongue to his top lip — split tentacles — like a sea creature of some sort, exploring. August shudders. Is this all some kind of Halloween show? Surprise drama that everybody is in on, except him?

The supposed doctor, a tiny man in a black satin cape and leotard, kneels down next to Lenore. He leans over Madeline, touches her cheek, and takes her pulse. "Fine, fine," he says to Roderick. "A light one this time."

Roderick nods and makes a sound of relief. He asks Ian and one of the big transvestites to take her upstairs. Her head lolls as she's lifted. Ian pulls her swimsuit cover-up into place on her thighs. August is disgusted by the lack of concern. "Roderick, she needs an ambulance. She's unconscious, for god's sake. The doctor didn't even —"

"August, get a grip. This is the tropics. People get hot and they fall down. Dehydration... too much to drink... It's likely to be that. She'll be fine in the morning."

"Dehydration from drinking too much? Really. What if she has a concussion?"

"No worries. The doctor will finish checking her out upstairs. If she needs hospitalization, we'll take her." Roderick frowns at August's clothes. "You're leaving? Already?"

He shakes his head and reaches for his cell to call 911, but Roderick takes his wrist. "Listen, it happens to us Ushers. A genetic quirk. The doctor has her medicine. Nothing serious."

"The ceiling falls in, your sister cracks her head on the floor, and that's normal?"

"It's connected."

"What? Madeline was outside with her friend —"

"Stay here, August. Just tonight. I'll explain everything in the morning. I know you don't love me anymore, and I can't do anything about it. But you might decide to take a chance on us, me and Maddy. We desperately need your help. You can see that, can't you? It will be good for all of us. I promise."

August draws his hand down his chin and breathes out hard. "Did you really invite me here to work on the house?"

Roderick nods. "My god, yes. You're our last hope. I mean it. I knew already — when we were together in New York — that you would be the one to save us from this curse."

"Curse?"

"I promise to tell you every bit."

"You kept track of me?" August wipes his eyes, trying to clear his vision. He needs to give it more thought at some point. He walks toward his suitcase and the door, Roderick following. He leans to pick up the bag and loses his balance, saving himself by grabbing the back of the chair. "I have a motel reservation. I'll call you."

Roderick takes his shoulder and guides him onto the seat. "August, please. This is silly. I'll help you to your room. Time to lie down."

"I haven't had that much." He straightens, but he's dizzy. He feels for his phone. "I'm calling a taxi."

"Wait. Just a minute." Roderick looks around. "Roget? Roget?" He appears. "Bring August a glass of the special Italian mineral water, please." He pats August on the forearm. "Where are you staying?"

He pulls out his wallet and opens the bill section, looking for the folded piece of paper. He searches his pockets. "I had it right here — what was it, the motel you suggested?"

"I don't know. I thought you were staying here."

August scrolls down the emails on his cell, looking for a confirmation. He remembers he made the reservation by phone.

Roget brings a tall glass, chopped ice to the rim, bubbles rising through. August drinks it down.

"Hits the spot, right?" Roderick sets the empty glass on the floor next to the wall. "Roget will give you a ride."

"It's Atlantic... something." Tired. So tired. Head swimming.

He can't think. "Give me a second."

Roderick looks vacant, waiting. "No idea, what I might have said. Come on, Augie. You have a lovely bed upstairs. If they charge your card, add it to my bill." Roget moves beside him. August reaches for the suitcase and his head dips toward the floor. Somebody takes his shoulder, and he lets them help him down the hall. The middle section of a ceiling-to-floor tryptic opens. An elevator.

Chapter 5

Madeline's decision

It's early morning. Madeline sits naked on the side of the pool, swishing her legs. She scoops water onto her arms and bare tits. She's dehydrated and nauseous, and the shitty mimosa hasn't kicked in. Glitter still clings to her nipples and midriff. Where is Lenore? She hears Roderick's footsteps on the patio. "Rod-eee," she whines. I need your help."

He turns her way, his annoying mirror glasses under a wide-brimmed hat. "Wow, so early, this must be a record."

"Can't sleep." She puts her hand on her washboard stomach, taking slight pleasure in the taut feel of it. "Nauseous — and itchy."

He pulls an umbrella table over to shade them. He rolls up his long pants and sits, plonking his feet into the pool next to hers. "What?"

She holds her breasts, one in each hand, admiring their perfection as she shows him. "Glitter. Lenore said she'd be over first thing this morning, but she hasn't shown, the little slut."

"Finally recognizing her for what she is."

"I use the word with much affection, Asshole."

"You don't love her. It's mean — the way you treat her."

"Stop it. You know nothing."

His smile is wide, showing his new teeth. "Anything Lenore can do, I can do better."

She hands him her towel. "Please, just wet the end and clean me off. I think I'm allergic."

"No rash. You're just spoiled." He dips an edge of the towel into the pool and strokes lightly down her nearest breast and underneath. "Turn toward me." He does the other. His head dips and he sucks the nipple.

She lets her head loll and opens her legs farther. "Honey, get me off, will you. It'll only take a second."

"So, now, I'm honey?"

"I meant to say *asshole* –with much affection."

Watching his long fingers reach inside her pubic hair excites her. His strokes apply the perfect pressure that only a twin can know. She lets out a groan as a pulsing rush trickles to its end. Her head sags on his shoulder. "That was nice, Bro."

"Now my turn."

"You know I'm not doing it."

"My swimmers probably drowned long ago."

"Never know. Anyway, I'm sick. Don't ask me for a blow job either."

"Then you owe me." He tucks a lock of her longer hair behind her ear. "Help me keep him here."

"August? Me? He's not the least bit attracted to women."

"Neither am I, except for you..." He touches her nipple with the edge of his little fingernail, removing another speck of glitter. "You're the devious one. Think of something."

She swats his hand away. "Lure him. Mesmerize him. I can't think right now."

"You've got all morning."

"You do it. He came here for you."

He scoots closer. "Mads, I can't. If I pressure him, it's finished between us."

"It is already. He's with that model."

"What model?"

"Hmm. Don't know. I was drunk."

He smacks his forehead. "It figures." He lets out a loud breath. "One can only hope that money still has power."

"Enough money. Sometimes." She massages her temples. "Where is that Lenore? Did you send her away?"

He gets up and goes to the chair to dry his legs.

She glares. "You did, didn't you? Fucker. Why should I help you?"

"Because you'll be helping yourself."

She has her own theory about what needs to be done. It's been in the back of her mind for years. "We'll see." She pulls herself to her feet and wraps up in her towel. "I need a nap."

She remembers August as eager to please and fearful of showing it. He'll try hard to avoid confrontation, like most people.

Chapter 6

A Bad Morning After

August wakes to a slash of light across his eyes and an ice-pick through his head. The ocean rolls, and he realizes where he is, but can't remember getting into bed. He's wearing his boxer shorts, instead of the pyjamas he packed. Only a few minutes come back to him after Madeline cracked her head. Roderick talking crazy shit about a curse. Walking through a painting into an elevator. All insanity. Did he agree to stay the night?

Gars. He never called Garo! He sits straight up then falls back down on the pillow. Groans. His cell phone and wallet are on the nightstand. Almost ten o'clock. Three messages.

Garo picks up on the second ring. "About time, Sweetie."

August can't read his mood. "I am so sorry. I don't know what happened. I was really tired last night — I felt drugged. Can you forgive me?"

"Maybe you were." Gars' voice is dry.

"Drugged?" He thinks about it. "No, too many mojitos. It's not like they were pouring them down my throat, but almost — I forget, what's the time difference?"

"Six hours ahead — I'm on a break. Already started shooting this afternoon. Anyway, I enjoyed some lovely wine and dinner last night and went to bed with my cell phone so I could answer whenever you called."

"Oh... I feel terrible."

"Augie, I wasn't worried, just disappointed that we didn't get to talk. But maybe I should worry. You might've been slipped something. Really."

"I never set my drink down once — I don't think. But it was insane. I couldn't leave." He gives Gars a speed version of the party, the damage, Madeline's fall. "A seizure, I'm guessing. Nobody seemed to care, except for me — and her girlfriend."

"Do you really know these people? Sounds like they have more cracks than the one in their ceiling. Give it up. Meet me in Paris. You don't have to go to Key West to find work."

"Unfortunately, I do. I haven't told you all the pathetic details. I'm sure there's no check coming, unless I sue. My career is at a dead end — mostly due to acting like a hot shot. New York is bleak, just bleak — except for you. You're all I've got."

"Augie, that doesn't sound like you."

"I've made bad choices. Time for me to stop dreaming. I'll lose you, too, if I'm a failure."

Garo sighs. "Never — neither."

"This project could be huge. It's an amazing house, and Roderick is desperate for help."

There's a pause. "You know I want whatever you want. But now I'm worried. Be sure to call me tonight. I might have to grab a flight from Paris to Key West."

"If only! Besides the fact that I miss you and love you, I wish you could see this place. Beyond *The Money Pit* — *The Money Canyon*, I'm guessing — and the Ushers have the cash, or the collateral, to fill it up, it seems. An architect's employment dream."

"Remember Tom Hanks' laugh?"

"Everything about it. That was one of our first nights at your apartment."

"I'm putting the film on my calendar, as we speak — for the night I get home — two weeks from today. I'll get some Veuve Clicquot, just like last time, and bring a luscious Roquefort —" Port would go better, but..."

"I'm buying Dom P., if I get this job."

"Well, don't forget the ending. These people could be swindlers. Let me know if I need to come down there and show Mr. Roderick my knuckle tattoos."

"Please, do!" August laughs. Gars, the tough guy. August hardly notices the tattoos anymore, snakes winding around Gars' middle fingers — from his younger, wilder days — soon to be lasered off. He remembers the chill when Garo took his hand to lead him into the bedroom for the first time, and he saw the snakes. Gars called his bad-boy self "The Imp of the Perverse" — also his penis.

"It's intriguing, the weird fissure and the... curse. I want to check on Madeline. We were pals."

"You have a lot to consider, Augie, but sometimes there's only one consideration that's important."

He doesn't know whether Gars means safety or love.

"Augie — gotta run. They're starting up."

"Sorry! I didn't even ask how it's going."

"Fantastic! I'll tell you all about it tonight. Love you."

"Love you!" He's not sure Gars heard. So much excitement. He can't fool himself. Money, looks, intelligence, personality. As things stand, Gars is way out of his league. A childhood with a grand piano and polo ponies. His own family claimed a rusted tractor and stinky goats.

Chapter 7

Worse and More

He finds a thick terry cloth robe in the closet, slips it on, and grabs his shaving kit. Desperate to pee. The hall is dark with all the doors closed. He follows light down the stairs to the second-floor, one partially open door. He pushes the knob, and the door creaks, swinging wide into a huge bedroom. Light through the curtains shows Madeline asleep, a white sheet to her chin. A black cat on the pillow lifts its head, its eyes green and glaring.

August pulls back, but there isn't a flicker. The cat slinks forward, stepping on her chest and ribs, and down her hip. It crouches facing him, deciding whether to spring. As he steps forward, it hisses and hops to the floor. August rushes past to lay the back of his hand on Madeline's forehead. It feels colder than the temperature of the room. Is that possible? He moves toward the door, and the cat leaps back on Madeline.

He rushes down the stairs, wishing he'd gone straight for his cell phone, trying to think where he might find Roderick. He covers the ground floor, kitchen, library, and he glances out across the breezeway. Roderick is by the pool, drying his hair with a towel, wearing a robe and a swimsuit. More clothes than expected. "Good morning!"

August points upward. "Madeline — she's cold! Not breathing!"

"She's fine." Roderick signals to Roget and takes a tray of drinks from his hands. "Please, check on Maddy." He holds out the drinks, but August refuses.

"Augie, she was already in the pool and went back up for a nap. We're having a late breakfast and a light lunch today."

"Roderick! Right now, she needs an ambulance!"

"Listen, please. I would've explained everything last night, but you —"

He knows she's dead. There really is no hurry. He collapses into a chair and closes his eyes, hoping when he opens them, he'll feel sane. It doesn't work. "Yes, last night — I think I was drugged."

"Good stuff?"

He puts his hands on his head to pull at his hair. There's nothing on Roderick's face, except amusement at his own cleverness. "Okay, tell me what's wrong with Madeline."

"What you just witnessed is catatonia, sort of the opposite of epilepsy. Unknown causes... "

He's pouring sweat and his head throbs. He puts his fingertips to his forehead. It's bullshit. He knows bullshit when he hears it. He has to piss like a racehorse. "I'm sorry. Is there a bathroom close by?"

When he comes out, Madeline stands barefoot in a scarlet kimono, leaning her shoulder against the dining room doorjamb, vaping. The black cat poses next to her like an Egyptian statue. August stops dead.

She exhales toward him. "My meds," she says.

The odor is strong, ammonia-like.

"I hear you were worried about me, Augie. Sweet of you, babe."

It's nuts. Impossible. "I touched you."

"Oh? Sorry I missed it." She winks. "I took a pill."

He doesn't believe her, but he gives in to be polite. He won't be here much longer. "Sorry to cause an uproar."

"No uproar. Have some breakfast. Enjoy. I hope you'll come to the judging on Thursday to vote for me and my kitty — the Fantasy Fest Pet Parade. We're both going as Carmen Miranda." She cups a hand near her head. "Turbans with fruit."

It takes him a second. "Both?" He imagines her mound of bananas, strawberries, and kiwis, above hoop earrings, and the cat's tiny matching turban perched between pointy ears with dangling rings. "Really?"

Madeline leans more heavily, her opposite hip jutting out. He wonders if she can stand when she's not propped up.

Roderick strolls in from the patio, extending fresh mimosas. Madeline takes one. "Ah, everything's hunky-dory."

Not. Alcohol is the last thing he wants on his stomach. Roderick pushes a glass toward him and he accepts. He points toward the cat. "Is this — Pluto?"

Roderick licks two fingers. "No, but excellent memory. Pluto was our old cat and also the name of this cat's father. There were always cats named Pluto in our family. I must've told you about the bad luck? No?" He shrugs. "Oh, well. Now that Pluto is no longer a planet..." He flips his hand, waving it away. This one's female, Maddy J., for junior."

Madeline exhales a cloud toward the ceiling. Roget steps next to her and motions toward breakfast on the sideboard, covered dishes, pastries, fruit.

August tightens the sash on his robe. "I'll be right back. I need to shower and put on some clothes."

Roderick chuckles. "No need."

"Diet Day for me," Madeline says, "but nice spread." She looks at Roderick. Leftovers from the party?"

"Of course not." He gives her a look. "Just a few extras since August is here."

"I'll grab a banana."

August notes her slow, careful walk to the buffet, sexy or light-headed?

She selects a couple of kiwi slices. "See you later, honeys."

Showered and shaved, August descends the stairs feeling professional at last in a short-sleeved shirt with his favorite mechanical pencil in the breast pocket. He has his portfolio, sketchbook, and laptop, ready for a serious discussion. He takes a peek into the ballroom before he heads for breakfast. The cleaning crew is finishing up. Amazing job. Even the nets of broken chandeliers are gone. Scaffolding is erected in the corner. Prep for a superficial patch job and paint?

His appetite returns when he focuses on the pile of croissants, heaped pineapple and papaya, and four steaming silver buffet dishes. All this for three people, now two. Roderick has his plate under the umbrella on the patio. August sets his stuff on a side table and takes a China plate and fills it, getting hungrier when he lifts a lid and smells the sausage. He stacks his plate atop his gear and heads out to Roderick.

"The croissants are baked especially for us. As good as any you can get in Europe."

The thought of a French café leads right to Garo, as if Roderick is baiting him. August is tempted to ask if the whole island is made to Usher specifications. He takes a sip of coffee. Exquisite. In the city he was never bothered by Roderick's snooty attitude. He bites into a croissant. Crisp and flaky on the outside, soft and buttery inside.

He brushes flakes off his shirt. "I'm eager to get a look at your foundation. Figure out what happened and who I need to get to fix it."

"Plenty of time for that."

"I wasn't planning to stay more than two days, this trip. I have other commit —"

"You might want to change your plans. This is a long-term proposition. How would you like to be ultra-wealthy and famous?"

August's eyebrows lift. More bullshit. "I don't think I'm up to it."

Roderick puts his hand on August's, flattening it on the table. "That's your problem, sweetheart — you mentioned bills overdue — you need to let yourself shine. Madeline and I have the means to boost your ego, as well as your wallet."

"Boost my wallet?" August laughs. "You'd get plenty of maxed-out credit cards."

Roderick chuckles. "You're a hoot. Poor choice of words — Madeline and I will fatten your head and your wallet. How's that?"

He studies Roderick's face.

"August, we're talking millions — not to mention, future

recommendations that will keep you working for years after that. If I have to spend that much money, I want you to profit from it, not some stranger. I trust you. Ushers are special people. This house is special. It takes a certain acuity, an artistic sensibility, to understand that."

August's sense of artistry has been complimented all his life, but he's never believed it. He polishes off a third croissant.

Roderick motions for him to get up. "Follow me."

He obeys, out the doors to the breezeway, then under the moving shadows of palm fronds, the sun in between burning his face and neck, sweat rolling.

Roderick stops in a patch of shade. "Have you read any Swedenborg?"

"His philosophy is connected with your book, right?"

"You remembered! My scientific and philosophic discoveries build on his original concepts." He motions toward the house. "You need to visit our library. I have the Complete Works. He's almost unknown these days, but he'll interest you."

Roderick walks ahead and points out a section of foundation, huge carved blocks of stone, precisely aligned like the walls of the pyramids. "Right there." Roderick kicks it with his toe. "Ouch! That's the area that causes the trouble — the heart of the house."

He can't see any problem. Strange way of referring to part of a building. "What do you mean? Location-wise, I wouldn't call it the heart."

"I mean, the source of energy, it's right in there, inside the foundation. I can't explain it without diagrams and going into complex theory."

Any logic there eludes him. "Okay." August's head is level with the top of the stones. He has never seen anything this size in a residence. The stone being blamed for the problem is exactly like the ones on both sides of it.

"No visible damage." He walks off the length of one stone and notes it in his sketchbook. He'll come back later and measure with the laser. "These are approximately fifteen feet long — could be ten tons each. Where'd they come from?"

"England. Great-great-grandfather — we call him G.G.G. — shipped the whole house and its foundation, which is under this wing, to Boston, chunk by chunk, over several years. He and G.G., his twin's son, moved out of Marlborough in 1832. It's sarsen sandstone."

"Like Stonehenge."

"Exactly. You're amazing. As a matter of fact, an archeologist claimed the foundation of the old homestead was built of rock stolen from another Stonehenge-like formation, some twenty miles from the one everybody knows."

"How would somebody manage that?"

"In England, Ushers were lords. Anyway, the archeologist could never prove it, and now he's long dead."

"How did the stones get to Key West?"

"G.G. had a dream — or a nightmare. He became convinced that the dank air surrounding the Boston house — a miasma, he called it — was responsible for his mother's death and his father's deterioration. The house burned — possibly he burned it — so only the foundation was transported to Key West. A fascinating story, by the way. It's all in his diary. After that, he lived in a rooming house, waiting for the current west wing to be finished, in 1849. He never made it here. Mysteriously, his body was found in Baltimore. His twin sister moved down and brought him and the older ancestors along in their coffins."

"I can't keep track. Lots of twins in your family."

"Ah, yes. Our Great-grandmother, Lenore, was pregnant with twins, too. Unmarried, of course, as were all the Ushers. She died in childbirth."

August nods. "Tough — in those days." He rubs his hand flat over the surface of a stone. It's smooth and warm, rosy in the sun. "Lenore, like Maddy's friend. Such a coincidence."

"No. She changed it — to make Maddy happy. Her own idea, for our mother's name to live on, or some crap."

"Sounds like love to me."

"Huh? More like a gold-digger trying to attach herself to the family. Maddy doesn't care one way or the other."

Roderick turns toward the house. "If you look it up in local records, the building date is 1896, but that's when he was connected and turned into a Victorian."

The blocks are fitted so tight that August can't get a fingernail between them. "He? Who?" Roderick turns toward the ocean, scanning the horizon.

August gives up. "Sandstone wears over time, especially in damp ground. I'll have to do some digging to find the damage." Let's go back inside."

Roderick leads the way through the ballroom and stops. "They had all kinds of bad luck and made wild expenditures, our grandparents. They sold the house to a judge and his millionaire wife, but still lived in part of it. A practical arrangement. Then, somehow, the house was back in our parents' hands before we were born."

"I see." He's hardly listening, enraptured by the prospect of renovating such a historic beauty. He can't let it go to someone who might disrupt the use of symmetry and asymmetry, the delicate balance between boredom and bewilderment. "What did you mean by its being "connected" in 1896?"

"Originally the house was actually two houses. Sister houses. Twins, of course — they should have called them brother houses."

August opens one of the French doors to look up into the breezeway. "So everything to the east side of the staircase was a separate house, the bedrooms upstairs and the ballroom below?"

"Exactly. The kitchen and downstairs living areas were later made into the grand ballroom. The third-floor hall above us is the only physical connection between the two wings, just a closed-in walkway really, an arm, supported by the west wing. The foundation and cellar run under both sides, but the original foundation is only under the east wing."

August studies the ceiling above the breezeway. "Incredible. I would never have guessed."

"The houses yearned to be attached." He laughs. "I'm joking."

August snickers to disguise a twitch. "Actually, I agree."

"In those days long pieces of timber were available. The Ushers have never spared expense. Ironwood was shipped in from Australia for the supports and to build the fire doors to close the connection, when necessary." He points to a wall at a distance in front of the breezeway. That's a turret attached to the west wing. It juts out from the front so you don't see the breezeway from the street view."

Roderick opens the three sets of French doors into the breezeway for August to take a close look at the inside walls of the ballroom in daylight. There's nothing new to see, only the crack in the ceiling extending from the corner, spider-webbing, touching each of the four seams between walls and ceiling. Bizarre. Tragic.

August shakes his head. "It's as if the eastern corner moved outward and pulled the ceiling with it, unbalanced tension and compression." He walks outside and looks at the back wall of the house. Nothing. He looks up. "That's my bedroom window."

"Yes, that would be your room."

"Why'd you put me there?"

Roderick raises his eyebrows. "It's the loveliest view. Once in a while, there's cell phone coverage. I didn't think he'd pick last night to act out his aggressions." He looks at the ceiling. "But I should have expected it."

"He? Who are you talking about?"

"Oh, you know. Boats are female, this house is male — probably gay. I don't know whether all houses are male. I've lived in this one my entire life — except for that short period in the apartment in Manhattan." His eyes go soft. "That divine summer."

August studies the stone.

Roderick sighs. "I have a little business to take care of — day trading. Really just a hobby. Let me show you to the cellar."

"The water table allows that?"

Roderick takes off at a clip and August hurries to follow. "Prohibitive cost, but again, much less expensive then, than now. I think that's where our problem lies, under the east wing in the area of the stones I showed you." He stops at a door in the hall near the dining room. "Hemingway's has a basement — and a pool — so why shouldn't we? Ours cellar is much, much bigger, of course. And we have the beach. Man-made."

"Oh?" Another incredible Usher achievement.

"There are no natural beaches in Key West."

August is dripping sweat as they enter the house and walk through the hall. He swipes under his chin, as the cold air-conditioning starts to revive him, and steps aside while Roderick pulls and jiggles the knob on the cellar door. They take turns pulling and jiggling until Roderick yanks it open. "We rarely go down here." He flicks the switch, and a row of dim bulbs light the stairs enough to show worn, crumbly, misshapen stones. If you continue right, it will take you under the breezeway and the east wing. Roderick points toward a handrail. "Hold on. But don't worry, we're insured." He motions toward the stairs. "If you run out of renovations..." He smiles to show he's kidding. "I'll see you at lunch. Three, okay?"

Sausage is heavy in his stomach, but August nods, already putting one careful foot in front of the other. He would normally have a flashlight. The door slams behind him. Will he be able to open it again? A small shadow flits past, nearly tripping him. Maddy J.? Did Roderick boot her down the stairs?

He goes back and tries the door, turning the knob both ways. He pushes, lifts, presses down. Jiggles. No pressure in any direction makes a difference. Balancing on the step, he can't get enough force behind it. He slams himself against the heavy wood, but it won't budge. Nobody in ear shot. He feels like an idiot. Hopefully, Roderick will get him out if he doesn't turn up for lunch. Garo was right. A den of insanity. He'll finish the preliminary inspection and grab the next flight to La Guardia.

He makes his way down. Roderick seemed such a different man in the city, not only charismatic, but intellectual — and sane. His book was in every bookstore window. The honorary dinner for "Advancements in the Field" was a huge, glamorous event. Were all those people Swedenborgians? He can't remember. He was young, possibly blinded by nearness to the limelight, but surely, he must have Googled them at some point.

Chapter 8

A Full Morning of Weird

Maddy J. is waiting for him halfway down. She sprints ahead into the dark. Automatically counting stairs, August finds himself on number thirty at the bottom. Amazing. An architectural miracle that there's no visible water. He passes four cases of wine stacked on a shelf along the wall, Thomas Garcia Amontillado — *Amontillado* seems familiar. Might be a vineyard Gars favors.

The dim light from above the stairs ends in cavernous blackness. How does Roderick expect him to see anything? There are many unwelcoming traits to the house that don't appear on the surface.

He's out of here tonight, even if he has to make a stopover. Gars should be home within the week. He pictures him, sitting in a café on a woven chair at a metallic table for two, like in the photo from a past trip. There's a tiny cup of espresso in his long, tattooed fingers, *crêpes* with caviar on a plate in front of him. There was likely to be a graceful Frenchman across the table, with thick, lustrous hair, snapping the picture.

He halts the self-torture, forcing himself to feel around the cold walls on both sides, spiders or not. There must be another wall switch, or at least a flashlight on a hook. Nothing. Just getting the place up to code could support him for years, let alone, the job of preserving its magnificence.

His eyes begin to see deeper into the dungeon. There's a glow. An egress window on the far side of the house? Doubtful. He makes his way toward it, feeling ahead with his foot before he puts his weight down. There's a peculiar smell, unfamiliar and unpleasant.

As the glow ahead brightens, he stoops to check the floor. Stone of some kind, not even damp. He rounds a high stack of wine cases and startles. Candlelight illuminates a woman inside a fancy wrought iron fence. As she turns, the light glows through her thin robe, outlining her body. "Madeline." She sets the candle on an elevated rectangular marble box and squints toward him.

"My god, a coffin?"

"August, there you are."

He walks slowly toward the gate. Maddy J. leaps up from the floor to the closest coffin lid, having gotten there invisibly. An identical black cat joins her and licks her between the ears.

"Augie. Finally. I thought you took off."

He puts on a calm voice. "You've been waiting for me down here?" He unlatches the gate. "Roderick never said —" There's a painful screech of metal grating on stone as he pulls. He looks at the hinges, grits his teeth, and swings the gate a few more inches to slip through.

"No worries. It's cool and quiet, although *dank* is the better word."

"I can fix that squeal if you have some oil handy."

"I doubt it. We're not handy people."

No truer words. He points to the cats lolling lasciviously. "Littermates?"

"Yes, almost twins." She lifts the head of the cat nearest her. "You met Maddy J. This is Roddy. If you look into his chest fur, you can see a splotch of white, almost an oval." She fingers it. "I know them by their attitudes, but sometimes they fool me."

She moves closer, tilting her head in an innocent way. She curls her fingers around August's neck. "I love cats, don't you?"

Goosebumps prickle the hair on the back of his skull. He stiffens. "I've never known any cats personally, as pets." He pictures barn cats dragging in their gory kills. Is she trying to freak him out?

"They're not pets, more like family members."

These Ushers are beyond him with their peculiarities. In the city, he thought Roderick's eccentricities were fun. He points at the coffin. "Is that... in use?"

"Very much so. This is our dear mama. She was lesbian, but she endured enough fucking to give us life."

He tries to look nonchalant. "Generous."

She chuckles. "The required fuck that I haven't fulfilled."

He gestures at the surrounding coffins on pedestals, in rows as far as he can see in the dark. "And these are all... relatives?"

"Ancestors from four generations, dug up and delivered from the old mansion in England, plus our grands and parents who were added more recently."

"Roderick told me. That's something."

"Yeah. It's a hell of a thing — rotting generations in the basement. I guess even Mom has turned to dust by now." She places his hand on the cool marble lid of the coffin. "Wanna peek?"

His head jerks. "I'll take a raincheck." He takes a breath and moves his hand down the side of the coffin, feeling its heft and the smoothness of the carvings. "Masterful work. Mind if I ask... is there one for you and Roderick?"

"Fuck, yes." She points out two at the far end. "Roderick won't spoil the family tradition. But if he goes first, I'm opting for cremation." She makes a broad sweep with her hand. "I'll haul out every damn bone — chuck them in the ocean. They're the cause of our problem."

"The cracking? From the weight of the coffins — down here?"

"The weight of the past." She laughs. "Let's go see the fucking fissures."

He follows her and her candle. Why not a flashlight, or better yet, an industrial-size LED? They pass a section of casks and bottles lined up in even rows, a dozen or more. *Amontillado* is stencilled on several more casks — an old-world vine? The Ushers must love the stuff.

After a few more steps, Madeline holds up the candle. From twenty feet away, a crevice is obvious, foundation stones broken and shifted, sagging. "Jesus, Madeline. How long has it been like this?"

She walks ahead of him, shining the light on similar breaks down the long east wall. "Um. I don't know. It's a little worse since the last time we looked, a couple of months ago. But we've had cracks for years. I think Roderick first noticed them when we got back from New York."

"This is extremely dangerous, especially if it's started deteriorating faster."

"We called a local company, but they weren't interested. Wouldn't even come to do an estimate." She puts her hands together prayer-style, touching her index fingers to her darkened lips. "Then... well, you know how it is. Dread turned into procrastination. 'Out of sight, out of mind.'"

He's thinking, yeah, if you start drinking before breakfast.

"It wasn't worrisome until recently. I don't know how to explain this, but I have a spiritual — or psychic — connection with this house. I sort of feel... *his* moods."

"*His* moods?"

"I meant *its*. Roderick always says *he*, but I don't know, could be she, or whatever." She chuckles, then clamps her lips. "I have to tell you this, Augie, whether you believe me or not. This house is upset."

He looks for a place to sit down, but not on a coffin. He doesn't feel like listening to another long, crazy story. He puts a hand on his queasy stomach.

"*Furious* might be a better word than *upset*." She crinkles her forehead as if asking him for a further explanation.

"Sorry, I don't know any structural psychology." He waits for a laugh, but it doesn't come. "Let's go up. I'll do the measuring after lunch." He cups his hand over his mouth and chin. "Seriously, we need to strengthen these foundation walls immediately, whether you decide to renovate or not. We're talking life and death."

She shrugs. "That'll help make my dear twin happy, but you can't fix this house."

"How do you know? You mean, *I* can't fix it, or nobody can?"

"Not by any kind of physical repair."

She sounds confident for somebody without a clue. "Then why call me?"

"Roderick won't listen. But maybe you can help him understand." She stares hard into his eyes.

"How's that?"

"If..."

He tries to wait her out, but she won't finish. Her eyes shift to the rough ceiling.

He points toward the stairs. "Let's go up."

Maddy J. — or Roddy — darts ahead as if knowing what the words mean. Madeline leads August with the candle. At the top of the stairs, she opens the door with one try. A cat leaps from nowhere and chases its twin down the hall.

Chapter 9

Extended Stress

Roderick is already high at lunch. Madeline pokes his calf when his flirtations toward August go too far, but August seems engrossed in his seafood salad. The possibility of making good money should be worth some suffering, but Roderick is likely to be shovelling on the BS too heavily when she's not around.

August soon polishes off his salad and excuses himself to continue the inspection. She wishes him luck.

She waits till he's gone. "I need more time."

"So far so good. He's still here. I knew you had it in you — the Usher charm."

"Not like you, Bro. His current plan is to find somebody to do emergency repairs. The house scares him shitless."

"Fuck."

She tosses back her hair. "You need to settle down. You'll run him off."

Roderick sips his scotch. "He's got that model controlling his head."

"Both heads. You make it worse with your slobbering." An idea comes to her. "I'll hide his cell phone. That should cause some trouble. He won't leave knowing the phone is somewhere in the house."

Roderick opens his mouth slightly, then clamps it.

She reads him. "I knew it. You still love him and you don't want him to suffer."

"I doubt it would work. And I do hate to ruin true love — if it exists — for anybody."

"You can't ruin true love, you know. What's that saying? —

let it go, and if it returns, it's fucking real?"

"That's the gist of it. A stupid saying..."

"Well, Augie returned to you, for whatever reason. Maybe he just needs a kick start."

"He'll ask to borrow one of our phones, or use the landline."

"I'll be out tonight with Lenore. You can come up with some bullshit."

She pushes a chunk of hair behind her ear and bites her lower lip. Luring Augie for her purposes will be tough, but keeping him in the house is a big step.

"I'll say I'm sick and go to bed. I feel sick already. Sicker than usual. I don't like being involved in trickery."

"Right-o, Lady Macbeth."

"Still flaunting that short summer term at Cambridge. How many years ago?"

"I loved British Drama. I would've gone for a lit degree if — she rolls her eyes upward — if he'd let me off this damned island long enough."

"You could do online classes — if we live."

Upstairs, she puts on a bikini. She hasn't worn a swimsuit for years, but nudity seems to scare the heck out of August. She admires her six-pack and tight ass. They're beautiful, nearly *au naturel*, with nature only slightly improved upon. If Augie wasn't gay, it would be simple.

She sits down on the side of the pool and watches him as he measures with his laser and inputs to his laptop. Such a hard worker, an upfront guy, although somewhat dull. He doesn't seem to notice her. He's wearing slim, fitted khakis, already sweaty around the lower back. There's no evidence of a cell phone in any pocket.

His door is unlocked and she finds the phone on the nightstand next to wallet, change, and keys. Such a trusting soul. The bed is made and his bag is packed and sitting on a chair.

What would be better, snatching the phone or his wallet? He might think Roget stole the wallet. No need to put anybody through that. Keeping him from talking to his partner seems a much better bet. Eventually, she'll plant the cell somewhere for him to find. There's a twinge in her stomach as she pictures him searching frantically and thinking he's lost his mind. Oh, well. She's not a softie like Roderick. She picks up the phone and presses the button. The screen comes on, not password protected. Of course not. On impulse, she snatches the keys. It would be like passing up a restroom if she didn't make copies, a missed opportunity she might regret. She opens the wallet to his Driver's License and uses his cell to take a photo and text it to herself. The more info the better. She deletes her text from his phone. There are unread texts from Garo — no doubt, the partner — that she'll need to look at, maybe delete.

Late afternoon, she finds August and Roderick talking on the patio. She stops and motions toward the beach. "Anybody for a swim? Nice and calm today." No takers. August is holding a mojito. Good boy. The more he drinks, the more he'll believe that he left his phone in some odd place. "Finished inspecting already?"

"A short break. Your brother insisted."

Roderick swirls his ice. "Key West. No rush."

"I expect to finish with the preliminaries by tonight and leave in the morning. First off, considering your problem with local companies, I'll need to bring some good people down here from New York."

She puts her hands on her hips. "You promised me your vote at the Pet Parade — tomorrow evening."

"I did? Sorry."

"If I win, the money from my sponsorships goes to help kitties, TNR — trap, neuter, return."

"Really sorry. I have to get back. Rod told me you're going out tonight, so I'll say my goodbye now." He dodges a mouth kiss and moves into a hug, bending far forward from the shoulders so there's no chance her chest can graze his.

"You'll be back soon?"

"That depends on whether we can come to some kind of agreement."

"I'm confident we can," Roderick says. "Let's talk at dinner."

Chapter 10

What Else?

August parks his butt on a case of Amontillado, all finished with the measurements for now. It makes sense that the sandstone is weathering and crumbling from Key West humidity and ground instability. A crazy choice to haul those slabs here — an insane choice — but it doesn't seem to relate to the ceiling damage, since the above ground foundation and the interior walls are fully intact. If there was deformation of the walls, loading on the ballroom floor beyond the capacity of the under-shoring might lead to deflection in the floor structure. That would explain why cracking takes place during parties. As is, he has no theory, which makes him nervous, but the first step is to repair and strengthen the faulty areas of foundation. Without tearing into it, there's no way to predict if the upper floor has been compromised and could bring down the walls.

The fastest and surest fix will be to shore up the foundation, below and above ground, with concrete. He'll need to excavate completely around the walls to add a water seal. Pillars from basement to floor and floor to ceiling, a heavier floor system above and below, and some exterior pillars at the wall line, regardless of what's causing the problem. Nothing creative about it, but an expensive project that he can handle, and something the Ushers need desperately.

He checks his watch. Damn. It's already after six, which means midnight in Paris. The romance in the words lands like lead in his stomach. He could be there right now. He hurries to gather his tools, eager to call. Gars is usually up late, but with unknown working hours, it would have been better to call sooner. He's been mesmerized, unaware of time, a good thing in general. Now, five minutes to walk from the dungeon up to his room or somewhere he can get reception — if he can get out. He should have left the door ajar.

When he reaches the top of the stairs, he's amazed to find the door standing open. Someone took pity on him. Madeline.

He passes through the dining room. Nothing is laid out for dinner, so he has time to call, shower, and have the required pre-dinner drink. Roderick has always been hard to refuse in person, whatever crazy suggestions he might have, so he'll hold back the details till he can verify costs.

Panic is instant when he sees his keys and wallet and no cell phone. He left it there. He's positive. He made a point of leaving it, since there would be no reception in the cellar. He moves the nightstand away from the wall to see if the phone fell behind it. He gets on his hands and knees and looks under the bed. Not even dust bunnies. The phone would have to fly to get any farther than that. He's looked in every likely place. He opens his suitcase and picks through his clothes and shaving kit. He runs down the hall and scans the bathroom. He rushes back and checks the pocket of the robe. He's building up a sweat.

He yells into the empty cathedral-sized bedroom, "Somebody took it!" For some reason, he's not surprised. But why? To delay him. What good would it do? So he can vote for Madeline in the Pet Parade? Surely, they're not that silly. He can't accuse them. What the hell is he going to do?

He heads down to find Roderick and ask to use the landline. He's not on the ground floor, inside or out. He smells garlic and pork and visualizes black beans and rice, a pile of plantains. He realizes he's starving. His blood sugar must be dropping. Soon he'll be frantic. He's already frantic! He pokes his head into the kitchen, feeling out of place. Rows of copper-bottom pots and sparkling wine glasses run across half the ceiling. Tall stacks of white plates float in vertical metal racks, and the chocolate fountain is a row of shining pieces on the drainboard. So, they actually own the fountain.

Latin music plays from somewhere. The cook is at the stove, stirring a big pot. He's wearing a chef cap embroidered with *Da Fortunato.*

"Excuse me, Mr. Fortunato?"

The cook startles.

August points to the cap.

The cook squints.

August struggles, "*Lo siento... dondé... está...* Roderick?"

"It's Italian. I worked at Da Fortunato in Rome." He stares into the beans. "Upstairs, taking a *siesta*."

"Thanks, sorry to bother you." August has no idea where Roderick's room is. Finding a phone should be easier. He hurries into the front hall and checks a desk and a table along the wall. Nothing. Surely, there's a landline, especially with cell coverage so spotty. He checks the patio and alcoves off the hall.

"Fuck." He opens a door. The library. Dark shelves to the ceiling, a rolling ladder reaching the top. Across the room, an inlaid desk with carvings and cubby holes, and a leather chair under a Tiffany lamp. Magnificent. Right out of the movies. He looks across the desk. There's a copy of Roderick's book, a pen, and notes, as if he's been working recently. No phone.

He turns toward the door and sees a phone cord. It's mostly hidden under a Persian rug, leading into a red lacquered Chinese cupboard. He must have stepped over it, almost invisible on the hardwood. He hates to snoop, but the cabinet's not locked, and he's desperate. Yes! A phone in its stand on a shelf. Hidden? Probably just kept there not to detract from the antique style of the room. He picks it up and presses "Call." No dial tone. They cut off their phone so he can't use it? No way. His paranoia is showing. He follows the cord and finds it connected at the wall. Possibly, the Ushers forgot to pay the bill.

Headed toward the door, he slams his hip into the ladder, and a book tumbles down, clipping him on the shoulder. He bends and picks up the thick tome. *Swedenborg's Theory of Correspondences: Revenge, Manipulation, and other Evil Spirits.* Some of Roderick's "scientific" research? August chides himself for being cruel. The cover is divided into quarters showing a burning face, a face covered with hair, a skull, and a set of vicious teeth. He jerks involuntarily.

An index card flies out as he lifts the book toward a space on the shelf. He recognizes Roderick's calligraphy:

> *Evil sentience caused by collocation and arrangement of stones. Aspects multiplied and strengthened by reflection and resulting in miasma. Panpsychism.*

He puts the card back and slips the book into its spot. He won't be around long enough to dip into this gem. He goes out and closes the door.

Roderick hasn't appeared in the dining room, but two places are set. He can't wait around. There are restaurants and bars within a short distance and maybe a pay phone somewhere. He barrels out the front door and takes a right on South Street. It's commercial up ahead. Nearly sprinting, he reaches Duval, the main drag, and dashes inside a little crêpe place. He's broken into a drenching sweat. The relief of cool air is instant. He has a primitive urge to crawl into a booth and take a nap. He weaves between the tables to the counter. The only man in sight is facing the back, putting together an order.

"Do you have a phone I can use? I lost my cell." No response. "I'll gladly pay."

"Local call?"

"Uh, no. Paris. Just a quick one. I'll give you a twenty to cover it."

The guy doesn't even glance over his shoulder. "No long distance. Sorry."

August is already out the door by the word *sorry*. This is how it's going to be. He stops two nicely dressed guys approaching on the sidewalk. "Can I please borrow a cell? I lost mine and I'm desperate to call my partner." Both pull out phones.

He reaches for one, pauses, scrunches up his face. "It's to Paris. I'll pay you whatever you think."

They look at each other, and the taller one shakes his head.

"Our plan's not set up for international calls."

"Sorry, sorry," they both say.

He nods and tells them he appreciates it anyway. Now he's running, sweat rolling down his back, no clear idea of how he'll make the call. He's almost had his quota of embarrassment for the night. He feels bad. They feel bad. He runs past several wide-open doors of T-shirt shops in a row, spewing icy air. He asks at the reservation desk in a tapas place, then an American café, an Italian restaurant, a bistro. It's the beginning of dinner rush and nobody has time to deal with him and his problem.

He just might black out from heat and dehydration. He's had no water this afternoon, only the lunch mojito. He sits down on a bench next to a bleached-blonde woman with a leathery tan, eating an ice cream cone. She's engrossed. He musters his most miserable, pleading voice. "Could I possibly use your cell phone for just a minute. I need to call my partner in Paris. I'll pay you." He pulls three twenties from his wallet. "Here, please."

She takes another lick and puts out her hand for the money. "You can give it a try." She stuffs the bills into her bag and drags out a clamshell phone.

He blinks, but says thanks and dials the country code and number of the hotel Gars left him, expecting the exasperating ding-dong of the "check-your-number" recording. The phone rings and Garo answers. "Hello."

"Sweetie! Finally. I'm having a hell of a time... My phone's missing —"

"Hello? hello? I can't hear you. Hello?"

"Gars, it's me."

"Hello? hello?" There's a pause. "Must be a wrong number."

"*C'est dommage*" — a sexy male voice in the background. Garo hangs up.

Enough words to conjure a hotel bed with a smooth torso rising out of the white sheets, dark sleepy eyes and thick curls. A comment on the call — as if it was his business. Was it really a bad connection? Or inconvenient? Gars would have been expecting his call. He snaps the phone shut. Ack! Of course, Gars thought it was a wrong number.

"Let me try once more," August tells the woman. He starts to dial, but she grabs the phone. "Another sixty."

"That's ridiculous." He hands back the phone. Gars isn't likely to answer the same number anyway. A computer is what he needs, an internet café. If he sends an email right away, Gars might hear it come in. Maybe he's already leaving a message on the missing phone.

He sprints farther down Duval, dodging couples, many of them men, but he's too disgusted with himself to interrupt their pleasant evening. No internet café, not a single pay phone, as expected. By now it's after one o'clock in Paris. Gars might need to get up early to model, and August can't be that inconsiderate. Or is he afraid of the truth? Gars in bed with a luscious Parisian. After only two nights? It must be the director or another associate working late, maybe practicing lines.

True, he slept with Gars on night one. But that was love at first sight for both of them. Then again, everyone falls in love with Gars, and who wouldn't fall in love with that husky French voice in the background? He visualizes a scene in black and white, smoke curling between them. Gars hates cigarettes.

He looks down the street. He's probably covered a swift mile during his anxious ruminations. Bed and breakfasts, private homes, T-shirt shops, bars, restaurants. He's sick of humanity right now, but it's stupid not to ask directions. He comes to the intersection at Fleming Street and sees the Old Island Bookstore a block away. Book people are nice people, and the lights are on.

"Crossroads Café," the woman at the cash register tells him, "The only one still in business." It's on Truman and Simonton, about half a mile south. She points in the direction he's just come. He lets out a deflated breath, and she looks at him with sympathy, reading his mind. His chest is soaked and his hair is dripping sweat into his eyes. A desperate gay man with romance problems. Probably a dime a dozen in Key West.

He types out an email, *sorry* and *love* many times, a detailed excuse about how he was working so hard in the basement, and "one of the fucking Ushers stole my phone!" It looks paranoid in print. <delete>. He doesn't say that he'll be getting home tomorrow. He's not sure what he should do. His options might have narrowed.

He goes straight to the pool area of the mansion. Roderick is lounging in a thick terrycloth robe on a deck chair, sipping what looks like scotch on the rocks and gazing out to sea. Pink-edged clouds mound over turquoise water, reflecting sunset from the other side of the house.

"Quite a sky, wouldn't you say? We celebrate it every evening." Roderick takes a deep, pleasurable breath. "Raining in town?"

August bites his lip. "Do you have a phone I can borrow? Mine disappeared."

"Disappeared? Really? I don't know where mine is either."

"Really?"

"I haven't seen it since the party. I'm assuming it will turn up."

"I can't reach my partner. I'm sure he's worried."

"You can use my computer to email. Up in my room on the north side. The WIFI works there. We'll get WIFI in your room by tomorrow. But have a drink first."

August explains that it's after midnight in Paris, and he already sent an email, but promised to talk to Gars tonight. He realizes he isn't hiding his anguish.

"I'm so sorry, sweetie. I don't know what to tell you." He sends Roget for a scotch for August. "It's just us tonight. Maddy went off with that stripper. How about a dip? You look frazzled."

"Stripper?" August flops into a chair like a rag doll.

"Whatever. Lenore."

The pool sounds good, but he knows Roderick will toss off the robe, and he's not going to join him naked. "We'd better talk about the house. I won't have time in the morning." He explains his theory of improper loading and foundation weathering and recommends the use of pillars and poured concrete with a water seal.

"You need a structural engineer to get an estimate, but be aware" — he grabs for a figure to see if Roderick will startle. "It could easily cost over a hundred thousand just to make it safe. There are always surprises with a place like this."

Roderick laughs. "You're finally getting it." He shakes his head. "But fixing isn't an option. I haven't explained the real problem." He points to the ocean. The three-story shadow of the house floats like a dark curtain. "That shadow has to go."

"Huh?"

"Of course, construction can fix the foundation and ceiling — poured concrete and whatever — but that won't fix *us*. It might even make the problem worse."

"Fix *us*?"

"Maddy and me. We are the House of Usher, the only Ushers left, and our lives are connected to the house. We should have had children together to continue the line, but we decided against it."

August leans forward. "Children? You with Maddy?" His upper lip curls.

"Let's not dwell on it. I knew I would have to admit it, sooner or later. The Usher family is incestuous. That's the root of all our problems, the evil."

Realizing his mouth is hanging open, August closes it.

"It goes way beyond the medical — nevertheless, the shadow of the house depresses us, or I should say, his reflection in the water, depresses our immune systems and creates disease that has aged us and will soon kill us. His shadow blocks any healing counter-power. Far worse than AIDS." He pauses, looking hard into August's eyes. "Sometime I'll explain in more detail, but what's important is that the entire east wing must be made of glass — in a hurry."

"Glass?"

"All the way around. And a glass ceiling to let in the heavens. Light must pass completely through. No reflection and no solid shadow can be cast by the building or its contents." He puts his hand on August's forearm. "Reflection creates symmetry. That's what's killing this family. We have to break the symmetry."

August looks at the wing and feels the enormity and the insanity of such a project. He knows little about light refraction. Is it even possible under the laws of nature? There's really nothing to discuss. "What about plumbing, electrical, interior walls? Also, it would have to be detached from the rest of the house."

"That's no problem. We've done some thinking on this. We need to modernize. The guest rooms would have to go, and upstairs plumbing, but we don't need those. We're thinking a forty-foot atrium with a two-story chandelier of clear crystal droplets at its center, something to break up the light into tiny, joyous sparkles. Glass stairs leading to a second floor with a couple of lofts — we might need to sleep there. We'll experiment to see how much habitation is required for our health. We'll have glass chairs where we can relax and view the sunset. Our bodies must be the only form of matter that light can't penetrate."

"Not possible. There has to be a floor line. You'll need ducts for AC and the electrical wiring would have to be —"

"Maybe 90 percent without shadow will do. I'm not sure. I'll have to figure out just what we can get away with once we're in there. Trial and error. It's up to you how to make it work. You're the artist. You'd better put in windows that open, in case we can't do air conditioning. If we can't have lights or bathrooms, then we'll do without. The rest of the house can provide those necessities."

"Trial and error in architecture is disastrously expensive." No hardware? What kind of fastening materials are translucent? "You'll have to give me more detailed specifications." A flicker of excitement builds as he recollects photos of glass skyscrapers and the pyramidal roof of the Louvre, but this is nuts. Maybe glass panels could slide on a base. Architectural glass has always been magic for him, but it's impossible. The expense, the risk. "It'd be a greenhouse in this climate. And we'd never get permits."

"I have friends where I need them. Friends I know very well." Roderick winks and pokes an elbow. "No worries."

"The cost will be in the millions, ten million? I'm guessing wildly. I don't even know what can be done or how to do it. It will take months just to —"

"Oh, no. It can't take that long. We'll never last."

"Rod, you're asking for a miracle. I can put together a design-build team, but even then, the planning will take — a year? Even if we simplify, down to the basics. There's nothing standard here. Normally, you start with a floor, four walls, and a roof."

Roderick starts to speak and August puts his hand up. "It can't work. A contemporary glass building won't fit with the aesthetic language of the west wing — the gingerbread trim and Victorian porches and turrets. Not to mention, the style of the neighborhood. It would be an outrageous misfit." As he says the word *outrageous*, he knows he's hit the button. There's no going back. Everything about Roderick is outrageous. He thrives on it.

"That's why I need an architect who's a genius as well as an artist. You, Augie. You'll make it work. I'm so excited to see your conception — I'm orgasmic."

"No way! Let's say it's ten million — you'd need to come up with 20% in a few months, just for the schematics. That's two million for starters."

"I can get the money. Cash? August, this is life and death for me and Maddy."

August has a flash vision of rounded seed-glass panels that slide within one another, and detached wrought iron shades that can be mechanically raised or lowered, a contemporary-Victorian blend. Steam punk architecture. Monetary and personal rewards... fame? Gars would get a kick out of that. The fantasy dissolves. The knife lodges again into his stomach.

"Fuck! Roderick, it's impossible!"

Roderick's eyes well up. "You won't even think about it?"

"Listen! I can't do fuck till I get my phone back —"

"Then there's a chance you'll do this?"

"No. I doubt it. It's impossible in less than two years, even with permits, a super design-build team, and unlimited funds."

"Get me the best guys there are. Let's build as much as we can in six months. If we have to cut it down to size, that's fine."

"We'd need to make size decisions up front."

Roderick flings out his arms. "We'll do it!"

"We need to work on the foundation before there's a collapse."

Chapter 11

A Whopping Mistake

The lobsters are saucy, spicy, and delicious. August wouldn't have dared pair Chianti with white flesh, but it's a scrumptious combination. He'll have to tell Gars... He heads upstairs, having had too much to drink again. He checks his watch. Six a.m. in Paris. He would call if he had a phone. He imagines slender fingers stroking Gars' cheek and running through his curls... a morning wake up. Stop.

He showers and falls into bed. Nothing can keep him awake on this night.

He lifts his head and glances at the clock on the nightstand. Three a.m. Something woke him, a noise in his dream, or a crack. He hears it again and sits up. A crack — from directly below. He slips on his robe and opens the door. Roderick and Madeline are a wing away. He walks barefoot down the hall. A louder rip. He runs down the stairs, half afraid the floor will fall in, half hoping to see a fissure in action in the ballroom.

He hears a sound behind him and glances back. Madeline on the landing. Cheshire cat smile. He runs the last flight and dashes across the hall and into the ballroom, searching the wall for a light switch. The room floods with the blinding glow of six chandeliers. His eyes adjust and he focuses on the far end, the area directly under his bedroom. There's a fissure, ceiling to floor, a coat of dust on the tile. He walks slowly, his eyes on the ceiling, expecting more damage to come. There, on the floor in the corner, is his cell phone, covered with plaster dust, flat on its back under the widest part of the fissure, in a beam of moonlight from an adjacent window. A shiver rolls from his skull to his toes. With a little imagination, the crack could be seen as a jagged arrow, pointing to the phone. Like the house coughed it up and wanted him to know it.

Roderick's insanity must be contagious. August can't recall being at the far end of the ballroom after the party, except to look for his cell. Maybe Roderick put it in the corner and somehow started the crack to convince him of urgency. But how? It's impossible. Or Madeline could have been down there when the cracking began and planted the phone to scare him. The reason she was watching him. They would do anything to convince him of their crazy stories. They did something. He's sure of it. Not the damn house.

He checks his phone for messages. None. Missed calls and voicemails could have been deleted. Would they go that far? The smart thing to do would be to head straight out the front door. It's quarter after nine in the morning in Paris. He dials, feeling the blood tingle in his chest. There's no answer. He's waiting for the beep, trying to compose his thoughts when Roderick comes sprinting across the room, black satin robe flying open, showcasing his bouncing pink cock.

"What a mess! *He's* in a snit these days."

August ends the call. "*He*? Oh. You heard it all the way from the other wing?"

"Hell, yes." He cups his mouth. "He's never done this before, outside of parties."

"Did you set my phone down there? On the floor under the crack?"

"What?" Roderick straightens his back and ties his sash. "Really? Why would I put your phone on the floor?"

"You would love it if Garo broke up with me!"

"Who?"

"C'mon, Roderick. My partner."

"No. I'm insulted you'd think that." He scowls and looks up and down the crack. "This event might not be over. Let's get some wine and take it into the other wing, the library, where it's safe — safer. We need to talk. I doubt either of us can sleep anyway."

August gives up. "You're right about that." He can barely think now, his mind paralyzed, focused on Garo not answering.

Roderick picks out Baccarat stemware and leads the way to the wine rack. He chooses a pinot noir and a cabernet and holds them out for approval. August reads the labels and shrugs.

"We'll take them both then."

In the library, Roderick flips on a Tiffany floor lamp and opens the wine. August moves to the corner and redials Garo. The call goes through, but voicemail picks up. "Please, call me, Gars. I have so much to explain. I'm so sorry. I love you."

Roderick pours August a full glass of cabernet. "Drink up. You don't want to hear all of this sober." He takes a book with him from the shelf and sits on the end of the leather sofa and pulls up his legs. The cavern of the robe opens to a few inches of darkness inside. He sips his wine.

August takes the chair opposite. He gulps a mouthful. Another. He should tell Roderick to shove it.

Roderick points to the book. "This is my treatise on some important tenets of Swedenborgianism. I believe you read parts of it in its infancy, but I never told you why I'm interested in his philosophy — its connections with my life."

August drinks and nods. He has a terrible intuition that he's lost Garo, or is about to. He needs to get this huge project in the bag, have something to show for his time. But it might be too late.

"It was my great, great grandfather's religion, but nobody else in the family believed in it except...."

Roderick's words drone in the background, behind thoughts of Garo, hurting Gars' feelings... losing his trust.

"... our love for animals. You know Swedenborg believed that animals are reflections of God's love and exist in heaven, that everything in nature reflects a higher universe, what people often refer to as God. Would you rather curl up and go to sleep, August?"

"Gars isn't answering. It's all I can think about."

"I'm sure everything's fine."

"He can have anybody. I don't know how I managed to hang on this long. Last week I made a huge stink about keeping in touch every day, and then my phone disappeared." He stares at Roderick to see if there's any reaction. Roderick stares back.

"He couldn't reach me. He must think... I don't know. That I haven't given him a thought. Or I'm back together with you."

"I could only wish for such a miracle."

"I bet they're all trying to devour him — men and women both."

"He's bi?"

"No. I don't think so. I mean, I'm sure he's not. But he loves women, and they fall instantly in love with him. He's worshipped."

"That unconscious charisma thing. You and I can only observe and feel its heat."

August looks at him. "You're right, damn it. He doesn't appreciate it. He was born with the whole world wanting to eat him up." He takes a long drink, drains his glass.

Roderick is quick with the refill. "Birth. The seat of all serious assets and defects. Nobody knows as well as I do. Except Madeline. We Ushers have hereditary diseases, multiplied and strengthened over two centuries. That's what I need to explain. The corruption of my great, great, great grandparents, inbreeding all down the line, has brought us to the point of spiritual and bodily disintegration."

He hasn't completely caught what Roderick is saying. "What? Seriously?"

Roderick dumps the bottle, turning it upright into his own glass. "Maddy and I are the end of the line, thank god. We haven't borne any children, despite the dictates of Dad and Auntie or Mom and Uncle — whatever you want to call them." His dry chuckle turns into a snort. "I can't keep them straight myself. We've added no incestuous offspring, with a little help from birth control." His wild laugh rips through the room, edging on hysteria.

August is thrown, the talk of incest outweighed by the idea of

Roderick and Madeline, using birth control with each other to avoid pregnancies.

"We've pursued lives of pleasure, you know, thinking we could beat the debilitating evil, or accept death when we were too old to enjoy our bodily pleasures. Until now. We're still young, and there's no time left. The demonic House of Usher is collapsing, committing suicide and perhaps murder. The grand old name and the family's birthplace — its living, rotting fungus — enshrouds us."

August takes a long drink. It sounds like justice, centuries in the making, but not deserved by Roderick and Madeline.

"I don't care about the family name or the house. I just want to live! Do you blame me?"

"Not for wanting to live. Of course not." It's clear now. Insanity by way of heredity.

"Maddy and I are physically connected to the house, and he's going down fast, taking us along with a vengeance." He opens the book and flips to a chapter in the middle. "All explained in here, how it works. 'Evil seeks evil and creates more evil. The collocation of the stones, the shape, the materials, they work together in a pattern of destructive energy.'" He moves his fingers as if feeling something in the air. His eyes almost seem to glow. "The stones absorb and reflect the evil created by centuries of Ushers. Not our evil — maybe a tad — but fault has nothing to do with it at this point. We are the final fruits." He hands August the book, pointing to a paragraph. "In a nutshell..."

August takes it and reads. Reads it again, trying to concentrate. His eyes are blurry. "Sentience in inanimate objects." He fumbles, turning the page. Roderick grabs the book as if from a child who might do damage.

"Yes, please, Roderick. Another time."

"He's sentient. That means he can learn. There are no homologies, like hands or opposable thumbs, so we can't expect his brain to function like a human's. But he's learned what's crucial for his existence. He's specialized." Roderick sets the book gently on the table and reaches over to touch August's knee. "You know, of course, as an architect, that form creates function and meaning. Maddy and I are the results of prurient construction, genes and stones repeated and reflected like mirrors within mirrors, from the roots of greed and pride. We are the scapegoats, or maybe the sacrificial lambs, depending... The dregs of evil have rooted in us."

"I'm sorry. I know this is terrible, but you're wasting your words on me right now. I need a clear head for this." He tries to get up. Sits back down. His legs are loose.

"I posit that evil is the precipitate of a chemical reaction between time and human frailty." Roderick stands and takes him by the shoulders, "You can't destroy energy, and you only lose a little when you reroute it. We'll preserve the lower foundation, as you advise, allowing the residual energy to circulate in a closed system. I can show you the formulas and the math model demonstrating how generations of reflected energy have created powerful sentience. This is how *he* was born. Matter gave rise to consciousness. If the mirror is broken, the power can't increase. We'll remain attached to our core, but we'll be safe."

August rouses himself. "But — why stay here? You could live in Manhattan. You had important work, a following."

"Tell me about it." Roderick opens the second bottle and pours both of them another glass. He sits down and shakes his head. "The first time the house cracked, I tried desperately to leave, just like great, great, great granddad. I knew about his problems, but I thought I could beat it all. When I went to New York I was testing. I had hope. For a while I felt fine — wonderful. Remember. We made plans — oh, god, it was bliss." He sweeps tears from his eyes.

"Sure, I remember." He could never forget the hurt and humiliation afterward. "Your book, great reviews — parties, lavish dinners. I was so proud to be with you. Then you disappeared... not a word. I checked hospitals, called the police." Anger rushes over him. "It took a week for me to realize..."

"Dear August... I was sick — I couldn't explain."

"You just plain dumped me."

"For god's sake, I didn't want to. I thought it might affect you too, if you knew about it — psychological contagion — but I've ruled that out. At the time, I even wondered if sexual transmission was possible. I was in total panic when I realized I had carried the disease with me."

"How do you *know* it's not contagious?"

"To my knowledge, no one outside the family has ever contracted it, but I think the great grands isolated themselves because of that fear. A vicious cycle."

It's bizarre, but he's beginning to understand. "That's horrible. But you should have told me."

"I couldn't — nor let you see me going down. I already had insecurities, being older. One morning I woke up with two loose teeth. Then a clump of hair fell out. Remember the last time you saw me? I was wearing that baseball cap — Mets."

August remembers. It was odd.

"I knew I couldn't keep it from you for long. Every sound was a roar in my ears, and the lightest touch made my skin prickle. Sunshine blinded me." He looks down. "I couldn't even get hard." He shudders. "I needed the power of the house. I had to return to stay alive. Maddy was down here suffering his wrath in lesser ways, begging me to come home.

"When you returned, everything got better?" August slugs the rest of his wine and sets the glass down on the Persian rug. He sees that his robe has fallen open on his thigh, but lifting a hand to fix it isn't worth the effort.

"Not altogether. I have sensitivities, painful at times, and tooth problems, and there was a need for some surgery and hair plugs — anxiety drugs for both of us. But we thought we'd be fine if we stayed here. Now everything is getting worse fast."

"The house is mutilating itself so you'll fix it?"

"I'd call it murder-suicide. If he goes, we go, and that's where we're headed. If I'm correct, there's no real human intellect, no decision-making. It's more like... a chain reaction." He bends forward and whispers into August's ear, making it tingle. "*He* doesn't 'know' I have a plan to make him powerless. I don't think he can understand words or use reason. He absorbs feelings from us and reacts." Roderick looks around the room. "I'm fairly certain this part of the house is not involved, only the wing with the original foundation. But I'm not one hundred percent sure of any of this."

August holds back comment. It's nuts.

Roderick squats in front of him, puts his cheek on August's bare thigh. His voice is child-like. "You are my true love, even though I'm not yours. If we work together you can save me and Maddy."

August touches the top of Roderick's head, his wispy hair, trying not to think *hair plugs*. Roderick, a desperate soul in need of comfort. He once worshipped him. If working on the house will help him regain mental stability, that's a worthy purpose by itself. Garo might already be gone from his life. He'd have no reason to hurry back. The knife twists in his guts.

"Please, August. I know this will work! You'll make a fortune, and Maddy and I will live and love for many more years." He tilts his head, looking into August's eyes. "Now that you've broken off with —"

"I haven't! Why would you say that? I just feel — everything's gone crazy —"

"Intuition rules in matters of the heart." Roderick's hand opens August's sash.

He stiffens, but doesn't move. Cool air wakens his cock.

"Don't pass up this chance." Roderick's fingers trickle up his thigh.

August pushes the hand away a few inches. Roderick is poised on his knees, his soft lips open, nostrils slightly flared. Does it matter? The fantasy of Gars is over. The familiarity of Roderick's touch goes deep, the grip of old emotion. Soothes, arouses...

Roderick bends closer and looks up into August's eyes. Inertia decides the rest. The wet warmth of Roderick's mouth locks onto the only part of him that August can still feel.

Chapter 12

Guilt Closes the Deal

The morning sun is an axe through his skull. His first thought is a rock in his stomach. He moves his eyes sideways and sees his wallet on the dresser. Thank god, he made it back to his room. He reaches for his cell. A text came in late, probably while he was drinking the second bottle of wine with Roderick, maybe exact timing... God, he can't believe he did that. A hot sweat breaks out on his chest.

Gars says to give him a call. No *please* or *love*. It's over, a Frenchman between them, finalized by his betrayal with Roderick. It's like something subconscious has sabotaged the relationship. Garo will tell the truth, and he can't lie to Garo. He's not good enough for Garo, will never be in his league, a simple fact.

The Usher walls are thick, old-fashioned plaster, and he rolls over and lets himself sob until the peaks level off. There's no place to go after that, back to painful reality, worse than unleashed anguish, a gut full of lead, unending.

When he wakes up, it's nearly eleven. His scheduled flight would have left. He doesn't want to live. He's still nauseous. Key West has dragged him into the mire. Or Roderick — or himself. In the shower, he lets tears flow until they stop. When he can talk without crying, he'll call to arrange getting his things. Not yet.

The hope of croissants and coffee still on the sideboard moves him to the stairs. After breakfast, he'll bury himself in research. The glass addition is either ridiculous or the challenge of a lifetime. He's not afraid of failure. He's become used to it, on a smaller scale. With a project like this, whether he's ridiculed or lauded — and there's always both — his reputation will go national, maybe international. He thinks of the Al Bahr Towers in Abu Dhabi, steel and glass phallic structures that blend local culture with technical advancement. The Blue Planet in Denmark... The Heydar Aliyev Center — where is that? He's headed off the deep end. Get a grip. The property size poses strict limitations, and Roderick can't compete with Arab oil money. But artistry can rival scale — the *Mona Lisa.*

Why not Victorian turrets and bay windows, steel gingerbread melding stylized asymmetry with contemporary flash and function? Mechanical shifting to allow light penetration and the creation of light at angles to offset shadows. He considers the use of Silverberg's electrostatic blinds throughout the interior, daylight round-the-clock automatic adjustment to prevent shadows. And solar-vacuum cooling? He's never had the chance to think big. It's a wild dream. He's been told he's got what it takes. Of course, he still doesn't believe it, but that won't stop him.

Roderick is at the table with Madeline when August walks into the dining room. Roderick looks triumphant. "Ah, our guest has arisen!"

"Back from the dead? Not a chance." He lowers his head and takes a bread plate to the sideboard. Again, it's piled high with goodies. "I haven't slept this late since..." He shakes his head, remembering exactly when — the first night he spent with Garo.

"I was just telling Maddy that you'll be staying here and starting our project."

He works at sounding chipper. "Yep. First thing, I need to make some contacts. Find an engineer to do the repairs on the foundation before we start talking about building an entire glass wing."

"Glass wing?" Madeline sounds startled.

"Yes. I told Augie all about it."

August looks at Maddy. "The demolition alone —"

Roderick drops his knife. "This decision can't be based on money. I told you. We need new construction."

"Last night... I had too much wine. Way too much." He bites off a mouthful of buttery croissant and swigs his coffee. "An architectural masterpiece like you want — we're talking many millions."

"So you said."

Madeline wipes her fingers on a napkin. She winks at August. "Realism isn't Roderick's strong suite."

Roderick flashes her a look. "Runs in the family. But, of course, we need figures before we go ahead."

"There are many impossible problems, without delving further. Even if the money is available." He points to the heavy drapes that are nearly closed, blocking the view of the ocean. "You seem to like it dark. Glass walls?"

"That's a symptom. It will improve quickly when the house is fixed, along with my sensitivities to certain sounds and textures. Maddy will stop going comatose, too."

"I wasn't aware —"

"Let me explain a few more details. The wing will be an energy demagnetization chamber. It will work to disperse the diseased molecules that have emanated from the foundation for generations into the miasma of the House of Usher. With the new glass, the accumulation of diseased particles will be released harmlessly over the ocean. It's the only possible solution to thwart the entropy threatening us."

"You're saying... uh, the foundation magnetizes molecules inside you and makes you sick?"

"Sort of. I'm speaking metaphorically. It's not the kind of magnetism that you know. Yes, everything is interconnected. But I had a lot of wine myself last night. We can downsize and get the same effect."

"Ho, hum" comes from Madeline across the table.

August shakes his head. He can't buy into the craziness. "I'll go ahead with the estimate for shoring up the foundation and sealing. It has to be done. You can't build anything on what you've got there. We can talk more later. I need the twenty percent though."

Roderick tosses back the last of a mimosa. "Look, Augie.

There's no time for all that repair. Demolition will be free if we don't get started!"

Maddy's chair screeches as she pushes it out. Her face is flushed. "Tonight is the Pet Parade. I need to finish up my costume. I hope you boys can spare some time to cheer for us."

August realizes what staying with the Ushers will entail. "Sure."

"Excuse me." Roderick heads in Maddy's direction, moving her along, and they have a sharp, whispered argument in the hall.

August finishes his coffee and pours more. He hadn't expected to need his laptop with all the software. He has the measurements on his notebook computer, but he'll want all his other gear, if he's really going to do this. More clothing. He'd better start a list. What the hell has he gotten into? He checks his pocket for the second time, always worried his cell phone will go missing. The mystery will likely never be solved.

Roderick returns with a hand behind his back. He bows and presents a check.

"I can't accept this. I don't know enough yet to set up a renovation contract. I need hard numbers."

"I trust you. Just put it in as a down payment on the foundation repair. We'll work it out. Consider it as assurance of plenty more to come. I don't have it all liquid right now, but I can get whatever it takes. I told you, there's no time."

August looks at the check. One million dollars. A local Chase Bank. He uses Chase in the city. He's breathless. "You really want to go ahead without a solid contract?"

"More than anything! It's only money. I'm trusting you with my life."

"You have my word then. I'll do my best to get the renovations underway." He doesn't feel right about it, but Roderick's face shines with hope. He puts out his hand, and Roderick grabs it so eagerly that he wants to renege instantly. But he won't. It's time he takes a big step. He'll never make a name for himself without risk, and what better cause than a desperate man's relief?

"Chase is right down the street. No need for a taxi."

August guesses that the Ushers live without a car, like New Yorkers. Is it because parking is scarce, or are they too ill to drive? He walks alongside Roderick to the bank, in and out of hot sun and blasts of cool air from open shop doors, dodging the reach of thorny, lovely, fuchsia-tipped branches in residential areas. The sway of feathery palm fronds against blue sky could become relaxing, might be paradise under the right circumstances.

The bank transaction is surprisingly smooth. In five business days the money will appear in his account. Real bank, real teller, but too easy. He needs to learn to ignore those feelings.

When they get back to the house, he makes a fast escape to the library, where he's told the WIFI now functions. He stops himself from calling Garo. Still not ready.

He opens his laptop, not sure where to start. It dawns on him that what he's doing is not completely ethical. If he should die unexpectedly or fall into a coma, Roderick's money will be unprotected. He sets up a simple contract with the amount and a guarantee to continue work until the funds have been spent, and if the renovation project cannot be started for any reason, the unspent portion returned. He feels satisfied with that until he can work up all the details. Of course, there's no printer. Another thing he needs to ship from home or buy.

Work-mode kicks in, and he starts churning out specifications for concrete and sealer. He considers calling the finest structural guy he knows, but the wait is bound to be long. He reaches a young, competent, enthusiastic engineer that he's worked with on small jobs. The guy is eager to give an estimate for the foundation work based on August's measurements. They set up a meeting at the site for the following Tuesday. He'll send approximate figures in advance.

Getting people who would join a design team for the full renovation would be much trickier. Good luck finding skilled people out of work, like himself. Nevertheless, August can't stop thinking about it.

Chapter 13

Less than Transparent Activity

Roderick opens the heavy drapes a crack and squints, scanning the pool and grounds. Madeline yawns aloud from her chair at the other end of the table, irritated by his constant agitation. She stretches and pokes at the plate of cucumber slices, carrot sticks, and celery. "I'm not even hungry."

Roderick closes the drapes. "Wonder where Augie is today. I don't think he ate breakfast. Now, skipping lunch?"

"Your little playmate wouldn't run off without telling you."

"Playmate, funny. He deposited my check. Just hope he's feeling okay."

She sits up straight. "You mean *our* check? *We* gave him a check?"

"I handle the finances, but sure — *our* check."

"How m —?"

"I told you! I had to win his confidence."

She's out of her chair, inches from his face, pointing a carrot stick. "How mu —?"

"A cool million. Like it or lump it."

She slumps against the sideboard and bites the carrot. "Christ!" She pauses and chews. "You can't be fucking serious."

"This kind of work doesn't come cheap. The million is just a start."

"Asshole! It's useless! What's your plan? We're mostly living off interest. We must've taken a major hit in penalties. Son of a bitch!"

"Mads, we won't need it if we're dead!" He takes a breath. "Listen. I know what I'm doing. There's still property in merry old England. Why keep it? We're the last of the tribe. I hear from our well-traveled friends that Cornwall is thriving. People watch these TV series filmed, maybe, thirty kilometers from our property and they travel there — *Poldark* and *Doc Martin.* Shows on the internet."

"Oh, yeah?"

"It's all the rage — location vacations. Our timing is perfect. Ooh, and some priest detective thing, *Grantchester.* That one's in Cambridge. We own property there, too — a small castle. It would make a fantastic bed and breakfast."

"We can't do that." Madeline shakes her head. "What are you talking about?" She'd like to smack him silly. He's got to be making this up. "Fuck. If there's property — a castle — why don't I know about it? Why haven't we dumped it? You need to show me those deeds."

"We haven't needed to sell. The lawyer has all that stuff. I'll get him over here beginning of the week. Let's invite him for drinks."

"Fine, Bro. Get some cheap stuff — Smirnoff."

"Oh, stop it." He clicks his tongue. "By the way, how did Augie's phone wind up on the ballroom floor in a heap of plaster?" He winks. "Pretty clever."

"His cell! I forgot about it. I set it on the corner table..."

Roderick looks up at the ceiling. "Oh, then it was *him.* I thought so."

"You're giving *him* too much fucking credit. Probably vibrated off. What would it mean anyway? Mr. Evil House wants Augie to be happy, so he returned his phone?"

"Quit mocking me. I can think of a few reasonable interpretations. For instance, he figured August would get scared and go home to Garo, and there'd be no one to do the renovations. Or, he's jealous of my attraction to Augie and wants to scare him off. On a simpler level, he's against anything we want."

To her it's all nuts. "You're saying *he* can see, hear, and reason, and has emotions. Not to mention, he's fucking in love with you?"

"I just threw that in. Emotions, maybe, absorbed from us. I don't think he can hear — or see." He looks around. "I don't believe he has any abilities on this side of the house. In the east wing, the root of his power, he could be siphoning from my overly acute senses. He's telepathically connected to both of us, like we are to each other."

"You never mentioned this."

"We are the House of Usher, extensions of the whole, as Mother reminded us on many occasions. That's why we sicken and die if we stray too far, like sprouts on a root, deprived of nourishment when severed."

She runs her tongue over her replacement implants. "Sprouts sometimes become independent plants. It's a means of procreation."

"If we ever had the option to thrive autonomously, it's gone now."

"Says who? This is all your newest theory?"

"There was no need to scare you — till now."

"You take dear old Mama too literally. She meant we should behave ourselves, be proper Ushers."

"What is a proper Usher? For god's sake." Roderick turns his back, looking up at the largest gargoyle in the room. "*He's* powerful, but no genius. And he can't connect to August's thoughts. With August on our side, we're one up on him." He faces her to show his smug look and nods repeatedly, as if emphasis will convince her.

She squints at the devious gargoyle face looking down from above him. The figures with their open mouths freaked her out when she was little. A different face peers from each cornice, but only this particular one has a sense of humor. "We better stop thinking about this shit if he's reading our minds."

"Only in the east wing. Is this your way of ending the discussion?"

"Just saying, in case he *can* hear in here, no more inside discussions about you-know-what."

"You mean the *an-play*," Roderick says, deadpan.

"Yeah, Bro, that." She stifles a laugh. Snorts. "Think *he* knows *ig-pay atin-Lay*?"

"Maybe *atin-Lay*. Lots of it is chiseled into marble..." He breaks into a giggle, the sound dribbling into wheezing, then a cough. "How in hell are we going to keep from thinking about it?"

"I would never give your idiotic *an-play* a thought." She angles her face toward the most cynical gargoyle and speaks in a stage whisper: "Renovations won't work, and we can't fucking afford them anyway."

Roderick winks. "You're right. I must have been high to think we could get that kind of money."

"You're always high!" She snorts loudly and pops a cuke slice into her mouth, starting down the hall. If valuable property exists, the deeds should be looked at in the law office downtown, just in case. Stop thinking! Stop thinking! She laughs.

Chapter 14

One More Chance

August notices it's nearly five. He's skipped lunch. His eyes are watering from concentrating on the screen. He hasn't thought of Garo till now, but the pain is instant. He backs up the files on his flash drive and reaches for his cell. He hadn't realized the draw of warm weather in Florida as the Northeast slides into early winter. He's gotten important call-backs on the foundation renovation, and by dropping casual mentions, some interest that makes him believe it might be possible to put together a design-build team, if he were ever to consider something that crazy. The right amount of available money can work miracles. But he hasn't revealed any of the outlandish factors, and there's no timetable that would suit Roderick.

He's at a dead end on everything without his software. With money, an expensive last-minute flight isn't a problem. Also, a great excuse for missing the Fantasy Fest debacle on the weekend. Of course, Garo won't be back home, not a chance. He Googles flights and gets the earliest one for the next morning. It will take an extra two hours, making a connection in Miami, but he'll have lunch, check out the gift stores, be home by afternoon.

He looks at the time. A parade of pets is not his choice for spending the evening, but he doesn't want to disappoint Madeline, especially now that he'll be seeing her daily. He'll need to set some parameters on socializing, or rent a place, if this stay is going to be long-term. Fuck all of it, if only he could go back home to Gars.

He checks his cell. WIFI working, but nothing new. He texts about the phone and how sorry he is, then deletes it and starts over. Guilt smolders in his stomach. Ten p.m. in Paris. It's been over four days since they've talked, too much and too long to pick up where they left off. But he has news to share. Before he can think too much, he presses the call button. His breath catches.

"Augie. Are you okay? What's happened?"

"I'm sorry. I need to start by apologizing for not calling or answering your text. I'm sorry. I'm so sorry."

"I am too. I got your voicemail, but I... gave up..."

"Do you have time to talk?"

"Nothing could be as important as us talking."

August tells the story of his missing phone, and all he went through trying to call, running the streets and the bad connection on the lady's phone, luck being all against him, and how the house seemed to cough up the phone the next night. A mystery, although Roderick was bound to be behind it, a ruse to keep him there... but it doesn't matter. The project is real, and a million dollars is in his account. He gives a few details about the great people he's talked to and the crazy possibility of creating a work of art in Key West.

"Wow." There's reserve in the tone. "You could be talking international fame."

August pictures those dark eyes, wide and huge, when Garo is impressed. August could often impress him, somehow, but it was never deserved, till now, maybe.

"I understand why you didn't call the first three nights, but why not the next morning? I left three or four messages and texted about when I'd be available. Didn't you get those?"

August hears the hurt, and maybe, disbelief, and his stomach clenches. "God! None of those calls were logged on my phone — no voicemails, no texts. They must have been deleted. It's hard to believe he would lie... I don't know."

"I even checked the hospital down there."

"I'm so sorry. I would have called when I found the phone,

but I couldn't talk without crying. I thought you were finished with me. That you had some gorgeous Frenchman in your room —"

"No — just my producer... at that point."

August swallows hard. "Oh?"

"I was so hurt — and... Later, I got drunk."

August doesn't want details, not now... not ever. They'd both gone down the same path, except Garo's liaison had not involved a madman. Pain constricts August's throat, but he squeaks the words out. "I slept with Roderick. Not slept...." He wipes his eyes. "I was hurt, too, but I was an idiot for not trusting you." There's a pause. He's afraid to assume anything. "I'm so sorry. How can I make this up to you?"

There's a long exhale. "I don't know. Augie, we're both idiots. At least, we're honest. Maybe we can get past that — but now...

I signed a contract. I thought, why not? August isn't worried about me. So... I'll be staying in Paris for the next two months to shoot my scenes. Right up till Christmas Eve. Then I'll probably fly back here next year, depending."

August drops onto the bed. "I see."

"It's for a film, a feature film. Not the leading man, but a real role. I wanted to talk it out with you. I thought maybe you could join me. But then... everything fell apart. I couldn't keep them hanging."

"Your chance of a lifetime. You couldn't turn it down. I know."

"The same for both of us."

He shakes his head. "We're on parallel tracks — heading away from each other."

"Kind of strange."

"It doesn't have to be like that, does it? I have money now, Gars, just not much time. I could fly over for a weekend, to make up."

Silence. August holds his breath.

"Augie, our careers are important. I'm thinking we need to stop worrying about each other. A long-distance relationship with boundaries.... look how quick we fell apart. I know it was mostly bad luck, but there are a lot more things to accidentally go wrong. It's always hard work to get things right. The time change alone causes all sorts of problems. I don't want to be worried and feel hurt all the time, even if it turns out to be for no reason. Do you? Know what I mean?"

"I would choose that rather than losing you. Maybe we learned our lesson."

Gars doesn't respond.

"I learned mine." August tries to make his voice strong. "Okay. I think you've already made up your mind."

"Don't be like that. I haven't. If you won't agree, I don't know what to do. But I don't have time to travel now, and you, coming from Key West, when you figure in the flights and jet lag... Fuck, Augie. We've already gone through the worst part, the shock of distrust. Two months is nothing. We'll have a lot to talk about when this is over."

"For me, it's true love."

"Augie, you're my true love."

August knows there's no choice, and at any second somebody is likely to call Garo back to work. Without an agreement, indecision will become a decision. "We have to keep in touch. Friendly emails, once in a while, no personal questions. Just so I know you're still alive — if that's the way you want it."

"I think we should only email if there's something important. If we don't fall into a pattern, we won't be disappointed. We'll be mature. Right? Our love will keep growing. We have a strong foundation."

A strong foundation. One that doesn't wear away. No hidden cracks. August manages to agree. Is this just the easiest way for Garo to get his freedom? Let him down slowly? He can't hear any tears in Garo's voice, but he's always been in control of his emotions. August tries to sound matter of fact. "I need to fly home — to the apartment — to get some things."

"Sure. Take what you need till Christmas, and leave everything else in its place. That way I know you'll be back."

For the first time, he understands that Gars must have thought he purposely dropped out of sight. He's felt that pain, calling hospitals. It was partly his fault that Gars let his defenses down.

Gars says something about the film, but August misses it. Garo has to hang up, and August tells him he loves him. Garo's "I love you" is distracted.

He wipes sweat off his face. Sweat and tears. Who can tell the difference in this climate? He scrolls back through his missed calls, Tuesday, Monday. Nothing from Garo, no voicemails. Why didn't they show up as soon as there was a WIFI connection? Garo has never lied. Having no security code was a symbol of trust between them. You're not in Kansas anymore, Dorothy. He goes to security settings and inputs a code. Yep, lock the barn door after the horse...

Chapter 15

Fitting In

There's a knock. "Yeah." The heavy door creaks open a bit. He notices for the first time that there's a grumpy face carved in the middle, more like... demonic. Roderick peeks in.

"Rod, I appreciate the knock, but you don't have to."

"That's the first time you called me Rod." He winks. "You have your privacy here. How's it going?"

He looks back at the computer. "Too soon to give you details, but I have an engineer coming down. I'm flying out tomorrow morning to get my stuff, so I can be prepared to meet him here on Tuesday." He glances up at Roderick's face and prepares for an argument.

"Roderick clucks. "Too bad. You'll miss all the fun." He's staring at August. "Your eyes are solid red from that computer screen. Ready to go? Maddy's after me to get your butt to the Casa Marina."

He hits save. "Huh?"

"The hotel. The Pet Masquerade. Madeline still calls it the parade, but it's a big production now, with a stage and chairs. We can stop at Louie's Backyard and grab a drink on the way. You haven't seen any of Key West."

"Most of it was here, at your party."

"Only one tiny facet, my dear."

August shuts down the computer. Socialize? His body yearns to get fetal in a dark room.

"Louie's is right next to the Dog Beach. Get you in the mood. The dogs won't be in costume though — all nude." He slides behind August and massages his neck. "The Maddies will be upset if we don't show up to cheer for them. It's a clap-o-meter vote."

He realizes he's Roderick's default date. Or is it just politeness to invite a guest staying at the house? He dredges up a name. "Maybe Ivan would like to go with you."

"Ian? I don't want to get into a long explanation of that right now. It's... He's a great guy... kind of a party friend."

A face hard to look at in daylight. Such an unkind thought.

Roderick suggests shorts and a Hawaiian shirt for the evening festivities. "I figured your wardrobe was lacking in Key West casual so I stocked your closet with a few Tommy Bahamas and *guayaberas*."

"*Guayaberas*?"

"A Cuban style. A little dressier, and just as comfortable as Hawaiians."

"Really? Okay — thanks."

They meet in the entryway, August in his new shirt and shorts, looking forward to the drinks. Roderick is dressed in a long-sleeved, pink pastel shirt and white cotton pants, a wide-brimmed woven hat, and dark sunglasses with side pieces.

"Should I have a hat?"

"No, it's near sunset. I'm particularly sensitive, especially my eyes. But you need to get something for daytime." Roderick moves to August's right side as they walk. "I hope you don't mind. I've got my plug in."

"Plug?"

"Ear plug on the left. That's my most sensitive side. I have a high pain tolerance, but tonight I'll suffer from all the clapping." He bends forward and uses his hand to muffle a guffaw. "What kind of plug did you think?"

August looks around to see who might hear. "For god's sake, Roderick."

"Great idea!" He chuckles and gives him a little push. "They've got them in the shop window right around the corner, a variety of colors. Also, decorative *braguettes* — codpieces. Of course, as you well know, I can barely fit my cock into my pants as is."

August avoids Roderick's face and points to a placard. "Key lime pie. I'd like to try that."

Roderick ignores him.

At Louie's they take a table on the deck over the surf. Roderick orders martinis for both of them. The air is fresh and the water slaps against the pilings with a lazy rhythm. Heavy rain clouds are heaped above the horizon, blocking the sun. A cool breeze off the water. It's almost comfortable.

The martinis arrive and Roderick toasts the sunset, even though it's impossible to tell if the glow is near the horizon. He's in high spirits, chattering about how much fun the weekend of Fantasy Fest will be, more costumes, more parties.

Ugh. Not a chance. Whether Roderick's mood is due to romantic fantasies or confidence that August can save their lives, reality is lacking. He points to the *Dog Beach* sign next to the restaurant. There hasn't been a dog in sight. "The pooches must be home getting dressed up."

Roderick smiles, looking pleased and relaxed. "For sure."

"Madeline will take the cat in a taxi?"

Roderick nods. "She's got Maddy J. trained to sit on her shoulder — or the cat trained Maddy to let her sit there. She likes to suck on her earlobe. Should be a hit with the judges, two beautiful lesbian look-alikes."

"Funny. Maddy J., a lesbian kitty."

"In appearance... strictly speaking, neither is Madeline." He slurps his martini. "I'm glad when she finds projects that interest her. The less Lenore comes around, the better."

To August, there's a hint of jealousy. "Why don't you like her? She seems to care a lot for Maddy."

Roderick imbibes his martini in a gulp and motions for the check. "She's snoopy, and sort of, uh — low-class. Plus, a know-it-all and a butt-in-ski. Let's get going."

August leaves half his drink. Better to start slow with the mood he's in. Wasting part of a drink is guilt-free now that he has money, his new way of life.

The beach and patio of the Casa Marina are packed. A wagon

of pirate schnauzers cuts them off. Ballerina Chihuahuas follow. Multiple leashes make walking slow, and Roderick claps his hands and laughs like a happy kid every time a clever costume blocks their way. August composes a letter in his head to Gars for the umpteenth time, while managing to smile on cue.

A temporary platform, fringed with orange and black crepe paper, takes up most of the deck on the beach. Rows of folding chairs in the sand are filled with people waiting for the show to start. August looks at darkening clouds on the horizon, realizing it's already late night in Paris.

The palms wave their shadows on clean-raked sand bordering the glinting ocean, a postcard view of paradise, mostly illuminated by artificial light. He's hoping he won't see any of the people from the party, or if so, they don't recognize him. He can't remember anyone but Ian and Lenore. A man with a ferret on his shoulder walks by. Roderick purses his lips as if to kiss it.

Ian is heading toward them. "Here comes your ape friend."

"Ian? He's rarely out before dark." He waves his arm above his head. "Ian!"

August swallows and tries to make his face welcoming. The plastic bumps under Ian's skin look like huge pustules dying to be popped.

"I don't think you two really met," Roderick says. "Ian, this is August, a genius architect from the city. He's down here to build us a new wing — replace those cracked walls."

Sweat drips from Ian's chin. His T-shirt has soaked through at the neckline and arm pits. "Hi, there. Nice to see you again." He puts out a hot, sticky hand.

August takes it and nods. "Roderick flatters me."

"He flatters everyone. That's why we like him so much." He winks at Roderick and looks back at August. "I bought an island a few weeks ago. Maybe you can help me with some ideas for developing it. I always take Rod's recommendations seriously."

"Yes!" Roderick throws up his hands in a silly-me gesture. "I forgot. Your new island. Perfect. You plan to have a bed and breakfast, right?"

"A hotel with diving rooms for each suite — so you can scuba dive from inside. Private, no need for a bathing suit."

"Ah." August attempts a smile. "Exposing naked flesh to sea creatures?"

Ian laughs, seeming to think he's joking. "There's a place like that in Largo, but I'll go a lot bigger, fancier."

"Sounds tricky with tides and currents —"

Rod flashes August a look. "That's why Ian needs the best."

Roderick grabs August's arm, pulling him to the side. "Look out!"

A Jack Russell in a polka-dot bikini dashes past, followed by a six-foot, fully-feathered green parrot. Not a close call. Roderick's sense of humor. The parrot bends down and grabs the leash for a woman in a bikini matching the terrier's. She's out of breath from trying to keep up the dog's pace in her high heels.

Roderick whispers in August's ear. "Call Ian later to make an appointment."

August presumes he's made a *faux pas*, maybe a few.

Ian gives Roderick a sexy look. He chuckles. "You'd do better than that in *your* heels, Rod." He points to the woman's feet as she walks away. "Remember?" Ian turns toward August. "He won the grand prize at the tea party."

Roderick groans. "I remember the hangover." He explains to August that there used to be a regular Sunday tea party at the Atlantic Shores Motel, and the men would strut around the pool in spike heels, to be judged on who looked the sexiest."

"That's the name! — the hotel I reserved."

Roderick frowns, then continues. "After each round, the contestants had to take a shot of rum for the next strut, until they were eliminated or fell into the pool. They tell me I outlasted them all and went back to the bar for more. I don't remember a thing, but the prize — a case of Meyer's dark rum — turned up at the house." He sighs. "Atlantic Shores will soon be gone, I hear — turned into condos — so sad."

Ian nods and they take a few second to mourn. A menagerie of people and animals continues to flow around them. Iguana, snake, parrots, opossum, sloth, all wear neck scarves or beads. The iguana and sloth both wear hats. Unreal. The possum would be skinned and roasted where he comes from. Dark gamey meat, lots of bones.

Roderick can't seem to get enough, but after a few minutes, Ian apologizes, saying he has work, and takes off. Roderick nods, as if it's a common occurrence. August notices that they're blocking traffic, but Roderick is shaking hands and giving hugs and air-kisses right and left. He pokes August's back. "Here comes another business prospect." An older man holds hands with a stunning young brunette who's walking a pink standard poodle in a tiara.

"Ah, fantastic to see you, Peter and lovely Dahlia. Have you entered the contest?"

"No, no." Peter fans his neck. Too hot to dress up."

Dahlia adjusts the poodle's head piece. "Flash likes to wear her tiara whenever she gets the chance."

"Flash Dancer is always a delight." Roderick scratches behind the pink ears. "I didn't get to introduce you at the party. This is August, a talented architect from New York. He's going to be building a fabulous new wing for me — all glass."

"Glass? What an interesting idea," Dahlia says. "That will certainly jazz up the neighborhood."

August swallows. "It's a thought. We're very early in the planning stage."

"It's exciting." Roderick clasps his hands in front of his chest. "It will be a showplace. When you see it, you'll want August to build you something."

Peter steps closer. "We've talked about putting in an indoor-outdoor swimming pool."

"You mentioned that at the party. You might have to fight Ian to get August. Ian's got that island to develop, you know?"

"Ian?"

Roderick looks around. Ian is long gone. "The orangutan at the benefit."

Peter's eyebrows shoot up. "Oh, no. I don't want to fight Ian."

"He's really a lamb." Roderick looks up at the stage. "They're about to start."

Dahlia takes Peter's hand. "We'd better claim our chairs."

They wave their goodbyes.

Roderick turns to August. "I can keep you working down here for years. Small island with huge money. Peter taught at M.I.T. He was one of my consultants for the Swedenborg physics book." He touches August on the forearm. "Hell, August! You should be exuberant. Trust my instincts."

From Roderick, a pep talk doesn't inspire confidence. August looks up at the stage. Maddy smiles down at him, her fruit-loaded headdress glowing in pink sunset. Her costume is two puffs of black fur adhered to her breasts, and a lower puff, indistinguishable from pubic hair. She turns to stoop and sport her fluffy black tail, the base of which barely covers the illegal six inches, required by Key West law, that he's heard about. Little Maddy, in exact headgear and hoop earrings, is perched on her shoulder, still as stone. She's not sucking on Madeline's earlobe, possibly put off by the earring.

It's a different world. He's not sure he fits. Or wants to.

Roderick puts his hand firmly on August's lower back. "We try to have a good time. What else is there?"

There are answers, but nothing he can explain in that moment. He looks at Roderick. In the city, he had a reputation as a brilliant scientist, a philosopher, a charming man. Yeah, always a charmer.

"Time to cheer for Maddy."

They add their applause to thunderous approval as the judge holds his hand above Madeline's head. To August, it's clear that the Maddies are winners, but the judge declares a tie. They'll have to compete against the "Chihuahua and his Matching Master" in a final round after the rest of the categories compete. Man and dog look amazingly alike under their Mexican hats.

"No fair! That guy always wins!" Roderick yells. "Not a chance!" There are boos from the audience. "The announcer is dragging it out for the drama."

They've been standing near the stage for almost an hour. August is ready to drop. "Is this going to take a while?"

Roderick gives him a look. "Shouldn't. I guess there are a few categories left."

"Sorry, please, text me who wins. I need to get up early for my flight. See you Monday." Before Roderick can say anything, he makes his break.

Chapter 16

Not According to Plan

August has never been so glad to get on a plane as on Friday morning. He sits down and takes a breath of jet-conditioned air. Fresh, compared with the Usher house. Already he's more relaxed. Spending the weekend in the apartment is sure to bring on bouts of loneliness and anguish, but having the option to suffer alone is a relief. He's resigned himself to the two months, a test of his own will, as much as of the bond between him and Gars. At some point, maybe he'll feel that bad luck has been good for him, forcing him to take a risk and see this through. Conscientiousness and perseverance have always come naturally. Obviously, from his mother.

The thought of his family triggers a memory from when he was ten. His father stealing his friend Wayne's 4-H goat for a scheme to sell goat milk ice cream. He tied her behind the barn and forgot her. August heard her agonized bleating, like a screaming child, and found her starving. She'd eaten the scraggly weeds she could reach, down to the roots. There was no water trough at all. He tried to walk her home, but it was too late. She fell down in the road and he had to leave her. By the time he got back with Wayne and his dad in their truck, she was dead. It was pure careless meanness. He saw later that she'd demolished a small cherry laurel tree, poisonous for goats. From that day on, he vowed to be a kind and honest person, to walk backwards over the footprints his father left on the world. So far, he's kept that promise. Helping Roderick will be a challenge. As for honesty... he'll have to watch his step on the shifting ground.

His flight is smooth and he arrives at his building in the early afternoon — Garo's building. As he steps from the taxi, there's a lightness in the frosty air. Maybe the effect of being drier or above sea level. In the long run, spending the winter in "paradise" will be preferable to the icy city, but for the moment...

He runs up the stairs, skipping the mail, getting inside before any of the neighbors spot him. No breaking into tears trying to explain the situation. His hope is to sneak in and out of town and resume his life with Gars at the end of January, never having undergone sympathy. They were the perfect, handsome, loving couple to their group of friends. People would be so disappointed.

The Hemingway Collection sofa with its antique styling and soft lines brings on tears as soon as he sees it. He recalls the Amini... Armani? sofa... underwear needed, their last fun conversation before this whole business started. The lack of a check and his inability to pay rent hovers in the background, his feeling like a loser, undeserving of Garo's love.

He sets down his bag. It's quiet out on the stairs, so he cracks the door and makes sure nobody's around. He opens the filigree box expecting mail crammed tight, but there are only a few pieces for him. Nothing for Garo. He must have set up online to have his mail held. But it seems like something would have come through before the order went into effect. Could Gars have known about the film earlier and kept quiet? Why would he?

For him, two life insurance ads, an Ikea catalogue, and a donation request from his former university. How did they always manage to track him down? Apparently, no check is coming from Fire Island. He makes a note to have his lawyer send a letter.

He writes a check for four months' rent, one a back-payment and three to get him through January. He sets it in view on Gars' desk, in case he happens to get home sooner than expected. There's no way to calculate groceries, dinners out, and bottles of wine that he didn't contribute to. If he can support the household, he'll be thrilled to do it when he and Gars are back together. If and if. Might be a jinx to think it.

He needs to calculate a fair salary for himself on the foundation work, along with a complete breakdown of costs, so he can get Roderick's approval when he goes back down there. He walks into his office — so small compared to his current residence — powers on the computer, and sits up straight. Garo won't want to cash the check, a genuine reason to email, to convince him that the money is there, to take what he's owed.

After a few tries, his first sentence still sounds like the lamentations of a lost soul. He gives up and opens Autocad. He boots up his laptop and starts inputting his notes on dimensions, roughing out his plan for the placement of pillars in the crypt — cellar. Not good to feed negativity, even in jest.

Work has always been his relief. He's never understood a stiff drink as an antidote for trouble. You'd have to drink until you're brain-dead to feel better — or stay half-looped most of the day. He sees how that works, their escape from paranoia... obsession... guilt? Making the house safe should relieve some of Roderick's symptoms if they're caused by stress.

He works until he notices that the room is dark. Dinnertime. It's good, losing himself and making progress. He shuts down.

A few bottles of Fuji water sparkle on the top shelf of the refrigerator, but there's nothing else. Garo did a thorough job cleaning it out, considering he only stayed one day after August left. It seems he would have kept the condiments, expecting to be home in a week or so. The freezer has some leftover goodies, neatly covered with foil, identified, and dated. Lasagna, beef stroganoff, chili. Each one sends a pang through his stomach, not only from hunger. He shuts the door. It doesn't feel right to eat homemade food that he can't replace.

A headache is starting behind his jaw — stress, dehydration, or both. He hasn't had anything since the bottle of water on the plane. He takes a Fuji water and downs half of it. If he can get out of the building without being spotted, there's his favorite little café not far. He puts on a long-sleeved shirt and finds his wool sports jacket, looking forward to the short walk, the spot where he eats when Garo is working late. A gut clench comes with the thought. He'll have to endure those.

He's in the bathroom when he hears a key in the door. He flushes and zips, his heart fluttering. Garo home early? He dashes down the hall and around the corner into the living room. "What the hell?"

"Jesus!" A dark-haired woman in a fitted black dress and heels is staring at him, her coat falling halfway off her shoulders.

He stops short a few feet from her. "Who are you?"

"Who the fuck are you?" She straightens herself back into the coat and takes a step forward.

"I live here." He points to the key still in her hand and asks a foolish, hopeful question, "Maintenance?"

She shakes her head and pulls back from the absurdity. "Nobody is supposed to be here. I came to water the plants and check the mail."

He'd forgotten about the succulents in the kitchen and Garo's beloved Norfolk Island pine. Of course.

"I'm supposed to be the only one with a key."

"I live here. Didn't you notice there was mail for me?" He's never met this woman. She doesn't know he exists.

She's frowning. "I thought it was a mistake."

He pulls himself together. "Sorry. I'm August, Garo's partner. I'll be gone again, as of Monday, so please continue to..."

She stares, her smooth face molding itself into a sneer. "Business partner?" Her voice is somewhere between fierce and breathless.

Sweat breaks out on August's chest. He shakes his head. "I've lived here for almost three years."

She stands frozen, her eyes wide and unblinking.

His throat tightens. He indicates the door so she'll leave. "I'm headed out." His hand thrashes at the lining of his jacket, not finding the sleeve. Finally, he shrugs on the coat. "Do you mind?"

She puts up her hand like she's stopping traffic. "Garo never mentioned you."

"I can see. I'm as surprised as you are. Probably more. For sure, more."

Her shoulders slump as the air goes out of her. She bites the corner of her lower lip. Her dark eyes turn glassy. "Can we sit down — talk?"

He takes in the perfect make up and artfully tossed hair, her svelte figure, like a model. A super model. Has he seen them together on a book cover? Working close together, sexual touching... holding back physical response, day after day. Visions of them posing together spin in his brain, working late, meals, drinks... He wants to sit down, but he can't talk. "No. Please, go. I don't want to know anything about it."

Is Garo letting him down easy to replace him with a woman? Or they've been sharing him all along? It doesn't make sense. Garo, who is he? Did he pretend to be gay, when he's bi-sexual, afraid August would think less of him? No way. Garo is secure in himself, and August will never be convinced that he's deceitful. He's heard of people being attracted sexually to a particular person, no matter the gender. He can't believe it. They were thrilled with each other.

The woman moves toward the door. August opens it and they look into each other's eyes. It's all there in hers, everything.

"I'm Raven, just so you know."

A model's name. Seems she's staking her ground. "August," he breathes.

He shuts the door behind her and counts to a hundred. Last thing he wants to do is pass her in the lobby.

At the sidewalk, he turns right, without noticing where he's going, his natural turning direction. When his senses start working again, he's in an unfamiliar spot. He can go back past the apartment to find the café, but there's an open door, right in front of him, and a placard on the sidewalk advertising specials. Anywhere he can sit down will do. He's past worrying about seeing people he knows. Truth is worthless in this world. He'll answer their questions like nothing has changed.

His appetite is gone, but the pain behind his left jaw has become a full-blown headache, pulsing from his teeth, like a sinus infection. Something he picked up on the plane? It seems too soon. Please, not now.

He needs to eat, regardless. A waiter motions him to a dark booth and he slides over to the wall, grateful for the feel of cold leather and the dimness of the hanging lamp. He orders an IPA and the roast chicken special with mashed potato and seasonal vegetable. He takes out his phone. A particle of his brain still doesn't believe Garo would deceive him like this.

The waiter brings the beer and a roll and butter. August sets the phone down and picks up his knife. He doesn't want to sound angry, irrational, suicidal, or any of the other feelings blinding him. The knife won't penetrate the roll, another goddamned irritation. He sets it on the plate and bites hard on the crust, trying to rip off a piece. Pain! Like a nail through his jawbone. He drops the roll and prods his gum. A back molar, the root, although he can't tell which tooth. Now what's he supposed to do? The trip has turned into a nightmare. His flight has a flexible return, just in case his fantasy came true. If he wasn't so miserable, he would laugh at such naiveté. He can't stay for a dental appointment. He has the engineer flying in from Philadelphia on Tuesday. No toothache is going to keep him from that.

He recalls Roderick's mention of recent dental work. He'll suck up the pain and wait to see Rod's dentist in Key West. His phone chirps and he glances at the text. Roderick — speak of the devil — hoping he's having a good time, "but not too good. Ha, ha!"

Sure, ha, ha, ha! My foot! The family expression always pops into his head. In other words, *bull shit*! Roderick can't leave him alone for a minute. He texts: "ha, ha, ha, ha, ha, ha!" Seeing how crazy it looks, he deletes. He sips gently at the beer and texts: "No fun. Toothache. Will need to see dentist." Roderick can probably reach somebody on weekends. He adds, "Hope the Maddies won contest."

A half chicken is set before him, glistening, and fragrant with rosemary and garlic, a good choice, comfort food. He's never been able to eat chicken without thinking of his mom's. When he was little, she made fried chicken once a week with mashed potatoes and milk gravy that she called wallpaper paste. The lumps of drippings added flavor, and you knew it was homemade. On his visits home, she cooked for him even when she had to rest in the middle of frying. He couldn't make her stop, couldn't disguise how much he enjoyed her cooking.

The phone chirps. He ignores it and digs in. He told Garo he was flying home to get his stuff. If Garo wanted to keep Raven a secret, he could have told her not to stop by on the weekend. Maybe she didn't get the message.

The chicken is tender. With concentration, he can chew on the right side of his mouth. Maybe she didn't listen, didn't want to listen. The shock and realization on her face were unmistakable. The waiter stops by. August orders a double Maker's Mark.

A bite of flabby broccoli and carrots slides right down. The buttery mashed potatoes are homemade, and he tries to appreciate them. He sips the whiskey and lets it warm on his tongue before bathing the molar, wondering if he might need a root canal. He checks his phone. Roderick has already made an appointment for Monday afternoon, and the Maddies came in second. The man and his Chihuahua won first prize again.

At least, he'll be able to afford to save his tooth. He remembers the bill for his mother's surgery. He was there when she called Dr. Albo to apologize for how long it would take to pay. The doctor told her not to worry, just be grateful when an illness can be cured with money. Three years later, when she was no longer cancer-free, August realized the doctor's full meaning. Nevertheless, not having to fret about cost for every decision is nice, a fresh beginning.

He buttons his jacket on the way home. The temperature has dropped and the wind stings his ears. He can't talk on the cell outside. He should have realized that he wasn't enough for Garo. But why would Garo hide his true sexuality? That isn't Gars. And Raven could have been kept a secret. Since August is so easily fooled, maybe the possibility of being caught hadn't occurred to Gars. How many others of a variety of genders might there be?

It's only 7:00. He must have gulped his food. Still, it's 1:00 a.m. in Paris. He'll never sleep if he doesn't make the call. He's a little high, despite the heavy food, and it gives him the strength to hit the call button. Time doesn't matter for something like this. If Garo isn't too busy with his newest lover, or lovers, to answer.

Gar's voice is hoarse. "Augie, something wrong? I thought we were going to limit to important emails."

"Are you sick?"

"Starting a cold." He barely gets out the words and begins hacking.

August waits. Gars hasn't been sick, except for a hangover or two, since he's known him, but obviously it's no fake. August's anger ebbs with each bronchial cough. What if he's wrong? It's not the right time for accusations. Maybe he doesn't really want to know. He wishes he could be there to bring Gar's ginger ale and heat up chicken soup. The cough continues, but with less volume, away from the phone.

"I'll call back. Gars?"

Twice Gars tries to say sorry, but can't get the word out.

"Gars, hang up! Please. Sorry. Call me when you're better. Just hang up! No worries." He's not sure how much was heard, but Gars croaks an "okay."

August hits "End." His emotions are frazzled. He should be there. Being there in times of sickness is what it means to be a partner. Maybe Gars was trying to split from Raven and she wouldn't let go. Too kind to give her the boot. That would be Gars. One bisexual affair wouldn't matter, if Garo never planned to touch a woman again.

Chapter 17

An Ending or a Muddle

Monday afternoon, August steps out of the pink taxi and runs fresh eyes over the mansion. He has some good ideas for Roderick, and his tooth has calmed down with back-to-back Advil. The sun isn't as oppressive as expected, and a cool breeze almost feels dry. The streets are silent. A few pieces of litter blow by. He steps over a puddle of dried puke in the gutter. He can't blame the inhabitants for not getting an early start on reality after their wild weekend. Reality sucks. But what else is there?

He and the driver unload the bags and boxes onto the sidewalk, and August is just about to take the first load inside when Roderick and Roget barrel down the stairs like puppies. You'd think he'd been gone a month.

Roderick grabs the smallest suitcase, calling over his shoulder, "Roget, you get the rest." He turns to August, free arm outstretched. "My poor baby! How's that tooth?"

Fuck. He would choose less fanfare, to huddle silently in his Gars-less universe, rationalizing, romanticizing, suffering. He thanks Roderick for getting the appointment, saying the pain is tolerable if he doesn't talk too much. Time to set some ground rules. "It's been a rough weekend. I plan to work and squeeze in a nap before the dentist, so I'm going to head straight to my room."

Roderick sets down the suitcase, looking forlorn, and motions for Roget to take it. He puts a hand on August's shoulder. "Your room is changed. We've started clearing out that wing. You'll be near me and Maddy on the second floor, west side. No view of the pool and less of the ocean, but I'm afraid we all have to make some sacrifices until the renovations are complete."

"Are you kidding? Complete? I've barely started the schematics. What if we can't do what you want?"

"Then we die. Might be messy, but won't take long."

"Jesus." August shakes his head. "I don't know what to say, how to get through to you. There're limits to what can be done."

"I don't know how to make *you* understand. Cut down the size, the amenities — whatever it takes. We need a place without shadows. Immediately!" He pulls back his cheek to show a vacant hole where a molar used to be. "This is the third one." He sticks out his hands showing bluish fingernails.

August startles. Carbon monoxide? A trick?

"I usually polish them, but I wanted to show you." He turns and strides into the house.

What the hell is that about? August puts a finger into his mouth to feel which molar is bothering him. It's in the same vicinity as Roderick's gap. He glances at his nails. Normal.

Roget is back. "Let's go up." He carries a box. On the second floor, he motions toward an open doorway between Maddy's room and a closed door he suspects is Roderick's.

August's suitcases stand inside. "Really?" He's relieved to be in the west wing, but it's the last room location he'd choose.

"Normally, we like to spread out, but only a few rooms are set up with beds. Guests will be put on the third floor."

"Guests? I'm a guest. I'd feel more comfortable out of the way."

Roget moves closer and whispers. "Mr. Usher thinks you'll be more comfortable here." He pauses and stares hard into August's eyes, obviously trying to convey meaning without words.

August blinks. "I can't choose?"

"If you want to move, talk to Mr. Usher." He gives an exaggerated wink. "Catch him when he's out by the pool."

Roget follows with the box as August goes inside and sets his laptop on a huge modern desk. The window above overlooks the ocean. Its smooth greenness is inviting, but too cloudy to know what's underneath. The edge isn't visible from here, but most likely the waves are smashing against the rocks near the road. This room is lighter than the first, with more comfortable furniture. The Usher odor is prominent. "WIFI?"

"Sorry, sir, the walls are too thick between the rooms — something like that. Mr. Usher is working on getting your router set up, but if you walk down the hall to the windows, you can usually get cell reception." He checks his watch. "You have a dental appointment at seven and we'll hold dinner for you."

"No need, please. I probably won't want to eat."

"Mr. Usher is expecting you."

Roget leaves and August drops down on the bed. Evening dentist hours in Key West. Who would believe it? His jaw feels okay for the moment — the Advil still working. He has plenty of time to nap and catch up with Roderick by the pool for Happy Hour, as they call it.

He hangs up his tailored shirts next to two pastel Cuban-style shirts, more gifts from Roderick. Hopefully, not left from a former paramour. Gars should see this new wardrobe. If they ever meet again... a slight catch in his breathing. He's always been teased about being shy and conservative. It's true, covering the fear of showing a lack of good taste. Poor Gars. So sick.

The sheets are cool and clean-smelling — fabric softener. He should get some room spray. The mild stench of mildew and decay lurks in every nook of the house, even on the patio and in the yard. The Usher miasma? Years of damp walls due to the breaking down of the foundation — possibly.

He turns on his side and closes his eyes, then sits back up. He can't let go. There must be an easy explanation for Raven, and he needs to hear it before he drives himself crazy.

He sits down at his laptop. He'll write it while he's feeling brave, then find WIFI. He has to get every word right, not to accuse, but to get the truth. One woman in Garo's past is not enough to give up on the relationship. Gars being sick saved him from the huge mistake of letting loose his hurt and outrage. How to ask if there are other lovers without showing doubt of Garo's honesty? Half his brain, or at least a third, tells him that Garo would never lie to him.

An uncontrollable part of his brain is scrambling to remember details of times when Gars was late or had an unplanned shoot. Still there has to be an explanation for Raven that doesn't include subterfuge. Maybe she's a friend — or a relative — who didn't know Garo is gay. He tries to recall her exact words and facial expressions. The outrage of a lover or plain shock? His first impression has taken over, a lover. He's jumped to the worst conclusion because he doubts his value as the one and only. An ego problem or truth. Why, in hell, didn't he talk to her?

My dearest Gars, I feel so bad that I called and caused you a terrible coughing fit. I won't call again. I promise to wait until you're feeling better and you call me. I hope you've been taking your temperature and have seen a doctor. The cough sounded deep and could be bronchitis. You might need antibiotics. I hope you're keeping warm. Can you get chicken soup? I wish I could be there to make it for you. Is somebody taking care of you? I hope so and I hope not.

It's stiff. He sounds like a needy person that nobody would want hanging on. He does hope Gars is being taken care of — by an extremely unattractive, uninteresting, old fart who's paid by the production company. He deletes the question and the "hope not."

My mother made great soup, but I never asked for her recipe. She didn't know I wanted to learn to cook. Anyway, I would figure out something, plenty of garlic, to get you better in a hurry. I hope you're not missing much work.

Superficial. Stiff. <delete>.

He doesn't know enough about Garo's current life to say anything meaningful. Tears fill his eyes and he can't see the keyboard anymore. Instead, Gars driving a red convertible on a curving mountain road... Then, the most handsome tourist strolling through the Gardens of Versailles. Then, like he first saw him, dancing under black lights in a pair of low-slung jeans, bare-chested, twirling a glowing wife-beater amid teasing hordes of toned men, all vying for his attention... Imagination is brutal. So is reality. Raven. Another slash of pain.

There's one thing I wanted to ask you. A woman turned up at our place. <delete> *your place. She said her name was Raven and she was supposed to water the plants. She seemed shocked that I was there. I told her I would take care* <delete>*I told her I was your partner.* <delete> *I told her I'm your partner. I hate to ask you about it because I know you wouldn't keep a secret from me, and I don't want you to think I could think that. I just can't think straight not knowing who she is. I realize there are many parts of our lives, mine too, that we haven't talked about, just because they haven't been important.*

Also, I don't know anything about your new work or where you're staying. I need to picture you somewhere. Are you in a hotel room or apartment? Is it nice? Even though we're apart, I would still like to be your confidant, and there are many frightening <delete> *weird* <delete> *troubling* <delete> *interesting aspects about this job that I would like to discuss with you, but I know you're busy, so I'll wait until you have time to write me or call. I don't care if you wake me up. I realize we promised not to communicate often, but in this case I needed to make an exception.*

Love, Augie

He walks into the hall, hits send, and in seconds the email goes. Must be WIFI in one of the rooms. Instantly, he regrets it. He should have waited. He shouldn't have written so much. He should have left it more open so Gars didn't have to answer. He falls into bed unable to move.

He wakes up wanting to stay there forever, but soon his eyes open. He grabs his cell and hurries into the hall to check email. No reply! The wait might kill him.

His tooth feels so good, he wonders if he should cancel his appointment. He's never had a rotten tooth in his life, only a few small cavities. The pain might have been sinus-related, the shock of frosty winter air up North. A cold mojito will be the test.

He chooses a light pink hibiscus-covered Tommy Bahama shirt and beige Bermuda shorts from the closet. Roderick is so full of surprises that the word *surprise* no longer applies. Hawaiian shirts are far from August's style, but the loose cotton is comfortable. Maybe his style needs to change. Might as well make Roderick happy when possible. Nothing to lose. There's a pair of leather sandals in his size, too, perfect for a casual night out at the dentist's.

"Wow-ee, look at you!" Roderick beams at him, a mojito extended in his direction.

"Keep it."

"You look like you need it. Everything okay?" Roderick calls to Roget for another and presses the cold glass into August's hand.

He takes a small swig. "Mmm." Swishes it around. Picks out a lime chunk and bites down on it in back. "The tooth is fine. I should cancel the dentist."

Roderick frowns. "You don't want to do that. Once they go bad, the pain will come back worse and worse until the tooth is gone."

"Really? I don't know much about toothaches. Never had one before."

"This is a special kind of toothache."

"Huh?"

He pulls the corner of his mouth back to show him the gap on the other side, the bottom gum again, a space for the second last molar. "Symmetrical. Same area as yours, right?"

It is the same. "Not sure. Nothing hurts right now."

"Trust me. If nothing's wrong, she'll give you a good cleaning."

"Oh, a woman dentist."

"Umm. I should have said *zie*. Is that the stylish pronoun? Last time zie was wearing a sundress, but I don't know..."

August nods and sips his mojito. There are no simple answers in this town, and that can be a good thing. He decides to save the discussion about changing his room.

The dental office is in a Victorian house only a few blocks away. Dr. Lee greets him in the waiting room. She is obviously a female. No telling what Roderick was up to.

She positions him in the chair and offers a beer or glass of wine. He declines, wondering about pairing alcohol with Novocain. August checks his email while he waits for her to get her instruments. Nothing.

She begins exploring his mouth with a mirror and pick. Her hands are delicate and gentle. Maybe Roderick likes everything off-kilter. Is all of this a bored-rich-guy game? Something that makes Roderick feel superior to the people he's freaking out, namely August. But he couldn't have engineered the cracks or any of the damage. He didn't cause the tooth problem.

"So, you're an Usher here for a visit?"

August grunts something he hopes sounds like *no*.

She frowns. "The crack and decay pattern is so similar to Rod's and Maddy's that I would've guessed you were related, maybe a son."

He chokes on a laugh inside his throat.

"I guess you're a little too old." She removes her fingers. "Sorry, I didn't mean to comment on other patients' teeth. It's uncanny." She drops the mirror on the tray and starts picking at the molar. "Hurt?"

"Un-uh."

"Oh. I've been down this path before." She steps back and presses the button to raise his seat. "Lower left quadrant, number eighteen. There's a crack that runs from the crown to the gum, and no doubt, farther. I'll need to take an ex-ray, but I bet decay has moved into the root. I predict number nineteen will be next. You Ushers must have high pain tolerance. I mean — sorry — you should be screaming when I touch anywhere near it."

She's exasperating. "I'm no Usher — no relation." He explains that he's an architect, hired to do renovations.

"Well, that should be... interesting... So — ya'll chewing on rocks over there?" She chuckles in an uneasy way.

He can't appreciate the humor. He tries to remember what

he's been eating. Croissants, ahi tuna... "No nothing. Nothing hard."

"Not trying to open oysters with your teeth, are you?" She smiles, showing most of her unnaturally white teeth, then looks into his eyes and stops.

She takes the X-rays and goes off to develop them. One person office. It seems to take a long time, and he realizes he's been dozing when the door opens.

She clips the film to a glowing square on the wall and points to a long crack in his molar, not unlike — as he remembers it — the fissure in the ballroom wall. He puts on a neutral face. Her advice is to have the tooth extracted before the jawbone becomes involved. "Deep seated bacteria can transmit disease through your whole system. Not to scare you, but I've heard of fatalities when the person had immune deficiencies or refused care."

He swallows. "Wow."

"We should do it tonight. A good night's sleep and you'll be fine tomorrow. You can get an implant at your convenience."

Is this for real? He has the intuition of being jerked around. Too much coincidence? A conspiracy? Why? It's crazy-think. He never quite believes anything Roderick tells him, but so far, the guy's been right. August checks the diploma on the wall in front of him. University of Florida, 2009, Andrew Lee. "Andrew." He didn't mean to say it aloud.

"I mostly go by Anna now."

August is directly under her — zir — neck. Andrew might have had a tracheal shave, but there's no scar. Laser hair removal? Such fine, smooth skin.

Anna goes into the adjacent room to prepare local anesthesia and nitrous oxide. It's his best option, rather than jeopardize the contractor meeting in the morning and risk further infection.

He checks his emails. Nothing. He texts Roderick not to hold dinner.

A kissy-face icon comes back. An I-told-you-so.

He feels tingly and light during the procedure, better than he has for days. In no time, he's on his feet waiting for the Uber.

He checks his email. He stops breathing.

It was stupid to ask that question. He doesn't want the answer.

Dear August,

This is disturbing. I didn't give anyone a key. I don't know a woman named Raven. I've been pulling out my hair trying to think of an explanation. All I can think of is that I've given out a few keys over the years, and I wasn't careful about it. The only time I can remember giving a key to a woman was a few years ago when I went out West. Her name is Joanne. I haven't been in touch with her since you and I have been together, and I can't remember if she returned the key, but she wouldn't have known I was gone and certainly wouldn't go into the apartment without my permission. She also knows that I'm gay! Even if I'm somehow forgetting another woman who has a key, and somebody told her I was in Paris and that my plants needed watering, which is ridiculous, all my friends know I'm gay. I thought you knew it! It's hard for me to believe that you can question that fact at this point. It hurts me that you doubt my word and my sincerity. I know it was a shock seeing a total stranger with a key, and I understand that anybody would jump to conclusions, but why didn't you ask me right up front when we talked? I thought you would have had enough faith in me to question your immediate interpretation of what happened.

I called the super and arranged for the locks to be changed. He also said he had not given a key to anyone. I'm sorry that you will have to go to his apartment to get a key if you get back there before I do. I asked him to water the plants also.

There's more, but August stops reading and wipes his eyes. He can't ignore the formal tone. He sobs. Now he can't even get into the apartment. Nothing could be worse. He doesn't want to ask the super for a key.

He sees a pink taxi waiting at the light a block away. Not now, please.

I know you are having a hard time with our short separation. So now we are both deeply hurt. This is another unexpected event, but it is exactly the kind of thing I hoped to avoid by keeping our communications to a minimum. You seemed sure we didn't need any rules, and I trusted your judgment. But I can't live like this. I have to be able to look my best and act. When I'm hurting this badly and trying to figure out what could possibly be going on, I can't center myself. I'm stuck in my own head and the pain affects my work. If I were a professional actor all my life, maybe I could, but this is hard for me. I'm sure you're having the same problem. We both need to concentrate on our jobs, so when we get back together we will have accomplished something and not wasted our time apart.

The only way this will work is what I said in the beginning. We will meet at the apartment for Christmas and see where we are. Six weeks is a very short period of time for two busy people. I'm sure we will still be as much in love as we always have been.

I spent too much time writing this email, and I have to rush off. Write back so I know you got this and agree that we will see each other at Christmas and not communicate again before that.

Love you always, Gars

Now he's done it. The worst he could have imagined. "To see where we are" puts more space between them.

He gets into the taxi. He's done it. He writes a quick answer, saying he agrees with the plan, and he's so sorry to have ever doubted his one true love. He knows he's pushing it to go any farther. Garo is either honest, sensible, and strong, or he's a great liar. August ends the email with all the love in the world. He hits "Send."

Chapter 18

Another Blow

Madeline keeps count of their Margaritas. Roderick looks to be in his usual functional drunken state. After declaring he's on pain killers and shouldn't drink, August allows himself one refill and doesn't notice the second. She puts the pitcher in the kitchen. He's half out of it, as expected. Madeline sees hurt in his eyes and even his posture. A terrible thing, but she had to seal the deal. She had no problem overnighting the keys to the lovely Raven. One slick chick, a wonderful stage actress. They only had a short relationship, but might have stayed together forever, soulmates, if it wasn't for the damned Usher leash.

August's tooth removal would seem detrimental to her plan, but he's in a looser mood than she's ever seen him, exhausted to the point of giddiness, and no doubt, having given up on Garo. A new devil-may-care August. Flirty even. If she's still fertile, this could be the night.

She excuses herself to go to bed and leaves it up to Roderick to corral him. She hasn't told him her plan, or he'd make a mess of it, but there's no doubt that he'll take advantage of August's swimming brain to lure him up to bed. Roderick, of course, made sure she knew that August had succumbed to his charm once. A second blow job should be easy to orchestrate.

As she guessed, they're not far behind when she reaches her bedroom. They stumble upstairs and into August's new room, to the left of hers. The walls are thick. She'll need to hear them in order to step in at the right moment. It's a daring plan and unlikely to succeed, but desperate times... She slips off her clothes and goes into the hall to listen through the door. From what she can catch, Roderick has brought a bottle of Prosecco from the fridge to "rinse out" their mouths. More alcohol could put August straight to sleep or render him impotent. She'll be tip-toeing the fine line between a cloudy brain and a limp noodle.

It occurs to her that she might need more than Roderick's saliva in order to slip onto August. She reaches under the gown and fingers herself, recalling a sweet memory of her and Lenore on the private beach, pretending they didn't see a boater with binoculars. Ah, the tingle.

There's the creaking of floorboards and soft compression of the mattress. "Sweetheart," Roderick says. "Slide your beautiful ass over here and give me a kiss."

No objection. The mattress squeals and she figures August has dropped ungracefully. This is her best bet, when total focus is on his cock. Considering furniture arrangement, the odds are fifty-fifty as to whether he'll be facing her direction.

The 3-In-One oil August suggested for the gate worked perfectly. She turns the doorknob silently and dares to pull the door open a crack. The dim bedside lamp is on. August's pale back to the door, he slouches on the bed, left arm propping him up. Couldn't be better. Roderick nuzzling his neck. In the glow, she recognizes what he's attracted to, the lean muscularity, no hair or tattoos, just a few freckles trickling down mid-back. Roderick's eyes widen from above August's shoulder. She's been spotted, naked, by the door. Roderick's face moves downward and out of sight. Her participation thrills him. He won't give her away.

She should have let him in on it, but he might have poo-pooed the idea, and she would've had to ignore his orders. Better just to join the party. It won't be the first time, but a first attempt without total cooperation.

She creeps up. Roderick is kneeling between August's thighs, fingers kneading, head bobbing. August is looking down at him, or else his eyes are closed. She crouches at the end of the bed in Roderick's peripheral vision and motions him to stay quiet and make room. He frowns, but complies, slowly replacing his mouth with a hand, and moving over. August starts to look up, but Roderick tilts his face with his other palm, guiding him into a deep kiss to block his view.

She leans into Roderick and opens her legs, keeping her weight on the foot on the floor, lifting the other leg like a flamingo, bending it outward like a ballerina. A delicate maneuver. Roderick removes his hand gradually as she slides onto August's stiff cock. August reacts with a tremor, but Roderick holds his face hard in the kiss. She starts pumping, flexing her floor leg. She can't last long, but he's rock-hard, near climax.

He jerks his head away and looks her straight in the face. His bleary eyes focus with shock and anger. She freezes, drops to both feet. The erection falls out. Roderick groans and straightens up, pushing at a kink in his back.

A crack of lightning illuminates the room. A strike sounding close outside. August shrieks and they all turn to look out the window. There's no rain and no other lightning or thunder.

"What the hell?" August stares at her and then at Roderick, disgust replacing shock. "The fuck, are you —"

Roderick tilts his head toward the ceiling. "He didn't like it."

"You can be damned sure I didn't!"

"Not you, *him*."

"Jesus."

"Christ! He can make lightning?" Maddy climbs onto the bed near August. "If *he* doesn't like it, then we need to do it!"

August is shaking his head, fending them off with raised palms. "Get away from me!" He puts down one hand, keeping his eyes on her to pick up his underwear.

She grips her hair on both sides. "Fuck. This is our big chance."

Roderick sends her a pleading look.

She's screaming at him. "New blood will save us! He fucking knows it! See? See! He stopped us. What else could that mean?"

"He didn't stop you, idiot! It was already over," Roderick says. "It was real lightning."

"Fuck! You know I'm right. It also means he can see us and hear us. Cocksucker! Right now, here, in the west side of the house."

August pulls up his pants. He zips and buttons and faces Maddy, glaring. "You thought you could trick me into fathering your baby? Really? No! Really? Is that what you're saying?"

"Yes! Will you do it, please? To save our motherfucking lives? Please, just let's do it fast. Tonight's the night!"

Roderick sighs, puts his hand on her shoulder. "Mads. Settle down. Where in hell did you get that idea anyway?"

She shakes him off and steps away. "Mother, of course. What's the harm? Why not give it a shot?"

"Not on your life!"

"Fucking literally," she adds.

"I can't even believe this." August clutches his forehead. "I don't want a kid, Madeline, not with you, or anybody. You must think I'm fucking stupid that you could get me drunk and..."

"Huh! It was damn close. I thought you wanted to save our lives." She tries to touch his arm softly, but he steps back. "I'm sorry, Augie. Most men wouldn't mind if I —"

"Most men? Gay men? They don't mind if you use them to get pregnant?"

"No, I —"

"Then why force me — since they're all lining up?"

Roderick clucks his tongue. "The entire idea is ridiculous, Madeline."

"Augie, you're one of us. We respect you, trust you. I wouldn't want you to act like a father to the baby. Nobody would know."

August turns to Roderick. "How could you do this?"

He throws up his hands. "I had nothing to do with it. I thought we'd have some drunken fun."

August makes a guttural noise. "I don't believe a fucking word." He gives Roderick a push toward the door. "Get out — both of you!"

There's a rumble downstairs.

Roderick shushes them. "Sounds like an avalanche."

"See! We're talking too much. He wants us to go back to our own rooms before I convince August to impregnate me."

August's lips are clamped in disgust. "I'm going down and take a look." He turns to Roderick. "You can come or not."

She doesn't get it. If he *can* kill them, why doesn't he fucking go ahead? He enjoys tormenting them? Or... could it be suicide for him if they both die? She bets Roderick hasn't considered that.

"I'm going to obey." She throws the door open so the knob bangs the wall and everybody knows she's enraged. The rumbling continues, but the volume lowers as she steps into her bedroom. She flips on the light and slams the door behind her.

Maddy and Roddy are curled on her frayed quilt, the one made by Great Gran. Their obsidian fur shines in the moonlight and part of Roddy's white circle is visible. He's licking Maddy's head, and she stretches her neck so he can reach under her ears, so sexual. But spayed and neutered, by necessity, the end of their line.

The roar below has stopped. Madeline sits down and pets them with both hands. Maddy J. stands and bumps against her wrist, purring and writhing. She flops down half across Roddy's haunch to get her belly stroked. So much like her and Roderick, lazy, decadent creatures locked together in their tiny universe. Not what she would have picked for a life. If only she'd realized at a younger age that she was making a choice. Her options were limited, but maybe she didn't try hard enough. Staying beautiful seemed most important and took up all of her time. Now it's worth little and won't last much longer. She still clings to it. The thing that has robbed her, but all she has left.

She remembers the fifth of scotch in her wardrobe. She turns away from the mirrored door, avoiding the gaunt cheeks and dark circles under her eyes, and lifts the lovely Dalmore 18-year-old from the shelf. There's less in the bottle than she thought. She tilts it, coating her glass, such a pretty, golden blonde potion, and sips. A creamy burn. One of her faves, but since there's all that property to sell — and so little time — she might as well finish it off and upgrade to something more expensive.

Two musky shots have soaked into her brain, and she curls between the cool sheets. Time for plan B. Roderick is desperate enough to try anything. All she needs is a dollop of live non-

Usher semen.

She hits her forehead with her palm. Stop thinking! Fucking stop thinking! She cackles hysterically.

Chapter 19

Hard to Ignore

August moves with heated purpose as he leads Roderick into the darkness downstairs. A loud thump, followed by something like skittering, seems to have come from the dining room. As he reaches the ground floor hall, he gropes for the light switch and flicks it on. The lighting is less than adequate, as always, only a few fixtures glowing. Roderick seems frozen.

He pushes Roderick lightly in the direction of the dining room. "Give me a hand, will you? No sense exploring in the dark." In a few seconds, the room is illuminated, the chandelier like fire to his wide-open pupils. He focuses. A chunk of plaster the size of his laptop is resting between the table and the back of a chair. The chair he occupied earlier that night, the chair that has come to be his.

Roderick gasps. "It's you! A bust of you. Headless!"

"What?" With some imagination it could be perceived as a headless male torso, but nobody in particular. "Why would you say that?"

Roderick shrugs. "My first impression." Plaster is dashed across the long table, as if the chunk bounced, leaving a white trail along with nicks and scratches in the finish. August looks up and sees a hole in the ceiling at the far end of the table. Nothing nearby disturbed. He walks over to it. The bottom of the hardwood floor above is exposed.

Roderick's follows. His eyes bulge. "Fuck."

August's head begins to spin. He steadies himself, leaning

against the table. He's never felt off balance until he entered this house. "I'm freaked, Roderick. Let's go out by the pool where there's nothing above us."

"About time you get it."

Roderick suggests a swim, and something about immersing himself in the warm pool is so appealing that August slips off his clothes without a thought. The house has made Roderick crazy. Madeline too, worse, thinking a baby will fix it. Now it's working on him.

They walk down the tiled steps and duck under. August exhales and sits on the bottom step with his eyes closed for a few seconds. He tilts his head back, pinches his nose, and surfaces. He wipes his eyes and tries to... what? Center himself. Garo taught him how to do it, but he can't do it without Garo.

When he opens his eyes, Roderick is staring at him. "I think now's a good time to tell you more."

August lets out a sound. "Do you have to?"

"Last night I had a lucid dream. Partly lucid. Swedenborg had them."

"What?"

"A dream you control." He takes a deep breath. "I was in the east wing during a luscious orange sunset, and the walls were radiant with reflected light. I sat down in the chair by your window, wearing my white satin robe, letting it hang open, a breeze teasing my cock. No worries, light of heart for once, no pain, enjoying an expensive Pinot — I could read the label. I made some duck liver *canapés* appear on the nightstand and ate one. I felt young — highly sexed. More than usual."

"Why were you in my room?"

"I was waiting for you." He clears his throat. "Then black ink, or maybe old blood, rose from the foundation and penetrated the floor, covered it. I tried to make it go away, but the dream wasn't lucid anymore. I was stuck in the chair. I squirmed and kicked, but my ass was glued to the upholstery. The blackness thickened, turned hot and molten around my ankles. There was music somewhere, but so faint that I couldn't make out the tune. Black wax rose past my chin, and I started sucking it into my lungs. It hardened and I was screaming for help, but all I could produce was a tight whisper in my throat. I thought I was in hell because I couldn't die. Something powerful pulled me out of the chair, ripping off the upholstery sticking to my ass...

Roderick's face changes. His eyes roll back like a shark biting prey, but his voice is the low strangled whisper of a victim. "I heard bells, the tolling of the bells — of the bells, bells, bells, bells, bells, bells, bells. The rolling and the throbbing of the bells, bells, bells... His voice is gone but he continues to form the word with his lips. "The moaning and the groaning of the..." He slips under water, bubbles rising in the same rhythm of the words. August realizes he's drowning. He pulls him up by the armpits. Roderick coughs and gags, spews water. "August!" He coughs harder. August takes his arm and leads him to the steps. Roderick sits down, his penis bobbing between his thighs, erect, the only part of him that looks alive.

"You okay?"

His skin is eggshell white around the orangish edges of his bottled tan. He's breathing hard. "St. Paul's Episcopal. The bells. The church has been restored — many times — but the coral rock foundation is from 1832."

"Yeah?"

"Everything went black after that. Bells were clanging inside my ears, *inside*." He stares off. "I was burning all over." He stares at his chest and turns his arms, looks down his thighs, as if checking for scars.

"What a nightmare."

"I understand now. They're the same age... They communicate."

"Who?"

"St. Paul's was warning me. He's a good spirit. "Silent Night" — that was the tune. Christmas Eve. I'm going to die on Christmas Eve! Less than two months..." His head drops to his chest and his arms go out to August. "I thought we had more time than that." His eyes are closed. He looks soft, worn. "Hold me, please, Augie. Please."

August is wary of a new game, but Roderick's penis is flaccid now, below the surface. He's not faking. August sits on the step next to him and puts his arm across his slim shoulders, covered in goosebumps. He leans his head on Roderick. His mind goes back to the chunk of ceiling... and his cracked tooth.

He takes Roderick's elbow and urges him upward. "Let's get you to bed." As soon as the words are out, he's sorry he said it, but Roderick makes no reply. August gives him a squeeze and kisses him on the ear. He walks him upstairs. Roderick lies down without making eye contact. August tucks him in and he rolls over and starts snoring.

Still feeling less than sober, August gets into his own bed. He pulls up the sheet and curls on his side. He sits back up, looks at the ceiling. When might a lethal chunk choose to fall out? Nope. Not going there. He won't believe a house is plotting against him. He lies down and curls up under the sheet.

He's beginning to doze when electric guitar chords seep through the wall. Low notes. Roderick? It's a gloomy tune, not really a tune at all. The rhythm seems vaguely like Roderick's droning in the pool.

He wills the chords to stop, wondering if he should do something. He wakes. Two A.M. Loud chords. Roderick might be in a trance again. Or it's a lure. Or a brain malfunction. Possibly his own. He throws on the Hawaiian shirt and shorts.

There's no answer to his knock. He turns the knob and pulls it a few inches. Roderick is slumped in his upholstered chair, silhouetted in moonlight. He's moaning along with the chords. Outside, dark billows roll across the full moon, a classic shot from a horror movie. He takes a step inside.

"August? That you? Sorry. I disturbed you with my awful playing."

"I was worried."

"Sweet boy. It is a dreary tune, passed down from one of the greats, of course, way back. When I'm depressed, solemn music puts me on an even plane. A kind of torment that feels good. Hard to explain. You know how art can be pleasing, even if the subject matter is horrendous? Everything working in perfect harmony to create a single effect. It's sublime. Even if the effect is deadly."

August recognizes depression brought on by alcohol. "Let's not talk about it till morning when you're feeling better." It's easier to be sympathetic when Roderick's down and not focused on cleverness and sex. Is this the real Rod and the rest is for show? August sits on the end of the bed and watches the clouds drift, wondering if the moon is waxing or waning. At the moment, he feels detached from everything that's happened, like none of it was real. "I've got a lot to do in the morning, but I want to be sure you're okay."

"You're the best, Augie. I'm fine. I'll never be able to thank you enough for taking on this job, no matter the result. And for helping me out... even after Madeline's behavior. The Prosecco did me in."

"We'll make it work." He pushes himself up from the bed. "Whatever it takes. You've got my word." He puts his hand on Roderick's shoulder. "I need some space for storage, and to set up a table. It would be best if I rent an office in town where I can concentrate without being interrupted." He waits for the argument.

Roderick smiles, his eyes coming alive a little. "I agree totally. Where you can work freely without the roof falling in. The sooner the better."

"I'll find a place tomorrow. Nothing fancy."

Roderick nods, pleased. "I know a good rental agent. I'll pay the rent, due to circumstances." He angles his head in the direction of the dining room.

Terrible timing for a financial discussion, but there will never be a good time. "I still have my office lease in the city, so this is additional. I'll add the new rent when I bill you again, starting on the renovation plans. You do remember that you've only covered my salary, the demolition and foundation permits, and materials, right? We still need full funding for the plans, new construction, the engineering and construction subcontractors, permits, and all the materials for the new structure, if we — when — we get there. I need you to sign off on the spread sheet before we go farther." He holds his breath.

"Of course, but knowing the details doesn't mean anything to me. I trust you. Dear August, just say the word. There isn't enough money in the world to compensate for what you're taking on."

August smiles and steps out into the hall. A chill spreads from his scalp to his spine, as if the lizard part of his brain knows truth when it hears it. He sucks it up. He's personally involved now. He chose it, whether he meant to or not. His tongue finds the hole where his tooth used to be. The gap feels huge, but the gum is pain-free.

There's no way he can sleep. He needs to cancel the structural engineer, now that the wing is going to be demolished, a complete change in direction. It's a terrible way to do business, notifying the guy at the last second. His reputation would suffer if he was in the city, but there's no choice. The structural components and foundation repairs needed for a glass atrium won't even resemble his original proposition. He writes an email, hoping to sooth any hard feelings by paying expenses and a ten percent bonus, with a promise to get back to him soon. It's double bad because he knows the guy was eager to get the work.

He'll call first thing in the morning to confirm, but it might be too late to stop him if he's in flight or already in Key West. Now he needs to find a demolition contractor who can fly down, pronto. He knows a few people who might be able to recommend demolitions companies.

Chapter 20

Too Much Thinking

Madeline wakes up early, too hung over to move, but needing to pee. She pushes Maddy and Roddy off her chest and sits up. Her brain sloshes against her skull. No time to nurse a headache.

She looks out into the hall. Both August's and Roderick's doors are closed. She goes directly from the bathroom to Roderick's room. His head is under the sheet. She touches his shoulder. There's slight movement. "Bro, meet me in five for a breakfast chat." She peels back the sheet and he sputters something.

She trudges down to the dining room, wondering if his lack of motivation means that August is leaving. She gets a cup of coffee from the sideboard. Her eyes are too dry for contacts, so she's wearing her glasses. They fog as she sips. Her life is mostly fog, boredom, and annoyance. Why is she so desperate to keep it? She grabs a croissant and bites out a hunk. Roderick creeps into the room and picks up a cup, ever so delicately.

She waits for him to pour coffee and sit. "So, that didn't work, did it?"

He wrinkles his nose. "What?"

"Wake up! Getting the jiz. Is August leaving?"

"No, but you were insane to try that."

"Not much to lose, Bro. So far there's no indication that your plan has a fuck's chance in hell. Our time is getting short."

"No kidding. Christmas Eve is coming right up."

"So?"

He lets out a long sigh. "The date came to me in a dream — like Swedenborg. Not like his creative dream, more of a nightmare. Without the remodel, which seems impossible, I'm done for in less than two months. I don't know for sure, but I expect the house will take us both out together."

"Maybe you'll listen to me now."

"Madeline, he's not going to father an Usher."

She grabs his forearm. "You can get it! Easy."

"What? No..." He inspects his arm. "I'm going to bruise there."

"For crying out loud, Roderick. Save me a used condom. Or blow him and spit it in a cup. I'll handle the rest."

"What happens when you're walking around here looking pregnant? He'll figure it out and scram, right back to New York."

"So what?" She winces. She's tried not to think about how she'll look. At her age — ruined abs, drooping tits, stretch marks, varicose veins, scarred perineum... Is it even worth living like that? She needs to stop Googling. "You say we'll be dead in a couple months. But if my pregnancy keeps us alive longer, there's time to do the renovation and flush *him* out for good. I'll name some local as the father. August will want to believe it."

"If he catches me — no way. Maddy, he's just now coming over to our side."

"Roddy, it doesn't matter if he's on our side. Use your genius brain. When the sperm does its job, we won't need your $1,000,000 remodel."

"Or... more.... Maddest, dearie, you've got no scientific evidence."

"Science, schmience. You change it every other day. The house tried to scare him off, so we must be on the right track."

"True. That chunk of ceiling in his chair was pretty obvious. I would run screaming into the sunset, if it landed in my spot."

"You always run screaming. August might be too rational for his own good, but it works for us."

"I don't know how much longer he can hold on to that."

"Exactly. No time to put our eggs all in one casket. Ha! What did the other generations have that we don't?" She sees he's coming around. The corners of his mouth want to flicker into a smile. She always gets her way. She makes google eyes. "Just think. A kid. Another generation — to take care of *him*."

"Mads, you think about it. We share the most condensed incest genes of any generation. It's taken centuries for our genes to get so evil. We're much worse off than they were. He's more powerful than ever. You would saddle your child with that?"

"Our genes will be diluted. The incest connection is his source of power. Didn't you just tell me that?" She takes him by the shoulders and stares into his eyes. "A mixed blood heir will free us. Maybe the kid will even have enough freedom to start a new line. Come on. He just needs to see a baby. He won't have any idea whose genes are in it."

"You don't know that."

"You don't know otherwise." She hunches her shoulders. "It's the strongest action we can take."

"We'll have to make sure he sees you and me having sex."

"I don't think so. No."

"What if the rug rat looks like Augie? Besides..." He puts his palms on both sides of his face and his mouth falls open, a good imitation of Munch's *The Scream*. "What are we thinking? You can't produce a baby by Christmas."

"Maybe your dream is all bunk. What's the downside? If we fail, we die. We can try to buy some time — set up a nursery."

"Madeline!"

"Maybe *he'll* sense the fetus early on. He's gone through the process for hundreds of years. He might recognize —"

"Stop it! Now!"

She follows the thought of a newborn to what comes next. Shopping. Decorating.

"For god's sake!" His eyes bulge and dart to the hole in the ceiling. "No, way! You're nuts, Madeline. Stop talking about this ridiculous idea. Get it out of your head! Got it?"

She gets it. Stupid! Stupid!

"No renovations either." Roderick takes her hand. "Come out to the pool where we can have a peaceful swim and forget this nonsense."

She's nodding vigorously. "Ack! OMG! You're right! I lost my mind here again. I'm with you now, Bro. Not another thought about idiotic theories."

She beats him out the door, dives in, and surfaces with her hair streaming. "Fuck, fuck, fuck." It's almost impossible to keep from thinking and talking inside the house. Has she already blown it, big time?

She gazes across the water, light coming up from the East. A coral-pink dawn edging low clouds. A nice color for the nursery. She drops down and pushes off the wall, does a feel-good lap underwater.

Roderick is standing in the shallow end. "Explain a couple of things to me, and then we never say another word about it."

"Safest way to go."

"Okay, why not get a volunteer? I know they're not lining up, exactly, but it would be much easier than tricking poor Augie."

"Naw. Not easy to find somebody we want. Augie's a solid citizen, a good guy. And we can use some architect genes in this family. Maybe our heirs can handle their own renovations."

He huffs. "I can't believe I didn't think of that."

She snickers. "Plus, he's cute. Might as well take advantage of that."

"Damn cute." He pauses. "What makes you think you're still fertile? At forty-four?"

"Ha!" She does a strut move in the water, like a football player who just made a goal. "I've got a dozen good eggs in the bank."

He clucks. "You sly devil."

"I figured you'd have a fit if you knew, thinking I was going to bring a brat into your life. I never expected to use my yolks like this, but hey —" She puts up her hand for a high-five. Roderick taps her palm with one finger. She gives him a smug look.

"Birthday presents — to myself — in case."

"Wait a minute. You have eggs? How? You were born a hermaphrodite."

"DSD, you mean? Wrong. All set. My eggs were screened for viability."

"More of Mother's bullshit then. Thirty-year panic?"

"Forethought. Thirty and thirty-five." She goes under and swims another lap, irritated that he won't give her the credit she's due. He can't stand it when she's right. She does a flip turn at the wall and swims toward his legs, then bursts up in front of him gasping for breath. "Be thankful, damn you! I'll be giving up my abs to save your life. Maybe."

"He motions toward the house. "Let's settle the details here and now."

"A week from now, Saturday, I'll find something to celebrate, and we'll have Cuban Night. Augie will love it."

"Is that enough time — to get the eggs?"

"They're always waiting for me. I'll order the non-toxic condoms and special freezer to be FedExed for the jiz. Let's change the day to Sunday. The jiz'll be fresher for Monday morning when the egg bank opens. I'll need to make an appointment."

He chuckles. "Egg bank — you're a hoot."

"A fertility center in Miami. How about garlic soup and *vaca frita* from Meson de Pepe? — and *tres leches* cake?" She licks her lips.

"You'll put him into food coma."

"No worries. That boy can eat. You'll revive him. As for me, I'm done watching my cholesterol."

"As if you ever did." He purses his lips. "Me too. I'm unlikely to block any arteries before Christmas Eve."

"Pooh on your nightmare." She climbs the ladder out of the pool and grabs a fluffy white towel from the cabinet. "No Prosecco after dinner, hear?"

Chapter 21

The Lure of Fame

It's only eight a.m., but August can tell from the empty cups and croissant crumbs that Roderick and Madeline have finished. Good. Maybe Madeline is embarrassed about her behavior enough to avoid him.

There's no sign of the plaster chunk, but a deep gouge in the chair back and a zig-zag scratch across the tabletop are obvious. He selects an unmarred chair at the opposite end of the room. His new chair. He scans the ceiling. He glances at his phone, just in case Garo has sent a text.

His plan for most of the day is to check out some rental offices online and follow up on foot. He'll want something serviceable and economical. No need to get fancy. From his figures and the tentative quote, the first million will cover the demolition and a year's salary of $200,000, some of which is already spent. He feels overpaid, but Roderick insisted. Now, sober, it's hard to imagine the glass wing as more than a pipe dream... Still...

He pours a coffee and slips back up to his room. There are no answers to his emails. It's probably impossible to get a demo guy down within the week. He pulls out his sketchpad. Strictures of time, money, and the needs of his client, a non-linear mass of interconnected details needs to be organized strategically. It's tough to get down to specifics, even flexible ones. The existing typography and surrounding style would challenge anybody's creativity. Having been told he possesses unique artistry, he still wouldn't bet the bank on it — Roderick is betting the bank. If he can actually pull this off, he'll have a landmark building to his credit for the rest of his life. The Ushers will live on, minus their paranoia. Possibly.

He's considering the idea of using detached turrets with ornate wrought iron to match the design language of the older wing and create a style connection. Maybe turrets of different heights, hugging the corners on three sides, preserving asymmetricity. No. A rounded look, half pillars holding the gingerbread, attached together on one edge, as if hinged, standing like open books.

Loosely sketching it out brings it alive. The half-pillars look snug, but will actually be two inches short of touching the glass walls to fulfill Roderick's demand for no reflection or shadow cast by the structure itself. Ornate wrought iron panels should work. They could span across the building, secured on the half pillars on all sides. With anchoring, they would provide stability for the pillars, plus mottled shade, some privacy, and a lovely, undulating pattern on a calm ocean. Or folding gates? Folded in quarters with mechanical means for movement. They could be unfolded and secured to protect the glass structure during hurricanes. A lot to consider.

Choosing the gingerbread style will be important too. Something curvy and leaf-like, classic. Sturdy, but allowing air flow. This is nuts. He's getting way ahead of himself. Spending so much time on a fantasy is unhealthy.

Christopher Wren, the famous British architect, is the source of his inspiration. The story of his legendary prank was told to him as a prospective student. When Wren was forced to add pillars to a domed ceiling at Eton College to quell investors' fears that it would collapse, he built them two inches short. Years later, a cleaning crew on scaffolding discovered that the pillars were freestanding. Wren was dead, but the world remembers him evermore.

Later, he read that the anecdote probably wasn't true. No matter. It represented the rightful courage of conviction. His own "prank" will be practical. The pillars and ironwork will provide a great amount of protection. The steampunk style will blend into Old Town, Key West. Goosebumps rise on his scalp.

He's eager to order supplies and start a detailed sketch so he can make a study model. Getting permits, or even contracting a demolition engineer by Christmas Eve is pretty much impossible, but showing Roderick something concrete should help. The glass, the magnetism, the church and house communicating, the timetable... none of it makes sense anyhow. He's trying to apply logical fixes to delusions. Not in his job description. His job is to eliminate the danger and please the client. And let Roderick pull necessary strings.

He thinks about the creepy stuff, the house hearing, seeing, understanding. *Him* watching the computer screen — can *he* interpret what it means? He almost glances over his shoulder. Stupid.

He refreshes his email. An email with "Demonitions" in the subject line has just come in from an unknown address — funny typo. Luca Montresori, a licensed demolitions expert, would like to meet with him at his earliest convenience. No Montresori was mentioned by August's contacts, but where else would this guy have gotten his email address? Probably legit, but he needs a recommendation. Montresori could have read somebody's email on an office computer and tried to get a jump on the job.

He goes back down to the dining room for a croissant. Roget serves him coffee and hands over a business card. A real estate office on Duval Street with a notation from Roderick: *Rentals right down the block*. Sounds good.

The patio windows are open and the sun is shining on the deck. Last night barely seems real, but the less time he spends in the house, the better he'll feel. He finishes breakfast in a hurry and goes back upstairs to check his email. Nothing from Gars, but there's an email from a colleague. Again, so soon, he can't believe it... "highly recommend Anthony Mentoni." There's a short list of demolition addresses that Mentoni has completed. He Googles the addresses. Mentoni has taken down an 1890s building that had become a squat. There was media coverage, a protest. "Historic Beauty to be Destroyed." The same guy who emailed earlier? He checks. No, wrong Italian. Must be a lot of

Italians in the demo business.

He calls Mentoni and they set a time for Thursday afternoon. Mentoni is in Atlanta, having been there to quote another job and would love a couple warm days in Key West. Good luck, for once. August can hardly believe it. It means he's doing the right thing.

As he heads down Duval toward the rental office, he notices he's more comfortable now with the humidity. The agent offers to drive him to several offices that are available, but he asks to walk.

The first office he's shown has immediate curb appeal. It's quaint, first floor, with a glass block window to let in plenty of light, without giving a view from outside. A tiny bit of gingerbread on the balustrade above adds a Key West flare. Inside the floors are carpeted in a tasteful and practical beige Berber, and the AC blows like a blizzard. A small bathroom even has a shower. He can put in a day bed and sleep there if he wants. Plenty of room for a table and chairs, a small refrigerator, and microwave. Cable Wi-Fi access. He'll set up the worktable for the Usher wing right inside the window.

No need to haggle or look further. He can move in the next day, so he signs the paperwork. All good. He takes his laptop down the street to a café to get a latte and start ordering what he'll need. In his old life he would have gone thrift-shopping on Ebay, but there's no reason to waste time now when he can order everything new and have it delivered in a few days. He picks out a table and types in his new South Duval Street address.

It feels good to take more control of his life. He didn't realize he missed it, until his stay with the Ushers. Not that Gars ever told him what to buy or do, and it felt right to let Gars choose what they ate, where they went, who their friends were. His tastes are wonderful and his routines were already established in the household. It was comfortable, for the most part, and Gars paid the bills.

The Utrecht site has the materials he needs to build the model. Utility knife, precision knife, titanium scissors, T-square, L-square, self-healing cutting board, foam board and a wood base.

He should've brought tools in his checked luggage, but no big deal. He scans the page. Micro LEDs will make a great impression for the interior lighting, but what to use for the glass? Clear sheet print is too thin for anything but small windows. For walls, Midwest polycarbonate sheets are claimed to be tougher and less likely to split than acrylic. He hasn't used the material before, but everything in this project is new to him. He's not worried about making a mistake that will cost him a few extra bucks, but there's no time to reorder. He uses his best judgement and goes for it. He chooses to draw his structural pieces on AutoCAD and have them laser cut for precision. Worth the extra money.

Hours have flown by when he closes the laptop, feeling a sense of pride, regardless of the low probability of bringing the project to fruition. Spending the time and money might be foolhardy, but many great people have been accused of that. He flings up his hands to fate.

Chapter 22

Financial Complication

Madeline seats herself in a tropical-print rattan chair near the glass-top desk. She's freezing in the AC and crosses her arms, impatient, while Roderick and Seabright Ellison, Jr., Esq., finish their gay-bud greeting routine. They babble on, the lawyer chuckling at Roderick's self-serving comedic remarks. "The house cracks every time I have an orgasm — you can imagine the damage!"

She can't take any more and cuts them off mid-laugh. "So, Seabreeze, let's get a look at those deeds."

Roderick glares. "Maddy, it's Seabright."

"What did I say?"

Ellison waves it away. "Common error, Sweetie. Just so you get it right on the check."

Roderick titters.

Maddy moves forward as Ellison opens a folder on the desk. "You're legally situated to sell with the Cambridge property, but... it seems, unfortunately, the Cornwall estate has a lien on it for 30,000 pounds, plus interest." He looks up, chewing at his lower lip.

"What?" Maddy scoots closer to Roderick and lifts the sheet. Legalese swims in front of her eyes, but she can read numbers. "Why didn't we know about this?

Roderick?"

Ellison points to the date. "You were children when the loan was taken — 1981. The Trust has been paying a monthly amount since then."

Madeline groans. "Roderick, you must have noticed the withdrawals. You've been handling the finances for years, since Mother died."

"I guess I knew at one time. An expense that I was used to seeing. At least, interest rates must have been really low in those days. We probably don't owe much over that amount."

"Hmm. Don't quote me, but I think rates were at historical highs around then. Close to twenty percent on property financed in the U.S. The Jimmy Carter era. It dropped by half, four years later, but your grandparents didn't refinance."

"Ugh." She knows they've never paid enough attention to finances, but this is uncanny bad luck. "I can't believe it."

"No sense in estimating. I'll get the exact figures. You didn't tell me that you wanted them."

"That was the point in coming here." Madeline raises her eyebrows at Roderick and gives a smug look. "Forget it then. Let's see what we can do with the Cambridge place."

"The Cambridge house has been vacant for about six years, so I would need to check on the condition, but the property is definitely in a great location." He finds a sheet. "We had an offer in 2011 for a mil and a half. That's dollars, not pounds."

Maddy looks hard at Roderick. "I never heard about that."

"We discussed it." He flashes his palm toward her. "Seabright, that amount isn't going to do it for us."

"The structure is in the midst of businesses and university buildings. I'm sure the value has increased. I'll reach out to our London office and get a new assessment. Then you can decide if you want to put it on the market. You can always renovate, as well."

"Renovation to finance the renovation?" Roderick sits down and slumps. "Not enough time. Not enough time to do anything."

Madeline flings back her head. "What a riot! We should send August to —"

"It's not funny. There won't be enough money to build even a one-story glass wing. We're doomed."

Ellison squints. "It can't be as bad as all that, Roddy. A mil and a half is better than a stick in the eye. Plus, you'll make something if you sell in Cornwall. I can help you locate possible investors." He evens the edges of the documents and slides them into the folder. "A glass wing?"

"Never mind. Let's dump both. How long will it take?"

"Not long to get them on the market as is, but I don't advise it. And I can't say when anything will sell. Pricing low will help."

Roderick turns to Madeline. His eyes are teary. "I need to get out of here."

Ellison puts out his hand. "I'm so sorry. Keep me posted."

Roderick pushes past. "Time for lunch. Don't ruin your conch fritters over it."

Madeline gives Ellison a 'sorry' smile on her way out.

On the sidewalk, she takes Roderick's arm and turns him toward Mallory Square. She checks her watch. "Yes, lunch. If we stroll, it will be eleven by the time we get down to Pepe's. And I can order the food for Sunday's mojito party.

"Why don't we just have José make dinner? Lobster Bianca pizza and a salad. We pay him enough."

"He needs the night off." She leads him into the interior of El Meson de Pepe and chooses a booth. "So. Everything depends on *my* plan now."

"You sound triumphant." Roderick slides into a chair. "Don't you realize the trouble we're in? August is wasting his time on the atrium structure."

"*My* little plan is going to work."

"We've probably only got enough for the foundation repair. If I tell him to stop the rest, he'll leave, and you won't be able to get the sperm."

"Roddy, he isn't going to split that fucking fast."

"Don't bet on it. I wouldn't be surprised if he took off for Paris tomorrow."

"So, hold off on the bad news for a few days, that's all. Get the jiz, and we're set."

A waitress comes to take their order. Madeline asks for two mojitos and *lechon asado* with black beans and rice and plantains.

Roderick looks to be in outer space. "Roderick?"

"Ian! For god's sake, Maddy. He'll give me a loan, whatever I ask for — instantly."

"The waitress has other customers."

He looks up and points to Madeline. "I'll share hers."

Madeline huffs. "Not a chance." She grabs the menu. "Give him the *palomilla* steak."

"Rice and beans and plantains?"

"And yucca fries. Oh, conch fritters for an appetizer. We'll share everything."

Roderick nods and the waitress leaves. "You're going to eat all that?"

"It's practice. Soon I'll be eating for two." She grimaces.

He runs his hands through his hair and lets out a sigh. "Ian doesn't know what to do with his billions. When the properties sell, I'll pay him back."

"Oh, yeah? If we make enough and it's soon enough. And you'll have to have sex with him — a lot."

Roderick cringes. "Maybe not." He looks at her. "I like Ian. I really do. Extremely. He's just doing his artist thing." The waitress sets down the drinks and he takes a sip from his straw. "Let's postpone mojito night and invite Ian for Sunday dinner."

"No fucking way. The jiz is more important."

"The money is most important." He fingers condensation on his glass. "I need to keep Augie out of the way while Ian is there."

"I'll go to Lenore's. Those subcutaneous horns... ack." She makes a grimace. "Can't he get those removed?"

"Please. Ian is a really nice guy. He has a purpose for the horns. I forget what."

"If you say so, Bro. But we're doing it my way. I'm ordering the food for Sunday. Let me know what night you're having Ian over."

"No worries. I'll get José to make us his lobster pizza."

Chapter 23

Clarification

August leaves Turtle Kraals feeling full and noticing the beauty of the night, the stars, the breeze and swish of palms. There's so much truth in Garo's words, as always, that he has to accept the situation, put on his big boy pants. If Garo is, in fact, letting him down easy, maybe he'll stay in Key West. Or not.

It was the perfect meal to lift his spirits. The Ushers have food as good as any he's eaten on the island, but it's mostly nouvelle cuisine, tiny portions, served alongside so much witty conversation that he hardly tastes the food. Nothing like guzzling a few beers and loading up on carbs and fried foods. Gars used to join him, on occasion, for a wild night of grease and salt.

Since the Ushers are dining with friends from out of town, he should be early enough to slip up to his room before they get home. He'll grab a book from the library on the way. Hopefully, Roderick has something besides dark philosophy.

He walks along Duval, glancing into bars, buffeted by the usual blasts of cold air conditioning. As he turns onto South Street, there's Ian, heading his way. No time to duck him without being obvious. He smiles, hoping he can get away with a wave and a hi.

"August! Nice to see you. Headed home?" Ian stops, taking up most of the sidewalk, and puts out his hand.

August shakes it. "How are you? Yeah, thought I'd make it an early night. Just loaded up on fritters and fries down at the Turtle Kraals."

"Oh, I thought I'd see you at dinner, but Rod said you had business —"

"Dinner? Yeah, I... Un huh." Moonlight seems to glint off of each horn on Ian's brow. August focuses there, avoiding the possibility of seeing the forked tongue. Why would Roderick have invited Ian and lied? Sex? He shrugs off a chill.

"Can I buy you a drink? We've never had a chance to talk."

It's the last thing he wants, but he needs to know.

"Been to the Green Parrot?" Ian takes August's hesitation as a go and points him back toward town.

Immediately inside the door, August regrets following along. It's a crowded, gay dive bar with a mixed batch of tourists thrown in. Loud. The kind of place to avoid.

Ian finds two stools at the end of the bar and orders IPAs. "You don't get out much, huh? Everybody knows this place."

"I'm on a tight schedule."

"I'm relieved to find out you're taking charge. Roderick doesn't need the stress. He's looking fragile these days. Besides that, the place scares me. Can't get those repairs done too soon, if you ask me."

"The work is long overdue."

"He's a special person to me. I wonder if he's told you about my project."

August shakes his head no and scoots closer to hear above the noise. "The island resort? Not much."

"Not that. Two years ago, I started a five-year living art installation." He points to the points on his forehead and sticks out his tongue.

August takes a gulp of beer. "Oh?"

"I'm an artist from upstate New York. Here temporarily. Henry Duval is my real name."

"Duval? Like the street?"

"Yep, descendent of William Pope Duval, governor when Florida was still a territory. But keep calling me Ian."

"Sure."

"I'm undercover to most people. I record the reactions of strangers to my visuals and the further effects on my personal relationships. I know you'll keep my secret. I wanted to tell you since we'll be working together on a professional basis. Also, you're so close to Roderick."

August points to his own forehead, already feeling relief. "So this isn't a lifestyle choice?"

"Only temporarily. It's for an LGBTQIA+ combination study in art and sociology, backed by The New School. Roderick immediately plugged me into his social group. I owe him bigtime."

"I see, in the city." He tries to picture Ian without the accoutrements, possibly a normal looking guy, a bear type. "Doesn't having Roderick introduce you skew your data? I mean..."

"It's more art than science. The sociology is only one thread of the experiment, or installation, whichever you want to call it."

"Something like architecture — evolving aesthetics and serendipity discoveries."

"I like that."

"Although, architecture is based on existing features, needs — and desires."

"I don't base my art on anything. No hypothesis. No bias — as much as I can help it. I'm putting together diary entries with video, a process to understand human nature. The reactions of strangers to my appearance. At the end of five years, I'll have the prostheses removed, my tongue stitched back together, and see what I've got." He touches his horns. "Almost done. I won't miss these."

"Wow." Ian's creepiness has dissipated, but he's still hard to look at. August scans the room. "Sounds interesting. I've never seen you with a camera man, though."

Ian points to the black center of a flower on his Hawaiian shirt pocket, explaining that it's actually a lens hole. He pulls out a small device and hands it to August. "I design shirts with an opening for a mini-cam. Two of my businesses combined."

August inspects the tiny plastic camera. He reaches toward the pocket. "Mind?"

"Not at all."

He fingers the inner fabric. There's Velcro on both sides to keep the camera in place. "Clever. You have these built into all your shirts?"

"Most." He pulls a tiny plastic box out of his pants pocket. "The remote. Of course, I can't incorporate any of the footage or I would need permissions." He drops the remote back. "I design digital faces, using the shape of the face, mouth, eyes, and brows."

"Interesting."

"I record their movements from when the person first meets me, and so on. The expressions are revealing when there's no distraction from other facial features or conversation. I'll show you my sketchbook sometime."

"That'd be great."

Ian laughs. "I saw some pretty good expressions on your face the night of the auction. Too bad my costume wasn't rigged for video."

"I'm sorry." Heat rushes to his face. "So, you purposely made yourself...?"

"Grotesque. And don't be afraid to say it — demonic." Ian swigs his beer. He says he also enjoys teaching, but not as much as creating. "I don't fit well with academics, or with my fellow trust-babies, not a bit. Except Rod. He's unusual. Both of us enjoy slinging a monkey wrench into the world to see what comes out of it."

"Rod does that?"

Ian shrugs. "Seems like it."

Something to digest. August admits to understanding the need to create, the main reason he went into architecture. "Personally, I like a predictable outcome... if at all possible."

He buys a round, and in a short time, he can look at Ian straight on. It's a good chance to bring up the subject of Roderick's fears, but he doesn't want to seem like he's talking behind his back.

Ian takes a long drink of beer. "So, I don't know if I should tell you... but..." He takes a swig. "Roderick asked me for a loan, a huge loan... to pay for the renovations. He has collateral. He just needs time. I told him I could help him out, but I want to be involved, in a small way."

August swallows hard. "I see. You want to keep an eye on the money."

Ian nods. "Sort of. I trust you and Roderick, of course. I just... umm."

August puts his hand over Ian's pocket. "Sorry. Is the camera on?"

Ian shows him a switch on the back and moves it to the off position. "I always run it, but I wouldn't use any of this. It's no good since you know the process."

"I hate to ask, but do you ever worry that Roderick might be headed for some kind of mental..."

"Collapse? Yes. He told me some pretty crazy sounding stuff."

August nods, not sure how far to go. "I have some... uneasy feelings. We should talk to him together."

"I've been wanting to clarify something."

August waits for a bomb to drop.

"Roderick and I aren't lovers anymore, not for, maybe, six months. That isn't to say we might not be again, but I won't step on your toes. I don't know what kind of relationship you have."

"I don't either. I didn't intend to get involved —"

"Oh, I know. I know. Roderick can be irresistible."

It isn't exactly the word August was searching for, but he can't think of a replacement. "I'm glad you told me. I was afraid I might be stepping on *your* toes."

"We never had a serious relationship. Not on his side." He proposes a meeting with Roderick on Tuesday afternoon.

August digs out a freshly printed card. "My new office. By Tuesday, I'll have a study model, nothing immutable, but a good visual to work from. My next step will be to hire a demolitions company. I'm meeting a contractor tomorrow, so that's underway." He takes out his cell phone. "I'd appreciate your input any time. I'm going to tell Roderick that we met up and you're in on the plans. No secrecy."

"He said he was going to tell you about the loan first thing."

"Great. We're all on the same page."

"I'm impressed with your honesty. I mean that, August."
August thanks him. He should be giving a warning.

Chapter 24

Such a Deal

August finishes touring Anthony Mentoni through the house and cellar. He leads him to the patio, and Mentoni takes a walk around the outside. August checks the time. Garo is probably having cocktails, or more likely, a creamy French Pinot at a café on the Left Bank. He could have tagged along if he wasn't so determined to make a grand statement about himself to the world. What's it worth anyway? Garo will keep him as a pet, regardless. Maybe that's been his status all along. He just hadn't landed on the word for it.

Why does he need more? Look at Roderick. A big name in the scientific community a few years ago, now a delusional alcoholic, borrowing a fortune to spend on his eccentricities.

Mentoni comes around the side of the building and stops to shield his eyes and gaze upward. As August gets close, he interprets concern. "So, can we write up a contract?"

Mentoni shakes his head. "I don't know yet. You really want to take down a huge chunk of this Victorian beauty? It needs foundational work, hell yes, but it's sure worth fixing. I don't know if I have the conscience to blast such a gorgeous page out of history."

"Listen, I can't explain all the details, but you need to decide within a day or two. Usher is adamant. If not you, I have to find somebody else in a hurry."

"I get that. I'm just not sure I wanna be the executioner."

"Jesus. That's a harsh word. I mean, really, come on, man.

You've taken down — at least — one unique structure. I read about it. The protest didn't faze you."

Mentoni moves closer to August. "I need the work, but I have regrets." He turns his back to the house. His voice is hushed. "This house has something like a... soul... and..."

"Charm."

"More like power. This wing with the ballroom is the heart of it." He puts his hand on August's shoulder. "Keep this to yourself. Somebody might think I'm a nut case." He puts his hands together, fingers pointed somewhere between his chest and abdomen. "Sometimes, here, I feel a primitive need to preserve strength, the strength under grace. Or maybe, it's an instinct against wastefulness. I fight it. This time..." He stares into space. "It's more like being repelled by an emotional force from... elsewhere. I don't know. I need to think the whole thing through, my principles."

"Principles." August's stomach clenches. Not something he wants defined. The heart... that nonsense again. "I see. How about — we build in a bonus? Say, 20% over your fee, and more for getting it done within the month? The owner is willing to pay a premium. You can let me know the figure tomorrow. I won't try to bargain."

Mentoni scans the house from end to end and focuses on the east wing. "There's no way I can get it done in a month anyway. I don't need to keep you waiting. You're a good guy, Augie." He puts out his hand to shake. "I hope we get a chance to work together in the future."

A flat-out no. "This is bullshit. We had a contract, an email agreement. Now you've taken up valuable time, and I don't know what the hell I'll do."

Mentoni steps forward. "Hey, fuck you! My wife came along for the weekend, so I won't bill you, but don't try to threaten me with lawyer crap."

August puts out his hand. "Sorry. I'm desperate. How about I cover the whole trip as a mini vacation? Double your normal fee? You name it. Just take time to consider. Stop back at your convenience."

"No, thanks. I'm never coming back here." Mentoni starts walking at a fast clip, then stops. "Tell me, would you take her down?"

August is thinking *him*, not her. He can't answer.

"That's what I thought." Mentoni turns toward the sidewalk.

August wonders if this conversation will ripple through his business contacts in the city. Normally, he's careful to hold his temper, not burn any bridges. The stress is contagious. He dreads telling Roderick the news. Is there enough money on earth to demolish this house?

The unsolicited email from the other Italian comes to mind. Montessori? He'll shoot a note to his contacts and see if the guy was actually recommended.

Mentoni drives off and August turns to the house. Stomps his foot on one of the pavers. "You won, didn't you? Son of a bitch!"

Maddy or Roddy scampers from a clump of red hibiscus, digs a hole next to August's toe, and squats. Pee sizzles into the sand. "Perfect comment." The cat leaps over his foot and cavorts across the patio.

Chapter 25

Desperate Measuring

Maddy grasps the handle of the sweating pitcher and pours herself the first mojito. She takes one sip and another. It slides down easy. She'll tell Roget to make the next batch stronger, in case August is counting his servings. Then again, being under Roderick's spell now, he shouldn't need many drinks. With her out of the house, he won't be expecting any tricks. Where the fuck is he?

She can't keep her mind off the plan. She steps out to the patio so she can think without possible eavesdropping. She takes a draw on her e-cig. Roderick in charge of getting the sperm, not great. She has to rely on him to use the special condom, knot it, and deposit it into the receptacle in her shower without August suspecting. Many ways for him to fuck it up. She'll be relieved when she has it in her hands in the morning and is on her way to the IVF Center in Coral Gables. It's a three-hour drive, but she hopes to be back by Happy Hour. Or maybe she'll add some nursery shopping in Miami, as long as she's up there. Picking out baby stuff might be fun. Some mother-fucking positive vibes.

She pictures the jiz and egg in their Petri dish, snuggling on their puffy round mattress. It's going to happen. It will be good for everybody. Best to go with a payment plan, so she won't have to listen to Roderick's bullshit about the $17,000 or so, which he'll say would be better spent on renovations. Anyway, there's no sense in paying the total balance when they'll likely be dead before the second payment is due. She drains her mojito.

Tonight might be her last alcohol for a long time. She'll have to prep for motherhood.

If she didn't need to supervise, she'd already be with Lenore in a premier room with a private pool at the H^2O Suites. Lovely Lenore, floating on her back, riding high in the warm water, her hair streaming behind her. A tricky maneuver she loves to show off. Her thighs split, her cute little clit peeping out as she moves forward, pushing with her arms until her feet touch the wall. Then she changes direction, moving her legs with imperceptible effort to glide head-first. She was born for the water. Madeline never saw Lenore as a mermaid at Weeki Wachee, her perfect job, ended by a manipulative man. Thank god for Lenore's grandmother's trust fund, so she never had to work again. The world would have ruined her, so much innocence, beauty, and love, packed tight into an out-of-control sex machine.

August better show up soon. She refreshes her drink and takes a napkin with a few plaintain chips to a padded lounge chair on the beach, turning it in the best position to view sunset. The crunch of August's dress shoes on the pavers catches her attention. He's dressed in a blue button-down shirt with a pencil holder in the pocket and light khakis with pleats, as if returning from a corporate office.

She calls to him. "Put on your flip-flops and Hawaiian shirt! The party's already started."

"Party?"

She salutes with her drink and points out her colorful sarong, festive and covering most of her body, so not to perturb him.

Chapter 26

November 21st

August passes Maddy and waves, heading to his room. He's worked a full day in his office, accomplishing what he'd hoped. He'll be able to tell Roderick that there's a demolition contractor on the way. Reputation unknown, but Roderick won't care. No one seems to have recommended Montresori. One construction engineer had possibly heard his name associated with something "unsavory." Pressed for details, he'd laughed and said he couldn't remember. Somebody probably didn't like the guy personally. In the past, August would have followed up, but this is the new normal.

The items from Utrecht have arrived, so he's into the first stages of the model. He decides to keep it secret until he can set the glass walls and floors. He's using a temporary adhesive since Roderick might want some input. He imagines Roderick's excitement and relief, seeing so much progress. If the glass building never comes to fruition, the model will stand as Roderick's wish list made concrete, for him to show to his friends. If it lifts his fear and despair so he gets through Christmas Eve without a stroke or heart attack, it will be well worth the effort.

Maddy J., he guesses, flits from the bushes to stand in front of him on the path, and he stops to stroke her, nose to tail, as she likes. Time for a drink or two and a garlicky, caloric Cuban dinner, as promised. Under the circumstances, he can accept Madeline's behavior as understandable. He sort of looks forward to the snide banter between her and Roderick. They put on a good face, despite their fear of imminent doom.

In his new blue *guayabera* shirt, he returns to be engulfed by the spicy incense of Cuban food, reminding him that he skipped lunch. He pauses in front of gleaming warmers spread across the sideboard along with a stack of white China plates, napkins, and utensils. It's a close call, but politeness wins out over gluttony, and he follows voices to the patio.

Roget is holding a tray of hors d'oeuvres toward Roderick. Roderick flashes his widest smile. "Here's Augie now!" He sounds breathless. "Augie, try the garlic shrimp."

August goes to the tray and toothpicks an extra-jumbo pink shrimp, dips it in butter and spices. As he's chewing, Roget slides a mojito into his other hand. Quite the life. He holds his glass up in a toast. "To the demo."

Madeline steps up to clink her glass.

Roderick's eyes are shining. "The demo! That means we have a demoli... a contractor." He indicates the house with his elbow. "Let's be careful. We're under the eaves."

"If you approve. He'll be here day after tomorrow."

"Sure! For the umm... demonstration. Enough about that."

Madeline giggles. "Yes, the oil painting demonstration." The conversation moves into art, and August stops listening, thinking that dinner is drying out in the pans, then wondering about Montresori, then rethinking window materials for the model.

Roget announces dinner. August and Roderick pile their plates with beef, rice, beans, and plantains. Madeline ladles garlic soup into an oversized cup, and Roderick needles her about her breath. Madeline gives him a disgusted look. "Lenore loves everything about me."

Roderick crooks a finger toward the patio. "Let's move to the chaise longues, to enjoy the sunset as we sup."

They settle into eating, unusually quiet for the Ushers. A rooster crows. Roderick rolls his eyes. "Oh, dear. Have you heard about the feral chicken crisis? They're taking over Key West again. Even worse, a rooster, Alvin, has moved in under our porch. I hear him at least three times a night, and worst of all, he wakes me at the crack of dawn."

"Alvin? Hmm. Could be that he's —" August shrugs, keeping rooster knowledge to himself.

"Better the crack of dawn than a crack in the head," Maddy says with cheer. "Or a crack anywhere."

"One doesn't preclude the others, unfortunately."

"I haven't heard any crowing," August says.

She shakes her head. "Me either. It's your sensitive ears, Bro. Wear your ear plugs."

"What if Alvin runs out on the sidewalk and spurs somebody? That's all we need, a lawsuit. Although, I suppose we're unlikely to live long enough to go to court. What about that chicken rescue?"

She tells him there might be a twenty-four-hour number. August settles it, volunteering to catch the rooster and deliver him, the least of their problems.

He's still working on his beef when Maddy stands with her plate and apologizes for having to meet Lenore. Roderick is unusually forgiving, considering it's supposed to be a party. "Don't mind her," he tells August. "No rush. Seconds are a must."

Madeline winks at them both, slugs the last of her drink, and says goodnight.

August goes back for another serving. He leaves off the rice, but the pile of rich meat still looks gluttonous.

He sits down. Roderick nods at the plate-full. "Good job, Aug."

He smiles, forking a tender bite of beef and soft, greasy transparent onions. He misses Garo's cooking, but he's not wasting away. He counts the days till he'll see him. Thanksgiving is only three days away, and that means thirty days until Christmas Eve, the overlap of Roderick's doomsday and Gars' arrival home. He'll be with Gars in the city that evening, at least until after New Year's, unless something goes wrong.

It occurs to him that Roderick will expect him to stay Christmas Eve night. Will he be able to leave when Roderick is sure he'll die? Madeline should be able to handle it. Maybe Ian can come over to keep Roderick's spirits up.

August puts his knife and fork on the plate, ready to head upstairs. "I'm stuffed. Thank you. Everything was delicious."

"It's so early, Augie. We need a nightcap, at least." He suggests a move to the library.

"Just a few minutes. I'm beat." He can't help remembering that he first betrayed Garo on the library sofa, thinking Gars had already slept with the Frenchman. Stupid. He still can't get it out of his mind.

He hangs back, but Roderick seems not to notice. The double doors are open and Roderick goes inside.

He drags himself up and follows. "I can't drink anymore. I have a full day of work tomorrow to prep for the demolition contractor."

"To be safe, you mean the demonstration contractor?"

"Yeah, yeah, slip of tongue."

"Ah, tongue." He smiles… then frowns. "Haven't you already met with him?"

It's too late to backtrack. "Oh, I was going to tell you about that after I hire the new guy."

In the library, Roderick falls into the stuffed chair. "Doesn't sound like good news. More money than expected?"

August sinks onto the edge of the sofa. "Nope. Worse. He refused to demolish, um... demonstrate..." He can't think. "I tried to offer a lot more money. He didn't want to hear it."

Roderick shakes his head. "I should have known. Nobody's going to do it! *He's* too strong. It's too late!"

"No, not at all. We're in luck. This guy flying in tomorrow. He'll knock down anything."

Roderick shoots him a warning look.

"Ack. Anything... in his way. I don't know much about him, but if you want it done..."

"Mafia?"

August takes a quick breath. "I don't think so."

"I'd like to see those wise guys *ump-day* an *oddy-bay* in there. He'd *ommit-vay* it right back at them." He puts his hand over his mouth. A snickery-snort seeps out through his nose. "You know Pig Latin?"

August laughs. "Maybe I should *eck-chay* further."

Roderick chuckles. "No. Go for it. Anybody who can *ake-tay* this *ucker-say* down-day — I mean *oun-day* — is fine with me." His eyes dart across the ceiling. "You're not thinking about this, are you, Aug? Stop thinking."

"I never thought of Mafia." Seems like somebody he asked would have known and told him if that were true.

"No worries, my dear Augie. You're trying your best, and you are the best. I dawdled around all those years while... you-know-who got stronger. I wasn't mature enough to believe that the future would come."

"Don't worry. I'm more determined than ever." August squints at the wall straight across from him. A hairline crack has developed from the ceiling to halfway down. "Was that there before?"

"I'm not sure. I didn't see it till now."

August crosses the room and taps the wall with his fist. "Hope it's not spreading."

"Cracks in this wing don't matter. The foundation is newer. The structures are only attached above ground."

August walks up to the crack and taps it. He whispers, "Can you feel this?"

Roderick covers his mouth. "Be careful. Just saying... Might be like conjoined twins."

August moves across, tapping to find a stud. "I'm going to learn all your secrets."

Roderick whispers, his hands cupped around his mouth directing the words, "Don't aggravate him, August. Too many mojitos!" He stares up at the ceiling and projects his voice. "Are you nuts, August? Any more talk like that and I'm throwing you out for good."

August puckers up and gives the crack a smacking kiss. "You'll be good as new."

"Stop joking around, for god's sake! How about a drink?" Roderick moves to the lacquered Chinese cabinet and brings out a bottle and two crystal glasses. He shows the label, hands shaky, a single malt scotch.

August considers. "A short one, if you insist. I don't want to be queasy in the morning." He sits in the stuffed chair across from the sofa.

Roderick hands him a glass, a double pour. It's glowing, beautiful. He takes in the funky, rounded aroma before he sips. If Montresori doesn't come through, this could be the last vestige of his millionaire lifestyle.

"Let's change the subject." Roderick leans on the desk and gives him the rundown on Maddy's evening, her meeting with Lenore at a fancy hotel with an in-room pool. August chuckles at the appropriate moments when Roderick pretends scorn at her behavior. August drinks the last drop of the scotch and sets his glass on a doily, thinking to check his email. Roderick's hands are instantly on his shoulders, kneading. He lets himself slump. Roderick moves up his neck into his scalp.

"I learned this from a *geisha*."

August is drifting. "You went to Japan?"

"I could never, but zie was dressed as a *geisha*. A local friend."

"Oh."

"Let's go upstairs before you fall asleep in the chair. I'll do your back with oil."

He barely has the energy to move, but the stairs have to be climbed sometime. They reach August's door and he gives Roderick a peck. "Thank you for a great dinner and evening. Let's cross our fingers that the meeting goes well in the morning."

"Oh, Augie. I'm so scared. This cheerfulness is an act. I'm trying to be brave, but I don't want to spend the night alone worrying about what happens tomorrow. Please come in. I'll get the oil and we can relax and fall asleep together."

He knows they won't fall asleep. Does it matter? Garo is lost. It's faster to appease Roderick than talk him out of it, accept a blow job. Maybe they can skip the droning guitar chords later. He puts his arm across Roderick's shoulder and draws him close, melting. "Sure. I don't want you to spend the night upset."

He follows Roderick into his room. The bedside lamps are glowing, and a red lava lamp on the dresser, unlike the last visit in cold gloom and spooky flashes of moonlight.

Instead of motioning August to the bed, Roderick offers a

chair. He rummages in a drawer and returns with scented oil. "Frangipani — you like it?" He doesn't wait for an answer.

August moans, as Roderick finds tight places in his shoulders. Without Garo, could he ever consider Roderick as a partner again? Be the mature half of the relationship this time, the half in control?

It's no surprise when he feels warm breath in his ear and the arousing touch of Roderick's fingers on his lower back as they probe tight muscles with exactly the right pressure. August pulls Roderick to him for a kiss, a whisky kiss, sweet and sharp.

The transition is swift to naked and bed. Kisses trail down his abdomen. He's aware of his own fast breaths as he caresses Roderick's fine, soft hair. All sensation draws into one tight center where Roderick's mouth removes the tension of the universe. Roderick breaks off and turns aside, fumbles in the nightstand. Taking precautions without a reminder.

"Give it to me hard, Augie. I have such a short time."

The words are out of character. Acceptance of death, passion in the face of death? Roderick's hand is on August's cock, rolling the condom over it, slathering on emollient, stroking, stroking. August rises to his knees and moves over him, taking Roderick's slim buttocks into his hands to slide himself inside. Fast, hard pumping.

"Yes, yes, yes, yes, yes, yes, yes."

Consciousness dims in the throbs of the moment. His groans share the rhythm of Roderick's *yes*, and the cadence of his trancelike chant repeats outside the window, the lapping and the slapping of waves... *the bells, bells, bells, bells, bells, bells, bells*, the lapping and the slapping...

He slumps. His cheek rests on Roderick's shoulder. He pushes himself to the side, not to flatten the delicate man he has just made love to. His hand trails near Roderick's forearm, such a fine wrist, slender, as is every part of his body. He could count the vertebrae in Roderick's back, barely covered with delicate musculature. He runs his fingers through Roderick's hair. "That was nice."

Roderick's eyes open. "I love you August, no matter if you

can't return it. You've given me hope."

"It's going to work out." He begins to move away. Roderick sits up, then drops sideways on the bed, struggling to untangle his foot from the sheet.

"You okay?" The condom sags between Roderick's buttocks. August reaches over and plucks it out.

"No, no." Roderick slides to his feet on the floor. "I'll get that. Please. I'm on my way..."

"S'okay. I'll use my own bathroom."

"No, really." Roderick's hand is out as if begging. "August, please."

August pauses in the doorway. "No worries. I've got it."

He drops the condom into the toilet and pees. He returns to Roderick's room to get his clothes and to say goodnight. Roderick is curled, fetal style. August turns off the lights and spoons him, putting his arm across Roderick's chest. Roderick lets out a whimper.

"Did I hurt you?"

He snuffles. "No, never."

"Why are you crying?"

He wipes at his eyes. "I'm going to miss you." His voice cracks. "So much."

"Not for long. I'll be back."

"I mean when I'm dead."

"Stop." He squeezes Roderick's smooth shoulder. "Don't worry, Rod. We'll fix it." He's thinking he can finish the study model tomorrow afternoon. "I'll have something wonderful to show you soon."

Roderick sniffs. "I'm excited to see it." He doesn't sound excited. "Stop thinking and talking now."

August awakens. The damn rooster is crowing outside the window. It's still night. The bed moves in the familiar Roderick rhythm. August raises his head. In the red glow of the lava lamp, Roderick is curled near the edge of the bed, his arm at work.

The man can't get enough. Great. As long as it makes him happy. August falls back to sleep.

Chapter 27

The Start of Something New

It's just after six a.m. when Madeline gets back from the hotel and looks into her bathroom. The shower curtain is closed, the signal that the jiz is in its mini-freezer. Fuck, yes! Roderick came through. She closes the door and pees. She can grab a croissant and make it to the Miami clinic for the 10:00 appointment with time to spare. Unless there's an accident that blocks A1A for the day, a looming possibility when you live at the end of a string of islands. But she doesn't think *he* has the power to pull that off, so it would have to be pure bad luck.

He wouldn't have any idea what's about to happen. She thinks how quiet it's been for the last week or so. How well she's been feeling. Hopefully, not the calm before a Christmas Eve shitstorm.

She rarely uses the car, stored in a public garage nearby. Roget has to give it a jump. She hesitates to pull out into A1A traffic, but there's no choice. It's a go. Soon, flying over bridges and sparkling water beneath frees her spirit. The chalky green blends to marine blue, as it flows to the ends of the earth. If only she were truly free, free of *him* and Roderick. She would keep on going, follow A1A to the tip of Maine, through snow and cold, to whatever destiny would bring. She could handle it, her and Lenore. A new possibility, a tiny glimmer to hang onto.

She arrives a little early. A young man in scrubs calls her into an office and leaves her seated in front of a metal desk. She's hoping she can manage the day without the tendrils of evil sending her into a seizure or catatonia. She's never had an episode outside the house, but she hasn't tested it much. She sits with the precious plastic freezer between her calves and texts Roderick, letting him know that salvation is underway. Roderick answers back instantly with a thumbs-up emoji.

The office is tastefully decorated, antiseptic-looking, except for the hodgepodge on the wall of smiling pregnant women holding distended bellies or happy babies in their arms. She can't imagine how the pregnant ones can flash those bright smiles when they're in such a vulnerable and unattractive state. Two look like they'll pop at any second. She pictures the skin, under that frilly blouse, stretched tight like the blue bladder of a man-of-war... Too gruesome. She tries not to think about it. And the flattened, overstretched breasts afterward, furrowed skin that never heals. She's seen plenty of ruined skin at the nude beach. Can plastic surgery fix that? Maybe laser. Probably not. At her age how long will it take to lose the extra weight? Evil mother nature. Then to care for an infant all day, all night... Will they still have the money for a full-time nurse? They'd better!

She hoists the freezer to her lap. She'll get out before leaving becomes an embarrassment. Maybe she'd rather die. Maybe it won't work anyway, and she'll ruin her body and then die. She stands up. The young man returns and goes to the file cabinet.

Then again, she went through a certain amount of deprivation to ensure viable eggs. Somehow Roderick never noticed those totally unpleasant weeks of cold turkey off alcohol and drugs.

The young man steps into the room, putting out his hand to shake. "Art Pym." He winks. "Please, relax, sit. Pretty soon you'll be sitting down every chance you can get."

She knows he expects a smile, but she can't manage one. She sits. "I might be too old to go through with it."

His eyebrows shoot up. "We don't hear that very often." His eyes rove over her a little too slowly. "You seem in great shape. What are your concerns?"

She rambles off a list of inheritable diseases, including epilepsy, migraines, and hemophilia, adding that she has never been around children and has no idea how to care for one. "Plus, I know it sounds selfish, but I don't want to ruin my body."

He takes an even longer look at her, tits on down, as if she gave permission to do an assessment. She's glad to have worn her thin cotton sundress. A tease might get her something. She crosses her leg and swings it.

He walks around to her side of the desk, watching her. "I'm confused. Why are you here? If you've changed your mind, I understand, but you don't seem to have any desire for a child."

"It's my duty." She explains it as a deathbed promise to her mother. It's not true, but her mother would have liked to get a promise.

He sits in the chair next to her and clasps his hands. His eyes are soft, barely leering. "I can understand that you don't want to pass along possible genetic aberrations, but your many physical attributes..." He leans closer. "It's a shame for you not to reproduce."

"Really?"

"I mean it. I've never told anybody that before. You're a beautiful woman in incredible shape."

She runs her finger from lips to cleavage and leaves it there. Her natural ability to exploit men's weaknesses always becomes a game. "I'm talking about inheritable diseases."

"I understand." He looks her straight in the eyes then glances at the door and lowers his voice. "I have to be careful who I talk to, but I might be able to help with your situation. The institute isn't licensed for polygenetic testing, but I'm connected with a lab that does private gene editing."

"Oh?"

"Have you heard of CRSPR? It's a means of altering genes. We just say Crisper. Google it." He puts a finger to his lips. "But keep it quiet. I can't let anyone on the staff here know about this."

She puts it into her phone. "Is it illegal?"

"No — but I would lose my job if anyone knew I recruited you for another lab."

"Is it dangerous?"

"Not at all. You've heard of designer babies? The kind we've been told only the very rich would be able to afford?"

She nods slightly, realizing there's a money angle, wondering if she still is, or was, "the very rich."

"Since the Crisper breakthrough, changing the genome has become fast and affordable. We can select diseased chromosomes and remove or repair them using bacteriophages. Beyond that, there's bridge editing, perfect for you. We can also heighten intelligence, beauty, and athleticism. Not that you'd need any of that. Of course, identified gene pairs are limited. I can't guarantee we'll be able to remove every risk, but it's a lot better than leaving it up to nature."

She's conscious that her eyebrows are frozen high on forehead, producing wrinkles. She looks down, bringing up information from Google. "CRSPR. Seriously? Looks like I could buy a kit online and do it myself. Not that I would."

"Oh, no. Those are hobby kits. You follow instructions and use bacteria they send you. Generally, E. coli. Nasty. For human gene editing you need an expert and the latest technology."

"So what can I do?"

"It's pretty simple. We already have your eggs, and you brought us the semen, right?" He points to the mini-freezer sitting next to her. "You write the check and we start work. The cost depends on how much engineering you want done. You'll also be contributing to ongoing studies."

It's a dream come true. Why hasn't she heard of it? "I want as much as I can get in a week. Timing is most important."

"A week?" He looks at the ceiling, as if calculating. "That would be a challenge — unless I can move you to the front of the line. Even then, I doubt it's possible. The faster the pace and the more you want done, the higher the price."

"Of course." She chews her lip. She has no idea what will work, how long the fertile egg needs to be implanted for *him* to know it exists. How will *he* know anyway? Maybe starting the nursery will be enough, or it might mean waiting until the pregnancy shows. If Roderick's death date is complete hooey, then rushing is unnecessary. Besides that, her whole plan might be complete hooey. But she has strong intuition. Now, her lucky day running into this guy. If she's going to do it, she should take the death date into consideration.

"Would you like to think about this and come back? Or" — he glances at the clock — we could talk it through more at lunch."

"No, no. Let's get started. I'll give you a check. Set the appointment for me to be implanted in a week."

"Not possible." He motions toward the freezer. "We do the insemination and wait to make sure it works before editing."

She shakes her head, feeling like she might cry. It's too much to think about, and there's no time to waste. "Can you just fix the egg and inseminate? Wouldn't that be faster? I know the sperm is quality."

"Only editing half would be faster, but health improvements can be made for both donors if we have a zygote."

"I'm the one with diseased genes."

"Can I ask you why this is so urgent? You'll get a better — excuse me — product, if you stick with the normal process."

She tries to think of something logical. Her brain is a vacuum. "Do I have to tell you my reasons?"

"If I know all the facts, I might have suggestions. I can tell them what to look for."

"Any disease. Also... early aging and exaggerated senses. Is there a name for that?" She pulls her check book out of her purse.

"I don't know. I certainly don't see you aging early, but I'll make a note." He looks hard into her eyes. "Just the ovum then. Let's see if we can get it done and be ready for implantation in a week." He motions her toward the door. "Meet me in the waiting room. I need to make a call." He hesitates. "It will be costly."

"I'm sure." Ian should have already made the big deposit, but this is really a fucking gamble. She swallows hard, tells herself it's just like buying a car. In fact, Art Pym reminds her of the salesman where they bought the used Mercedes. "Get me the price."

She hands over the freezer. A brilliant idea makes her flush. It's so obvious. The answer to a major part of her dilemma. "My best friend would like to be the surrogate mother. Is it a problem?"

"Oh? Fine. As long as she's healthy and signs the forms. More tests and paperwork."

She nods, hoping she doesn't look too thrilled and unmotherly. Of course, Lenore will do it. She'll do anything Madeline asks. She'll love having a baby, and her luscious, young body will spring back like a Tempur-Pedic pillow.

"Tell her to cut off alcohol and any smoking or drugs immediately." He hands her his card. "Call my cell with any questions. Would you have lunch with me anyway? There's a nice place just across —"

She laughs. "Will it get me a discount?"

"No, sorry." He turns red. "I wish I had the power to do that. I'll need the full amount today." He leaves the room, now in a hurry. When he returns, he hands over an invoice, a nice round $50,000. "Just to be sure — this is not according to normal protocol. No specific guarantees. You can't make changes to our agreement. You can't sue. And please, hush, hush. This lab is not aware that I'm sending your DNA out."

She writes the check.

Chapter 28

November 22nd

The heavy drapes are open to the west, and subtle morning light illuminates the dining room. August clinks his champagne flute against Roderick's and sips his mimosa. "I think you'll be pleased."

Roderick winks, an unusual sparkle in his eyes. "You always please me, Augie. Saving my life goes way beyond that."

"I'm not claiming your salvation just yet, but this is step one toward a new beginning." He looks at his watch. "We better get going. Can't keep our big investor waiting."

Roderick laughs. "You nailed it. He is big."

August lets that slide and opens the door for Roderick to pass in front of him, hoping to avoid hearing in how many ways Ian is big.

Roderick looks back at him and winks. "I mean, he's huge."

"Okay, okay. It's nice to see you in a good mood, but I'd rather not be distracted when I'm showing the study model."

"You won't get distracted by his huge cock. That's my territory — just kidding."

August grimaces, despite himself. What does that mean? Roderick will be distracted by Ian's dick or he owns Ian's dick? One of those just-kidding-not-really-kidding remarks? He opens the wrought iron gate. They pass through. "I'm meeting the demolitions man later this morning."

Roderick holds up his hand, two fingers crossed. "Great." He stops under the drooping leaves of a banyan tree and faces

August. "I had a realization when I woke up this morning. There's no way anything can be built by Christmas Eve. You were clear about that all along, but I thought if I pushed hard enough, you'd manage to do what I want." He motions to his cock and smiles. "It usually works."

August waits.

"There's no guarantee, but I'm hopeful that if the east wing is destroyed before Christmas Eve, his power will be knocked back far enough that he can't kill us, and we'll have time to build the new wing. There's no choice anyway. We have to hope."

"I'm thrilled to hear you say that."

"Clearly, he has influence in the west wing now — maybe he always did — but without the original foundation working for him under there, he can't regenerate, or not as fast."

"That's wonderful."

"Like I said, I'm hopeful. But if the demolition can't be done in time, there's no chance at all."

August has to ask the burning question. "Do you actually need another building? Why not continue to live in the west wing and put in a tennis court?"

"Oh, no. We can't risk it. If the original foundation doesn't continue to function, our roots will be gone, and that would be the end of us. To thrive, we need limitations, not devastation. Besides, we want a glorious glass architectural wonder, right?"

"There's nothing I'd like better."

Roderick gives him a hug. When they pull apart, August turns aside to swipe away tears, not sure what they mean.

Ian is waiting on the sidewalk outside the office as they approach. He has on a golf shirt, jeans, and a wide-brimmed sun hat, pulled low over his horns. Appears normal. Amazing what a little information can do.

"Good morning, Mr. Usher and Mr. Dupin, on this momentous occasion."

"Well, aren't we formal today, Mr. Duval," Rodericks says.

Ian looks around. "Yes, sir. But not too loud. I'm still in disguise."

Roderick cups a hand across his mouth and they all chuckle.

August turns the key and opens the door. He's positioned the model on his worktable in an area of sunlight and covered it with a white sheet. "Get ready for the ta-da moment."

Roderick and Ian straighten their shoulders and clasp their hands. August lifts the sheet. The sun catches on the panes of acrylic and tosses beams across the ceiling. Exactly the effect he hoped for, as if flecks of gold have been flung into the sky.

"Oh, my." Roderick feels for the chair behind him and collapses into it without taking his eyes off the model.

Ian steps forward. "Wow. Amazing."

August looks at Roderick in the chair. His face is pale, mouth open. "You okay?"

Roderick doesn't respond. August turns back to the model. "As you can see, I designed the wing to have two floors, more economical than three, and with the advantage that the bottom panels can be removed so the tide will safely flow through the ground floor as Key West becomes lower than sea level, due to climate change." He removes the panels. "The original foundation will be surrounded with sealed reinforced concrete on pillars, as tall as necessary, to anchor into the natural coral rock." He slides the simulated wrought iron walls closed and locks them on each side. "No shadows from the structure itself. Also, hurricane protection."

Ian moves closer, studying the detail. "Really? Brilliant. Right, Roderick?"

"I'll give you all the dimensions if you want." August folds the sheet and drops it onto his chair. Roderick hasn't moved. Could he be concerned about the apparent connection of the glass tower with the main house? "Let me explain how this works. The glass structure is self-supporting and detached from the solid west wing." He points to the corner pieces. "Hinged pillars, each with rolling panels of decorative wrought iron, camouflage the space in between the structures and hide the entrance to the elevator. The gingerbread will tie into the Queen Anne style of the main house, also providing some coverage from the neighbors, as well as shady spots in the morning and lovely vine-like shadows on the water in the afternoon."

"Clever," Ian whispers.

August points out a thin space between the elevator shaft and second floor entrance. "Two inches. Per your direction, nothing that makes a shadow will be touching the wing. There will be glass sliding doors on the east side and heavy-duty exterior elevator doors to the west." He moves away to give Roderick the full view. "We can get the pillars brought in fully constructed after the glass atrium is in place. We're still calling it the atrium, right?"

Roderick is mute, eyes glazed.

Ian turns to him. "He's done it so beautifully. It not only fits the neighborhood, it's an elegant enhancement."

Roderick swipes his hand across his mouth, replacing his expression with a less horrified look. "No, it is lovely." He points to the ceiling. "But the light is reflected. We can't have any reflections."

"Refractions? I'm sorry. It won't be like that outside. The flecks will fly off into space. I thought you'd like the drama of the light show. My mistake, so sorry!"

"What if there's low cloud cover?"

"The refracted light won't be strong enough to appear on clouds."

"I'm not so sure about this. You don't know what we're dealing with."

August shrugs. He thought Roderick would be completely enthralled. It's so fucking perfect. His arms flop to his sides. "I don't know what to tell you. I guess... I don't have the knowledge to be the architect for this project."

Roderick covers his face with his hands. He sighs. He looks into August's eyes. "I didn't mean to offend you, Augie. I'm just trying to delve into the possibilities of what can go wrong."

August realizes that his ego is out of hand. "Roderick, sorry. You're right. That's the purpose of the study model, to give you a chance to express your concerns and suggestions. I got too wrapped up in admiration for my work. I'll do some more thinking on it. Okay? But I have to say — I'm not sure I can do any better."

Ian walks around the model, studying all sides. "It's amazing. If you don't want to build it like this, Roderick, I'll find a way of integrating the design with my hotel. A restaurant maybe. I'm thinking it can be ultra-green and retro at the same time. A striking twenty-first century landmark for my island."

August steps closer. "I would love to give that some thought."

"What's your estimate per square foot?"

He shoots a look at Roderick. "I would have to go to your site and rework the plan to give you an estimate. Building on an uninhabited island has multi variables."

Roderick stands up. "Just wait. You're not going to grab it right out from under me, Ian."

August squints at Ian and gets a grin in return.

Ian pats Roderick on the arm. "Buddy, I'm just expressing my thoughts. The time and effort in putting together this model needn't be wasted. It's amazing, even if it doesn't meet your personal requirements."

Roderick shakes his head and the movement continues down his body, almost like a dog throwing off water. "I guess I... I guess... I'm sorry I doubted you, Augie. I see what you're saying. It is a viable option, considering our limited knowledge — and beautiful. There's no time for me to question every detail. The sooner we get started, the better." He puts up his hand for a high five.

August touches his palm. "No problem." Roderick high-fives Ian, and Ian high-fives August.

Ian looks back at the model. "Stunning." He winks at August. "Then you'll do something just as elegant for me."

"I promise." He looks at Roderick. "I'd better get moving to meet the demo guy."

"Okay! I knew you could do it. Once you take that sucker down, the future is ours."

August smiles to give him a feeling of confidence. He hasn't managed to get any credentials on Montresori, but he's the only hope. The mystery will have to be cleared up when he sees him.

Chapter 29

November 23rd

He has time to scarf a *croque monsieur* and toss down an espresso on the porch at Croissants de France. As he turns the corner by the house, he sees a guy step from a pink taxi at the front gate. Short and Italian looking, a heavy gold chain around his neck glinting amid curling black hair. He must have flown from Miami instead of driving a few hours. Pretty high on the hog. Could Roderick have guessed it — Mafia? August puts up his hand to get his attention.

The Italian stops the gate, craning his neck to see the turrets.

August pulls himself together, ready for another losing conversation.

The demolition contractor hands over his card, an Italian flag in the corner. Luca "Boom" Montresori, Licensed Blaster. "Seriously, pal. You really wanna take this place down?"

"Mr. Montresori, nice to meet you."

"Boom. Short for *kaboom.*"

"Ahh. No, sir, Boom, just a piece of it. Follow me around back. I can see you don't waste time." He increases his pace. Boom can keep up or not. He's decided to tell Roderick it's a go, either way. When Christmas Eve passes and everyone's alive, the schedule can be reworked. He shows Boom the huge sandstones rising out of a fringe of grass and explains how they're starting to crumble underneath, causing a dangerous situation.

Boom makes a disapproving noise. "It should be condemned. The whole foundation will have to go. Is there a basement, so I can —"

"Hang on —"

"Lucky for you, I've got just the thing. Betonamit. We drill holes on the inside, fill em with the glop, and let it work. Silent and deadly. In a few days, these rocks will be tunneled like ant hills. We hit the top and it all falls down, right into its own footprint. Beautiful."

He knows Roderick won't go for it. "Afraid we can't do that. The lower foundation has to be strengthened and preserved."

"Really?" He rubs his hand lightly over the surface, almost a caress. "Okay. You're the boss. How you gonna do that? Hell of a job." They walk the length of the house. I've never seen anything like this stuff before."

"I know, but let me worry about the lower foundation. I only need you to take down the surface structure." August points across the breezeway between the dining room and the wing. "Everything on the left stands and on the right —"

"Whoa." He looks at the upper stories above them. "Uh... so you only want to take down the east section? That's complicated. Everything needs to be completely detached and separated. You'll need to build a new wall on the raw side of the other wing."

"Not a problem. There were originally two houses. The hallway where they connect, above us, was added later and attached by beams. You only need to remove two short pieces of the façade to cut the beams and drop the hallway. Fire doors pull completely across to close off the west side. Refinishing can be done later. I know something about structural engineering. If you're worried, I can show you the bearing walls and the main roof and floor supports, and where the explosives should be placed."

"Umm. There are laws about the distance." Boom squints. "Do it yourself then."

Crap. Touchy guy. "I'm sorry. You're the expert. I'm only trying to clarify that there's no problem. I'm not licensed in demolition. I can't apply for permits, and I don't have access to nitro or dynamite. I just want to get it done as soon as possible for the client."

Boom scratches his chin. "There's no way to speed this up much. The plumbing and electrical have to be ripped out. We need to check everything for asbestos and lead, do special hazard removal for those, take out interior walls, brace some areas, eliminate glass... With my whole crew we're talking a few months prep, minimum."

August crosses his arm and props his elbow to hold his chin. At least it's not a *no*. "So how much would the labor cost for a two-week deadline? Extra-special service, double or triple the crew, whatever is necessary."

"Two weeks? No kidding?"

"I'm asking you to name a price."

"Your client will pay whatever it takes?"

"He's highly motivated. And he assures me that permits will not be a problem."

Boom pulls out a cigarette and lights it, scanning the empty beach and open water. "We can do without permits." He hooks a finger into his gold chain and holds it out from his throat, studying the wing, turret to turret. "There's a limited number of guys that can work at one time."

"We need permits."

"It'd be a miracle to get it done in less than a month. But — working 24/7 with four full crews. Hmm. It's a challenge." He nods, looking up and down the wing, his lips moving. "Lucky you found me. Nobody else would try it. Let's say a rock and a half, in that neighborhood, till I can get a better look. Lots of legalities involved, some risk. We can start day after Thanksgiving, finish on Christmas Eve. How bout it? Can your guy come up with it?"

Christ. Not a minute of wiggle room. "That's? A rock —?"

"Well, maybe I can probably go a mil and a quarter."

August's mouth drops open. "You're saying one million, two-hundred and fifty thousand dollars?"

"An estimate, so far. I'm thinking two-hundred Gs of that for tips. Yeah, it's high. I'm not eager to do this job, but that amount would tempt me."

August recovers, puts out his hand to shake. There's no doubt in his mind that Roderick will go for it. "You got it, bud — Boom."

"I'll apply for permits through the normal channels, but there's another way to —"

August waves his hand like he's fanning away an odor. "I don't want to hear about it. Talk to my client. He'll get them."

"You're the boss. Just saying — might cost you extra."

"How soon can you have the contract?"

"I can tweak one by tomorrow afternoon. We'll start as soon as the check clears."

"What about the permits?"

"You want it done a month from now, that's how it has to go. Most of the work is interior, and nobody'll know the difference."

August's stomach is queasy. His guts say stop, but there's no choice. "What does the interior work include?"

"Like I said, cutting pipe, yanking out wiring, taking down walls."

"What about the noise?"

"Normally we'd check the paint for lead and look for asbestos — but that won't be a problem. We'll start off removing bathroom fixtures and taking out non-loadbearing walls."

"How do you know there's no asbestos or lead?"

Boom gives a smug smile. "Because it's impossible to get rid of it in a month."

August gulps. His eyebrows feel stuck near his hairline. Black spots appear. Boom looks nonchalant. August steadies. "Okay."

"Depending on how long it takes for the permits, we can go ahead and drill the bore holes and have the explosives delivered in a storage magazine. We'll set the charges and hook up the blasting wires, but we won't take out the windows or tear into the façade till we post the permits. That can all be done in a day."

It's starting to sound real. He should stop right now. He can't. He can't do it to Roderick... or to himself. "Setting the charges in advance isn't risky?"

"Hey, what za dif? We're gonna blow her sooner or later anyway, right?"

"Huh?"

Boom chuckles. "Just kidding. Done it many times. We won't hook up to the blasting machine till we're ready to drop her." He scrunches his eyes, staring at the house. "Or him." He sniffs. "Yeah, double shifts, around the clock. As many Cubans as I can find. Hard workers. Good at keeping secrets." A wink. "No *Inglese*."

Workers without green cards. "Ninety miles to Cuba," he sees it nearly every day on the buoy at the corner. It's taken on significance. He's being sucked deeper into the pit. But this is for Roderick to decide. It's his life. He'll be the one to pay. He takes a deep breath. "What about the noise?"

"Your client will have to do what's necessary to fend off the neighbors."

"Yeah, I get it. Whatever it takes." Lies, promises, money. "So, everything will be ready when the permits come."

"Yep, the permits."

"What if you do all the prep and don't get approved?"

Boom laughs, tossing his head back. "You're fucked. That's why I recommend —"

"Nope. Never mind." August swipes a hand across the back of his neck. Sweat is rolling down his backbone. "You're on, Boom. Tweak your contract." He hands over his card. Meet us at my office. Noon tomorrow?"

August leads the way out through the ballroom, pointing out bearing walls and cracks. Noticing several tiny new ones. Boom knocks on the walls here and there and listens, as if they'll tell him something.

"Yeah, we'll take this sucker down. No problem."

Prickles rise on August's neck. He stops himself from shushing Boom and moves him toward the front door.

They step out on the porch and August reiterates the time and place of the meeting. "My client will be there with the check."

Boom asks about a good Italian joint for dinner. August can't think of anything that qualifies as a joint. La Trattoria has sparkling glasses and white tablecloths. He looks online, finds nothing familiar. Boom says he could settle for a burger so he points him in the direction of Sloppy Joe's and recommends a rum runner at Margaritaville along the way.

"They're homemade, not a mix like everywhere else. Friendly place." He smiles. Making a connection can never hurt. "Be sure to get a splash of Meyer's dark on top."

"Will do."

That's what August has been told, although he's never been there himself. He massages the indentations behind his jaw bones. An ache. He forgot to ask Boom how he found out about the job. It's going to bug him. He dials the cell number. No answer. He leaves a voicemail.

Chapter 30

Freedom Glimpsed

Madeline rents a red Mercedes convertible to pick up Lenore. They giggle like over-sexed teenagers and fly like gulls with the wind across the first bridge, heading for the nine o'clock appointment.

"Girls, gulls, girls, gulls, girls, gulls. Can you say that?" She sneaks a look at Lenore's lovely, innocent face, bubbling with happiness. Lenore didn't question the sudden need for a child. She immediately suggested that Madeline's medical conditions might cause complications for pregnancy and said that she would love to be the one to carry the baby. August as the father seemed to satisfy her curiosity.

Lenore winks. "Nice gulls' day out, huh?" She aims back those lovely blue eyes so blinding that Madeline swerves in the lane. They are very different women, but able to share the feeling of motherhood. Who'd a thunk it?

Lenore angles her lovely chin toward Madeline.

"Lenore, what'ya thinking, Sweetie?"

"It's a surprise to me that August wants to be a father. He's a nice guy and all, but I thought he'd head right back to New York when the work's done. Not that I really know him."

Madeline hesitates. Since Lenore is going to be around the house, she'd better be in on the secret. "Actually, he doesn't know. Roderick tricked him. I don't want a fucking man trying to tell me how to raise my child. I just want you. We're the perfect parents."

Lenore looks pleased, then frowns. "He'll be there a while, finishing the new wing. What if Roderick tells him? August could have the DNA tested. He might try to make you get an abortion."

"Roderick won't. Guaranteed. No reason to check DNA. Like you said, he'll be out of here as fast as he can, maybe flying back and forth, paying no attention to us. I bet he'll be gone by Christmas. He's got an angel of a partner waiting for him. He won't even know that this is my baby if you don't say anything."

Lenore zips her lips with a flourish. "Won't he think it's odd, putting the nursery at your place?"

"In his mind, everything to do with me and Roderick is fucking bizarre." She waits for Lenore to digest. "He knows how close you and I are. Even with a chunk of the house gone, we have plenty of space, so of course, I would want you there. Trust me, he'll understand. Whether it's my genes or yours hardly matters, does it?" The worst lie she's ever told.

"Okay. We don't need to talk about it now." Lenore flashes her smile. Her face is glowing already. "Yes! It's *our* baby."

Madeline takes her hand off the steering wheel and places it on Lenore's thigh. She'll have to decide how much to tell her. Plus, she hasn't quite convinced herself that *he* will sense Usher genes in Lenore's womb. If Roderick's death date is correct, the embryo will be the size of a... nothing — microscopic. Besides setting up the nursery, they might need to talk loudly about it being her baby, to be sure *he* gets the message. Pooh. It all sounds like Roderick BS. But she hardly cares. So, what if it's all for nothing? And it's not. It's something *from* nothing, a thing in itself. A new life. A free Usher.

She glances at Lenore again and they giggle. This might be the best moment in her life since she discovered orgasms. "Want to get married?"

Lenore widens her knockout smile. "Sure." She raises her tan, toned arms, slicing the wind, and leans her head back, stretching, touching the sky.

They take seats at the desk and Madeline hands Art Pym the phony notarized paperwork, giving August's permission to use his sperm. Pym skims the signature page. "Normally, we meet the semen donor in person, but I can waive that since he's overseas in service to our country." He slides the papers into a file folder. "All set here. By the way, your choice of having the CRSPR done was well worth the cost."

Madeline sits up straight. "What do you mean?"

"It's always best, of course, if the client can afford it, but in your case many epigenetic mutations that correlate with diseases of aging were found in the ovum. Extremely unusual."

"I was afraid of that."

Lenore frowns at her.

"Tell you later, sweetie."

He looks at the report: "DNA methylation was targeted, and senescence that causes inflammation removed. I can't give you a copy, for legal reasons, but I see that the Cas9 protein system was used to boost activity of cells that had stopped necessary production of certain substances, like GDF-11, and others, a long list." He holds the report out to her. "Would you like to read it?"

"No. What about the sperm?"

"You only paid for the ovum."

"I know. I just thought maybe you learned more. I'm thrilled. Believe me. I can't say how thrilled I am."

Lenore is all smiles as he explains the procedure of implantation. Madeline pats her hand. "You can still change your mind."

"She'll need to stay here and rest for at least three hours after the transfer."

"No problem." Lenore checks the time on her phone. "You do the shopping. We don't want to hit any Key deer driving home in the dark."

Nursery shopping was next on the itinerary, getting the most obvious pieces of furniture. Madeline nods. "Fuck. I thought it would be so much fun together, picking out the crib."

Lenore smiles and touches her arm. "Another day. We can shop for baby clothes and a stroller. It's fine."

"Don't you want me to stay and hold your hand during the

implantation?"

"I don't need a husband, silly."

Madeline tells her to pick out an expensive place on South Beach where they can have a late lunch. Pym hands Lenore a gown. She waves as she's shown into the hall. Madeline sets the GPS for Nini and Loli, a stylish baby boutique located in the design district. She wants to impress Lenore and keep her happy, and she can't imagine anything but the best for the perfect Usher baby.

The sky is still clear blue as they zip back to Key West. A good thing, since the top can no longer be closed with a crib, changing table, and rocker wedged into the back seat. The sooner the furnishings are installed, the sooner *he* will take notice. Maybe.

Chapter 31

December 21st

Three weeks have flown by working on the nursery with Lenore, stripping off old wallpaper, painting, and moving the baby furniture around to decide where it will work best. She's been wondering if *he* is tuned into the process. She hasn't filled Lenore in on the details yet. Since the house has been calm, she's put off staging a loud conversation. Although, an unusual outbreak of palmetto bugs in the ballroom a week earlier is worrisome.

August had motioned her in from the pool to see the northeast wall, thick with them. Hundreds — maybe thousands — of cockroaches scrabbling over each other with their thorny legs, toppling on their backs when they stacked themselves too thick across the baseboard. Motherfuckers dropping like rain as they tried to cross upside-down onto the ceiling. Not harmed, just starting over. Survivors. She pretended to be girly and left August to deal with that shit.

It might have been the natural result of demolition commotion, but intuition tells her *he's* trying to use disgust to move August out. Somehow, August seemed unfazed. Roaches in that quantity should freak anybody, especially somebody not used to tropical insect infestations.

Lenore has been banished for the last three days to avoid paint fumes, and now Madeline can't wait to show her the final product. She's painted two walls pastel peach and two almond, background for Lenore's original animal decals, realistic jungle animals for the crib wall and sea creatures across from it above the changing table. She's never put in such long days of sweat and labor — she almost enjoyed it. The room is a calming combination, suitable for any sex or intersex. It would have been interesting to be a hermaphrodite. Would that be considered a hereditary defect to be "corrected"?

She has a quick breakfast and returns to wait in the rocking chair, admiring the arrangement of the crib under the herd of elephants gathered around a watering hole. Lenore sketched out all the animals, and they found an online service to transfer the images to adhesive vinyl. Tears pool in her eyes. Why hadn't she done this when she was young enough to enjoy a baby? Why was she so unlucky to be born into this fucking depraved family? She catches hold of her emotions before she ruins her eyes. She wouldn't have enjoyed a baby when the glamorous world was hers. Traditional baby stuff — and Lenore's artistry — has made her melodramatic. Seeing Lenore's ecstatic face will bring her more pleasure than she could have enjoyed in her youth.

She opens the frilly curtains for plenty of light in this special room at this shining moment. She's made up the crib with the matching ruffled sheet set and blanket and laid out three newborn-size kimonos and pairs of tiny socks on the changing table for *his* viewing pleasure — and Lenore's.

She's asked Roderick to let Lenore in and direct her upstairs to the nursery, but to stay away. She doesn't want anything to distract her from watching Lenore's eyes light up at the sight of her animals on the walls.

There are sounds of voices below, and she listens while Lenore's steps climb to the second floor. She walks out into the hall to greet her, teary-eyed, and not embarrassed about it. She's found a way out of the hell she never deserved.

Lenore's eyes are liquid, too. They hug and kiss like long-lost sisters. She asks Lenore to wait in the hall so she can stand inside the nursery to watch her reaction. She motions.

"Voila!"

Lenore nearly swoons. She's a vision, her face golden, her radiance and murmurs of pleasure filling the room, further brightening the peach walls. She fingers the smooth painted spindles of the crib and brushes her hand over the striped pastel blanket. She bites her lip, her eyes taking in one wall scene, then the other.

"Nice set up for the rugrat, huh?" Madeline had no idea she was capable of this, that life could bring a peak moment beyond the languorous self-indulgence she's always craved. More satisfying than alcohol- and drug-laden sex. Completely out of control. She's light-headed. Her eyes lock with Lenore's in the paradise of their own creation and the realization of their possible future. Her knees go weak.

Lenore's eyes open wide, and Madeline realizes that Lenore is alarmed by what she sees — her. Madeline drops into a disjointed pile on the hardwood floor, unable to arrange herself, unable to get up.

Lenore is screaming, screaming for Roderick, screaming

"Call 911!" Feet pound the stairs. Madeline can't blink. Her eyes are stuck open and burning, but she's blind. Her torso and limbs marble-heavy, she's a bag full of bones, unable to move.

Lenore is sobbing over her, holding her head off the floor.

She smells alcohol. Roderick. He feels for pulse, listens for breath. "Help! Help!" There's no answer.

Lenore sobs. "She's gone... gone."

Footsteps running.

"Roget, call Tarr! Quick! I've never seen her like this."

Across the room, the rocker is rocking, Lenore's sobs mingling with the sound. Roderick has pushed her into a corner, as always.

His breath is in Madeline's ear. "I couldn't get his," he whispers. "It was mine. I thought it would appease *him*. Pure Usher heir. But now... it was a mistake. *He* doesn't need us anymore."

She's exploding, screaming curses inside her head. A mistake! That's what you call it? Asshole! Asshole!

He whimpers. "You've made this so beautiful. I'm so sorry." Tears drop onto her forehead. She's so cold, she thinks they might turn into ice. He whispers, "I tried hard. I thought I did the next best thing. I'm sorry. I'm so..."

"Move!" Lenore is back, putting her arms around Madeline,

crying into her chest.

Roderick hangs there, breathing. Madeline needs to get his scrawny fucking throat in her hands, to wring the fucking goddamn life out of him. What was he thinking? Appease *him*! She should never have trusted his terrible judgement, not for a minute, and his pseudo-scientific crap that wasted so many years of their lives. She tries to scream in his face, bore her eyes through his sockets and into his skull. Maddening! Maddening!

There's no feeling in her tongue, her lips. Her face is detached, a mask, like she's drunk, numb. Underneath it, a volcano unable to spew. Poor, sad Lenore. What kind of monster is growing inside her? She must tell her to get an abortion.

When will this end? Is she dying? Her senses are at their peak. She languishes in Lenore's gardenia and musk. Can Lenore hear her heart palpitating? Is it? It's broken, Lenore! My heart is broken. Regrets, fear, love. She needs to speak. The best day of her life turned to the worst.

Roderick snuffles. He tries to close her eyes with his fingers, one and the other, but they fly back open. He pulls at the lids until he succeeds. If only she could bite off his fingers at the second joint.

She's worn down when the slimy doc arrives. Roderick shuffles Lenore aside. Tarr feels for a pulse. His stethoscope moves across her chest, pausing, moving again, lifting. His fingers move inside the opening of her shirt, toward her nipple — a pinch! What! A new means of diagnosis? If her nipple rises, that means she's alive? If his dick rises, what then? Lenore, say something. Isn't anybody watching?

"She's passed."

Of course. The doctor has somehow forgotten that the disease suppresses breath and heartbeat below the range of human detection. *Et tu*, Roderick? She knows he's there. Speak up! She's been at this point before. They carry her, Roderick breathing in her face, the doctor at her hips, Lenore holding her feet and keening.

Roderick orders Lenore to turn down the bed. They arrange her body, head on the pillow, hands folded across her chest, the fluffy white bedspread pulled up to her waist. It's a viewing pose. Really? Really, Roderick? She's wearing a red fitted t-shirt and short-shorts, not the outfit for a funeral. She won't go this fucking easy — not under-dressed for her own wake. She won't take this crap lying down!

It's a long afternoon of Lenore crying into the pillow next to her and Roderick floating in and out. He tries to send Lenore home, then allows her to sit in the chair if she'll "stop blubbering." As if blubbering isn't appropriate. August pays a visit and leaves in a huff, shouting that her brother and the doctor let her die.

They know she's not dead. Roderick is scared to revive her, as he should be. She's spent hours pondering how she can repay him. The baby, a product of incest, after all. If only she could shriek and move! She would kick holes in the walls and throw the crib across the room. She would strangle Roderick and then take *him* down, wall by fucking wall with her bare hands. She would rather die by fire than bring another damaged Usher into the world. Worse than that, planting the seed in Lenore — loving, innocent Lenore. An abortion will destroy her soul.

It's morning and she wakes alone in her room. Laughing gulls screech. The sound of traffic that always starts before eight is in progress. She tries to move her fingers and toes, make her eyes fly open. What the hell!

Her senses have heightened more as the day drags on. She tastes the salt air from an open window and smells decay seeping from the cellar, the Usher miasma, almost delectable in this state. Tunnels are carving themselves into the foundation, grinding it to sponge. Does Roderick know? Is it a good thing? She can feel it in her skin, tremors moving from the old east wing through the new. Fissures light up in her head like a map. The fuck! What is *he* doing? Through her eyelids, relentless Key West sun broils, but she can't move a toe, a finger, a lid. Her tongue is plastered down.

Footsteps and whispering near the bed. How is her internal mania not obvious? She can't get anyone's attention. Roderick's fucking *faux* friends with their platitudes. Ian whispering how sorry he is.

I'll be back, motherfuckers!

When they're gone, Maddy J. tiptoes over her chest and crouches, purrs and paw-taps her chin, an attempt to wake her. Maddy J. knows she's still in there. Salmon is strong in warm kitty breath. At least, Maddy's being fed.

Why is she still wearing the stupid shorts and t-shirt? Lenore would put her into a romantic gown. How long must she wait for muscle movement to kick in?

By evening she's played countless scenarios in her head, horrendous possibilities resulting from the baby being Roderick's. As soon as she can move, she'll murder him, leave a note for Lenore, and kill herself. Poor Lenore. The next generation of Ushers can't come into the world. There could even be twins. She would die right now of misery, but she has to hang on to end it. What that will do to Lenore! Oh, poor Lenore.

Chapter 32

December 23rd

She awakes. Still rock-like. Fucking morning again. The day before Roderick's predicted doom. She's lifted from the bed onto something flat and hard. No sign of Lenore. Maddy J. hops onto her chest. It's not right. This is the second solid day of catatonia and she still can't move. That's never happened before.

They're taking her down the stairs, Roderick and August. Surely, not to the cellar. The bastard! He's going to seal her up. She's thrashing inside, but can't muster a flutter of a lash. Claw his eyes out, Maddy J.!

It seems a long way, a bumpy, twisting path, some stops to rest, the stretcher unlevel, sometimes teetering. A grinding screech means they've reached the family cemetery. The nerve, Roderick! They set her down to discuss how to move her body from the stretcher. Roderick, you must be terrified of me. It will only get worse! The words are burning pain inside her throat.

Grunting, they dump her on her side into cold billowing cloth, and Roderick rolls her onto her back. There's rustling of a plastic bag. "We have to put this on her" from August. "Lenore made me promise. Why isn't she here?"

"Oh, yes. The white gown. Almost forgot."

August gasps and his footsteps move away. Her shirt is being cut straight up the front, a dull scissors, or a knife, sawing at the stretchy fabric. Cold air falls on her breasts. Surely her nipples are puckering. Are they blind? Her torso is rocked side to side as her arms are freed and the shirt yanked away.

"Come over here, August. I need help with the shorts."

There's a pause, but soon her legs are lifted and the shorts slide to her ankles and off. She'd like to see August's face since she's not wearing panties. Boredom relief.

"Hurry up, please."

Roderick sighs.

Bastard!

"Sorry to embarrass you, August. It's my last look."

He can only hope!

Roderick finishes yanking the gown over her head and into place, and she feels Maddy J. settle back on her chest, then move up to suckle an earlobe. Such a little trooper.

Air moves over her neck, Roderick shooing the cat. August folds her hands on her chest and arranges her hair behind her ears. Maddy J. lands on her chest again, purring, whiskers tickling, short snout snuggling beneath her chin. Warmth. Roderick tries to lift her, but Maddy J. catches her claws in the gown, pulling as he lifts, and he sets her back in the same spot. Ha! Maddy knows what Roderick is up to. Does he think he can sacrifice his twin and escape?

"She'll move when we close it. On the count of three... They grunt and the top piece of marble scrapes, but the cat is clinging tight to her chest. They stop. Chilled atmosphere settles over her lower half under the lid.

Roderick blows his nose. "She was a hermaphrodite."

Madeline can't believe her ears. Why is he telling that lie?

"What?"

"Tarr delivered her and made the decision to remove her penis. Likely, the female organs were more robust, or since I was born first, he knew a female was needed to insure Usher descendants. He was best friends — maybe even a lover — with our father/uncle/whomever."

"I don't need to know..."

If anything can get me out of this box, Roderick, it's your idiotic chatter! She can almost feel her ribs cracking with the pressure inside her chest. She'll build up the energy. She'll drag him down and strangle him with her last iota of life.

Air moves across her. Maddy J. dives between her thighs and scurries down to her ankles. Roderick clucks. "Let's leave it partway open. When the cat comes up for her dinner, Roget and I will close it. We don't want a cat stuck in there." He shudders. "I've heard about that happening."

So, Roderick! You can't finish me off? I'll see you soon.

Both men are sniffling. Roderick kisses her lips, dripping a tear on her nose. It tickles, making her crazy. To bite off the end of his tongue would be worth her last move. Another of his tears dribbles down her cheek. The gate screeches. No prayers. No last words. Footsteps crunch. Quiet as a tomb. Fuck me! Fuck them! To bite him won't be her last wish!

Chapter 33

Last Minute Doubts

Light from the windows above penetrates every corner of what used to be the ballroom, now that all the floors have been removed. Carrying Madeline, he hadn't noticed. He follows Roderick at a clip, crossing under the scaffolding and over the layer of rubble, heading toward the stone stairs into the hall, back to the real world. He suspects Maddy J. is following them, and he watches every stair step expecting her to leap underfoot. They'll both land on their heads and Boom will find their corpses when he comes to hook up the blasting machine.

They reach the top of the stairs and he closes the door. No cat. Roderick goes off for a scotch, resigned to heavy drinking to get him through. It's the sanest he's been all day, a relief from his repetitious ramblings about blowing the house themselves, before *he* has a chance to finish off the last Usher. And something about the demolition team suspecting a layer of lead paint? Did Roderick hear that from Boom?

Suspects, what does that mean? They know it? Boom assured him up front that the building will implode perfectly into its footprint, and if there is any lead mist, it will settle with the plaster dust to be vacuumed up before the wreckage is removed. The rest will blow with the prevailing wind harmlessly out to sea. Harmlessly. As of now, a breeze is blowing in the right direction not to endanger anyone in Key West. What about Cuba?

He doesn't know enough about harm. Only what's been decided by court cases and government agencies that create laws, a majority of flawed thinkers like himself, using limited knowledge. Should he trust them, as opposed to his feelings for the well-being of a person he knows — or thinks he knows, sort of, sometimes? What the hell is he supposed to do? Clearly the choice isn't something he has the knowledge or intellect to make. In fact, his power to choose is already lost. Provided the permit arrives tomorrow, the windows will be taken out and the hall beams disconnected and dropped. Well before midnight, the deed will be done. Jesus. If only the permit doesn't come. Roderick will survive, and a hazmat team can be called in after the holidays.

And what about the old lead piping that fed all the pipes in that wing, his wing? He saw it himself when they passed within a few feet of it, carrying Madeline through. It's useless to say anything to Roderick. The other wing is likely to be fed by the same kind of pipe. They have all been drinking water of undetermined lead concentration, bathing in it...

He heads outside, trying to throw off the gloom. As he walks behind the house, he notices furrows in the above-ground sandstones. He pokes with his finger and makes a hole. Christ! Betonamit? He thought Boom understood that the foundation stones had to stay. If it's only in the top row, will it matter? He's not going back down to check the base. Lord almighty. Nothing he can do now but keep quiet. He sits down on a lounge chair facing the horizon, centering, telling himself it can all be fixed with another injection of Ian's fortune.

He needs to call or email Gars. Tomorrow is Christmas Eve, and he hasn't made a flight reservation. He can't leave Roderick, as planned and yearned for with all his heart. He can't believe he's going to postpone the happy day, the warm moment that he's huddled inside when doubts and pressures nearly overwhelmed him. There's been no communication with Gars within the past month, the way they left it after the Raven issue. He's followed the rules. This is an emergency.

He taps Gars' number on his cell, guts twisting, wondering if Gars will even answer, much less how he'll take the news. He'll understand. Knowing Gars, he won't show disappointment, not wanting August to feel guilty doing what he feels is right. The call goes to voicemail and he waits through the message, checking his watch. Mid-afternoon, probably working. Or not wanting to talk to him. His brain never misses a chance for sabotage.

He should already have gotten a flight. What exactly was he hoping for, that Madeline would come back to life and Roderick would suddenly be mentally stable? He leaves a brief message, saying how sorry he is and that he won't be home till Christmas Day. He asks Gars to call him back so he can explain and give his flight information. He goes to Google Flights and books the only flight available from Key West to LaGuardia on Christmas Day, 5:00 p.m.

With a layover in Charlotte, Christmas dinner will be late, but still wonderful. Now he's in for a torturous wait, plagued by wondering whether Gars will call back, and what he should do if he doesn't.

The workmen will return in the morning to knock out the windows and finish detaching everything. Roderick has again been promised that the inspection will be done and the expensive permit posted before dinner, allowing for all previous work, and for the demolition to take place before sunset. He lies back and closes his eyes.

He wakes to the sound of Roderick's guitar coming from the upstairs bedroom. The staccato rhythm and low chords. The bells, bells, bells, bells — he puts his fingers in his ears. Thoughts of a burger at the Half Shell and the futon in his office turn his feet toward the sidewalk.

Chapter 34

December 24th

It's late afternoon when he returns from his office. There's no permit in any normal posting place on the front of the building. Nobody's on the job. What a relief. He wonders what state Roderick is in, having failed. He'd rather put off finding out a little longer.

He gets his construction hat and respirator, following the rules, and crosses the breezeway from the dining room. The French doors have been replaced with plywood since yesterday, except for one, giving access. He opens it, preparing himself for a hard look at the war zone they stumbled through with Madeline.

He steps back, a shiver clinging between his shoulder blades. The explosives are there in the corner on the scaffolding in a heavy-duty container. Boom assured him that nothing could cause the container to fail, nothing could detonate the explosives. But that would be within the realm of the known laws of physics... Boom has assured him of many things.

He tears his eyes away and looks up into the hollow shell, all the way to the turret. Floor edges are jagged fringes between each story. He recognizes the flowery papered areas of his old bedroom and bathroom above. He's seen the truck on the back lawn at night, sitting full, tread-marks ruining the zoysia grass, but hadn't realized the quantity of material being hauled away. Amazing Cuban work crew, like elves. Eerily quiet. He's spent his days at the office, but only a couple nights. With them working every night, not a sound disturbed his sleep.

He checks to be sure the electricity is disconnected. The box is torn out from the wall next to him, nothing but frayed ends. Altogether a painful sight, the whole wing mutilated by insanity. The house must be dead already, if it ever had a life. Disemboweled without a struggle. Roderick should be at ease. No workmen were threatened by chunks of ceiling or otherwise. None that he heard about.

Areas of the concrete walls are tunneled-out with wormholes. Firing wires, dangling from each wall, are fastened together in the middle, and run toward their individual spools, standing on end near him on the platform. The wires will be cut and spliced to the blasting machine. He walks closer to a tunnel. The red cylinder inside is startling. Its shining blasting cap is attached, looking alien and dangerous amid the grays and whites of stone and plaster and dust covering everything.

Disconnected pipes gape below his feet. Farther down, the sandstone walls of the cellar bulge inward, etched with wormy designs. They look to be standing upright only through sheer determination. It's clear that there will be no foundation left to repair or build on.

He lowers himself to sit on the edge of the scaffolding, dangling his legs. He can see straight through to the front of the house where the ground floor windows are already boarded up. Odd. For security, he guesses. Easy to remove when the permit comes — sometime next year. He looks at the windows above. So clean and bright after storms of plaster dust? No glass! The glass is gone. The permit must be posted somewhere. Amazing. He should congratulate Roderick right away.

He pulls himself up and brushes off the seat of his jeans. Where have all the shelves and cases of wine gone? The shaft leading to the vaulted area where Madeline resides is a dark gap on the far side. He walks to the end of the platform. He can only see a short distance into the vault. When the house falls into its footprint, the entrance to the cemetery will be sealed off, a cave somewhere under the lawn. Nothing's been said about moving Madeline to a final resting place. Roderick must be planning for the crypt to be hidden forever.

Chapter 35

The Beginning of the End

It's Happy Hour and Roderick hasn't come down for a drink. Not having a drink would be appropriate, so unlike Roderick. August checks his phone. Nothing from Gars. It's out of his hands at this point.

He climbs the stairs to see how Roderick is doing. Midway, the familiar eerie chords penetrate his brain. He grabs the banister, halting an instinctive U-turn. The last thing he wants to do is listen to more of Roderick's unearthly music and watch him fall into another seizure.... He checks his phone. Still nothing. Buck up, buckaroo.

He stops in at his room before knocking on Roderick's door. The louder droning makes him even less eager to go over there, but he has some detailed drawings of the interior of the new wing that Roderick hasn't seen. He pulls them out, something to take the poor guy's mind off Madeline and the upcoming event.

Roderick's in his usual chair, silhouetted in front of the window, against a heavy sky, his head slightly back, as if meditating into the ceiling. His fingers seem to work on their own energy, arrhythmically plucking.

August steps into his line of sight, but Roderick's eyes are closed. "Roddy, I brought some sketches."

Roderick turns his head and looks through him. "I couldn't do it to her." His pupils are off center. "Now it's too late." He lets go of the guitar and puts his hands over his ears. His chin droops and his cheeks stretch, as if he's ready to scream. He shuts his mouth. "Did you hear that?"

"No."

"I didn't close it up. She's conscious, damning me to hell, as if I'm not already headed there. When she gets the strength, she'll climb out from under the lid with Maddy J.

"Roderick, she's gone."

"I hear everything now... even the cockroaches mating in the walls."

"What?"

"Their creepy little courtships, the male caressing pairs of antennae, until he identifies a female. Then comes the bubbling ooze of sweet, sticky candy on his back to lure her. Ah, yes. She laps it right up, her slip of a tongue vibrating in and out, making slobbery noises."

"Roderick?"

"She's crazy for it. She sticks herself on top of him. I hear his chuckle and her terrified squeals, then her claws, endless scrabbling, dragging him around. She knows she's been had. Finally, she settles into her fate, and he fucks her, a single hard penetration. There's been a lot of that."

Roderick cocks his head, listening. "I'm fucked. Probably, you too."

"I'm glad I can't hear it." August holds back the mating results that he witnessed earlier in the ballroom. The despised egg capsules, clustered on the bindings of his books at the homestead, aren't worth a thought now.

"Do males mate with males, ever? Do you think so, Augie? Is there sex just for pleasure in their world? Any pleasure at all for those hard-shelled little lives?"

"I need a drink. Would you like a drink? Or — let's go down on the patio where we can discuss the drawings."

There's a long pause. He isn't sure Roderick is taking anything in.

"Did you know that female mice have clitorises?"

August locks eyes with Roderick's wild stare.

"Apparently, they enjoy sex. I'm happy for them. Aren't you?" His face relaxes. "A drink on the patio might be nice." He gets up, stiff, and stretches his back. He leads the way.

"Just a sec. I'll catch the light." August steps back into the room. He checks Roderick's battery clock against his cell phone and sets the clock back ten minutes. He turns off the lamp and closes the door. There might be some advantage to Roderick's not knowing exactly when his doom is scheduled.

Roderick waits on the landing, scowling at the delay. August doesn't expect any thanks for staying in Key West on Christmas Eve, even though it's the biggest sacrifice of his life, but he could hope for a better attitude.

In the dining room, Roderick tells him that Roget and José have been given time off and aren't expected back until the day after Christmas. "We'll have to get our own drinks and order Chinese, if you want to eat. The remaining calories for my life will be liquid." He puts two short crystal glasses and a bottle of Dalmore scotch on the table. Its austere stag glares at August.

They sit. Roderick points at the label. "For the occasion of my death. Twenty-five years old, almost old as you, huh? I nearly bought a thirty-year-old Balvenie, the most expensive bottle they had, but it wasn't as pretty." He looks at August. "And it seemed wrong to drink something that will last longer than you."

He raises his eyebrows at Roderick. "I expect to last a good while longer."

Roderick is focused on the scotch, cracking the seal and pouring a splash into each glass. He sets the bottle down in front of them a little too hard, and August suspects he's several drinks along. They clink glasses and slurp. The aroma engulfs him and the alcohol clutches at his inner lip, then slips over his tongue and down his throat like cream.

"Won't be long now till we blow him." Roderick gives a short laugh. He looks at the wall clock, shaking his head. "Six o'clock. It'll be dark shortly. The permit was due over an hour ago. I know they're not working this late on Christmas Eve."

"It must be posted outside. The windows are gone."

"Yes, but they were supposed to hand it to me, so I can put it up after dark without drawing attention, as if it's been there."

"No!" August stands and screeches his chair away from the

table. "It must be outside. I'm going to take a look before we panic. Before *I* panic."

He cuts through the breezeway, headed counterclockwise around the property. Who's he kidding? He knows the truth, and Roderick is insane. The sun is a last flash, disappearing on the horizon, its orange glow reflected under dark clouds. Red sky at night, he'd call it. He wishes he was a sailor... far out at sea.

He walks slowly, knowing it's useless. His reputation is on the line. Does demolishing the house truly mean the difference between Roderick's life or death? Weighing everything, he can't say for sure. He approaches the dining room. Roderick and Boom aren't the least bit concerned about the permit. He'd be forced to call police to stop them.

Roderick stands at the sliding door. He takes a look at August's face and pulls the drapes closed. August enters through the side door. The room is dark except for a candle. Roderick's growing preference for gloom.

"We need to get plastered as quickly as possible. That way there's a lot less pain... in everything. Trust me."

August pours himself a half glass and sips. Roderick is right. The mouth-feel takes his mind off everything else... briefly.

Demolition is scheduled for eight. Boom will show up soon. He tries to drill through Roderick's skull with his eyes. "I can't let him take down the wing without a permit. We'll be arrested."

"Not a chance. But I knew you'd say that." He takes a long drink and holds it in his mouth, sucking in his cheeks. Swallows. "Who do you think we're fooling anyway?" Takes another. Holds it. Swallows. "With Ian's help I was able to pay all the right people."

August slurps across the liquid, mixing in air, feeling the smooth burn above all else. "Ian was okay with that?"

"Please, Augie, stay with me until it topples, then you can run. I'll tell the investigators that you had nothing to do with it and didn't know what I planned."

"I wish it was that easy. I'm your architect. My name is on the contract and that makes me, at least, partly responsible."

"For god's sake, burn it."

"The contract? Boom has a copy."

"Boom?" He scoffs. "Anyway, I still have judicial strings to pull."

"I guess your permit strings were broken." He feels sorry as soon as he says it.

Roderick flicks the words away with both hands. He nods slowly, seeming to have found new peace. "I'm likely to be dead. If I'm dead, it will be even easier to blame me. I told Roget to make a list of my lawyers and friends in Monroe County government and the Key West Building Department, in case you need it. It should be in your room."

August swipes sweat off his forehead.

"Such a worry-wart. It's there. Go up and see."

He hadn't noticed anything on the desk, but he didn't look. His legs are already rubbery from the scotch. "I'm sure it's there. As long as you told him."

"Of course, I did. August, you know I love you. I wouldn't leave you in the lurch."

In the lurch... what exactly is a lurch? He hasn't heard that expression since home. Left in the lurch when the rent was due. He will definitely be in the lurch...

There's a tap on the sliding door. Roderick looks into August's eyes, pleading. The door slides open and Boom pulls back the drapes to step inside. His eyes zero in on the scotch bottle. "Mmm. Mind?"

Roderick motions toward the kitchen. "Get yourself a glass."

Boom is on it. August shakes his head at Roderick. "Do you really —? Never mind."

"Are we okay, August? Tell me we are. I don't want to turn you against me."

Boom is back with his glass. August picks up the bottle and pours him a short one. "We don't have the permit. I can't let you take him down."

"I've been paid to finish the job." He takes a taste and smiles at Roderick. "Wow — better than pussy. I mean..."

Roderick turns to August. "Please. We need to do this now. It's my only chance."

Boom gestures toward Roderick. "Technically, I should listen to the owner —"

"I mean it! I'll call the police."

Boom's face hardens. "Motherfucker... cocksuckers. I can't deal with this."

"August, stop it, now! It's all set to go. The police will see that anyway." He reaches for August's hand and squeezes it. "Leave now. Boom will say you knew nothing about it. Right, Boom?"

Boom slugs the rest of his scotch and smacks down the glass. "Boom's not saying a damn word. Work's done. Gotta go. Sorry, no fucking money-back guarantee." He opens the sliding door and slips out.

Roderick smashes his forehead on the table.

August sips his scotch. "Let's take the bottle and go upstairs. I'll sit with you till after midnight. It'll be Christmas soon and all your fears will be gone. After the holidays, when the permit shows up, I'll call Boom. We'll get a hazmat team first thing in the new year and finish the job. There won't be any need to rush or break the law."

Roderick looks up, eyes bulging. "We can blow it."

"Not a chance!"

"I saw the blasting machine. Everything's there. You attach the wires to posts on top and push the plunger. Fuck, I can do it myself." He jumps up with new energy and heads toward the door. August catches him by the arm. "That's nuts! I'm not letting you near it."

Roderick tries to pry off his fingers, and August lunges forward to grab him around the back, pinning his arms, pulling him tight against his chest. Roderick jerks his torso and bends at the waist, using his full body weight, trying to break the hold, but August hardens his arms into stone. "We're going upstairs. If I have to tie you to the bedposts, I will."

Roderick cackles. "Finally!" He jerks hard, trying to elbow him, but unable to connect. He breaks into sobs. "I'm going to die, August. Tonight. It'll be all your fault."

August holds him tighter. "None of this is my fault. I have no idea whose fault it is, but not mine." He manages a few steps into the hall. Roderick is dead weight, his feet dragging. It's tough going. The stairs will be a challenge. He remembers the camouflaged elevator and turns toward it.

Roderick stops struggling. "All right. You win. We must look ridiculous. Let go."

August is sure there's a trick coming, but he loosens his hold, ready for a chase. Roderick straightens his legs and stands up.

"I can't get away from you long enough to blow him. I give up. It's all on you, lover. All on you."

"I take full responsibility. I'm sorry I let it get this far." He straightens his shoulders. "Rod, Sweetheart. You'll feel much better in the morning."

They walk to the dining room and August grabs the scotch bottle.

Roderick picks up the glasses. "If we live, we'll be horribly hung over." He snickers. "We'll wish we were dead."

"Won't be the first time." He motions Roderick to lead and follows him upstairs. At the landing, Roderick turns to give one last beseeching, hang-dog look. August kisses him on the cheek and nudges him forward.

Chapter 36

Another End

It's a slow, tender blow job. When Roderick moves up the bed and puts his head on the pillow, August slides down to reciprocate. Roderick touches his shoulder. "Save it for later... if there is one. I can't concentrate."

August moves back up to hold him.

"Can't you hear it? The rattling sound? He's charged up to a hundred percent from the new incestual legacy. He's manipulating Maddy to do the job."

A screech from below. August startles.

Roderick glances at the clock, rolls into fetal position, and pulls the sheet over his head. "You heard that. Now she's outside the gate, clawing her way through the rubble to us."

Betonamite? August looks at the clock. Eleven-thirty-five, only fifteen minutes to go, according to real time. He chews his lip. "She'll never make it. There's a long way to go." He turns to spoon Roderick and puts an arm across his chest, centers himself. All is calm. Almost over. Roderick seems comatose.

A thump below. A rumbling noise gathering volume. Roderick stays curled, his body stiff. "Oh, my god! My time is up!"

"Eleven-fifty-five! Easy, Roderick. You made it — I changed the clock. It's after midnight." He talks loud over the noise. "The house is settling. There's a chemical eating through the foundation. Boom made a mistake."

Roderick flings himself onto August and digs his fingers into his back and arm, as if trying to climb inside his skin. "No! It's not over." He yells into August's ear above the rumble. "Hear it? *He* won't go down without a fight."

He tears himself off and pins Roderick flat on his stomach. Roderick's back is clammy. "It's okay. Trust me. If he was ever alive, he's dead, eroded." He pries at the fingernails still gouging his arm. "Loosen up, buddy! It's past midnight and you're alive. You're free!"

"Can't you hear her? She's dragging herself up the stairs. Listen, her gritty hands on the banister, her feet... shuffling."

He listens hard, but can't make out anything beneath the rumbling. "It's settling. You're safe."

"He's not settling. He's gathering power for the fight."

August slips off the bed and feels for his pants. "I'm going down to take a look. Relax."

"August, please, close the door!"

He pulls on his jeans. Maybe, Boom came back. "I might need to call the police or the fire department." He slips on his shirt.

The rumbling is lower. He hears creaking on the stairs. Boom wouldn't enter the house, would he? They hadn't locked the slider. He puts on his last shoe and looks around for a weapon. Roderick leaps from the bed and slams himself against the door. "She's here! Now! Where's the key?" He spreads his legs, bracing. "I can't lock it. August, get the key! — on the nightstand."

August sees it on the other side of the bed and dives to get there.

The door flies open. Roderick screams. He flings himself to the side as Madeline walks into the room, staring at him with flat black shark eyes. Gray dust covers her dress and skin. Her face is papery.

Roderick turns whiter. "No, oh, no! Mads! I didn't know what to do. I thought you were dead!"

"No, you didn't. Not a fucking chance." Her voice is furious, but her face frozen, without expression. "Did you tell Lenore? Lenore has to know."

August gets to his feet on the other side of the bed. A gray powder-puff of plaster dust jumps onto the bed in front of him, hissing.

"August, get paper and pen." Madeline points to the desk. "In the drawer."

He opens it and sees a pad. Call R — 212-462-8745 on the top sheet. He tears it off and drops it back into the drawer. "Ready."

"Tell Lenore the baby is Roderick's."

"Her baby?"

"Mine. She has to abort it." A tear streaks her marble face. "It will be a monster. An innocent monster, doomed to a life of suffering and ridicule."

She looks at Roderick. "Tainted. Controlled by *him*, a double shot of our evil inheritance."

August stops writing. "Maddy, you're alive. The house is dead. The east foundation is crumbling." He needs to give her a hug. "I don't know how, but look at you... you're... fine! Everyone's safe, no harm done." He points at the clock. "It's after midnight. Roderick is alive. None of it was true. You're... fine. You and Lenore can be together." He moves toward the door. "I'll go and get her. Right now."

More tears flow, cracks down her marble face. "No. Don't. I'm not fine. Neither of us can live."

Roderick's eyes are riveted on hers. He nods slowly.

"Tell her I loved her more than my life. Write it, August."

She waits until he finishes and gives the address. "Take it to her. Promise me."

"I will, but..." He slips the note into his back pocket with his phone.

Madeline is a foot from Roderick's face, holding him tight by the shoulders.

"Because of you, we're as guilty as the rest... almost. He's given me the power, but I won't follow his plan. It's *my* power now — the will to die, to break the cycle and end the fucking Ushers, the family so evil that it seeped into rock. You die now, Bro. We both do."

Roderick stands straight and solid as she puts her hands around his throat, softly like a caress. He encloses her neck with his fingers. "I'll see you in heaven." He leans forward and gives

Madeline a long kiss on the mouth. When he pulls his head back, she shows her teeth in a grimace.

Their hands locked onto each other's throats, Roderick collapses backwards, bringing Madeline on top of him to the floor. She lands with head face-down on his shoulder. The cat leaps onto her back and hisses at August.

He's beside them, brushing away the cat, pulling Madeline off Roderick and turning her on her back. Lifeless, side by side, they're mirror images. Neither is breathing. Madeline is bloodless. How could the split-second pressure Madeline used on Roderick's throat have killed him?

He moves Roderick to make space between them. He kneels and feels for a pulse on his wrist. He can't find it. Might be the wrong spot. He touches the side of his neck. Maybe something there. He presses harder. It might be his own pulse in his fingers. He cocks Roderick's head back and blows into his mouth. Air whooshes out. It's cold and saturated with good Scotch. He gives a breath to Madeline. The returning air is dank. Plaster dust and mildew, refrigerated.

He gives Roderick another big breath. It returns cold. Maybe he shouldn't be breathing for them. No longer recommended by the Red Cross? He puts his palm on Roderick's breastbone. Hard compressions. He knows the beat — doot, doot, doot, doot, "stayin alive." Over to Madeline, doot, doot, doot, doot, losing his mind. A hysterical laugh swells to fill the room. August clamps his mouth shut, but he's not sure the sound came from his own throat.

There's a rattling noise from the east wing, traveling through the walls. He would feel safer outside. Four pushes for Madeline. Is it working? Four for Roderick. Two breaths for each. Four pushes for Madeline. Is that right? What the hell is he doing? It's not working. He's done. He wipes his mouth on his forearm. He needs to call 911. His phone is in his room. He crawls from between them.

As he reaches for the phone, he sees the contract on his desk. A contract with a dead man, his own name on it. He snatches it up and stuffs it into his pocket, chiding himself for such a selfish consideration. He doesn't see a list from Roderick, but papers are scattered. He puts the phone down. He's done his best and they're dead, were dead instantly. Calling 911 isn't going to help anybody. How will he explain Madeline? Will it be bad for him if they find out he was here?

Noise is louder from the direction of the other wing. Almost like human groans. His imagination's gone wild.

He puts the phone in his pocket and runs back into Roderick's room. They're both whiter than plaster now, twin statues — unexplained coincidental deaths. He needs to finish it. Finish off the east wing to make sure that if a curse ever existed, it's gone. He will blame Roderick for the demolition, as instructed. Roderick *is* to blame... sort of. He gets to his knees and tries to raise him by his shoulders into a fireman's carry. No way. He pulls him by the ankles and rolls him onto a woven rug. He grabs the edge. A hard tug doesn't budge it. He puts more shoulder strength into it and gathers momentum as he drags him backwards across the polished floor. Out of the room and down the hall. The elevator is conveniently waiting with the door open.

Roderick is too long to fit, so he sets him up, propping his back against the wall, holding him in place so the door can shut. He looks more relaxed than he's been for a month, two months. August's eyes well up.

It's a long haul to the dining room and there's cracking from the wing. He wants to drop the rug and run. The hall bridging the two wings has not been severed. The blast is sure to cause damage to the west wing, but he can't go back. The connecting arm will have to stay.

He drags Roderick into the dining room and slumps him against the sideboard. He goes out to the blasting machine. How to connect the wires to the terminals is obvious. He wheels it inside the dining room for safety. He goes for the first spool, unrolls it in a backwards run, and places it beside Roderick. He does the same until all four are lined up in front of the machine. Wire cutters. The Ushers own nothing like that. He runs into the kitchen. A heavy butcher knife. There are many. He takes the biggest one and a cloth napkin for wiping prints.

"Okay, Roderick. For you and Maddy. May your souls be released." He saws the wires and pries them apart so he can twist the ends around the terminals. If he holds Roderick's palms on the plunger and lets his body drop, it might seem he detonated the explosion and died of shock or heart attack. Maybe he did. Something internal. There's not a single mark on his neck.

He wipes down the blasting machine and the spools and drags Roderick close. He pulls him to his chest and squats, holding Roderick on his knees in front of the machine, and puts his hands over Roderick's. He can't hold this position. He closes his eyes and takes a breath. "Help me out here, Roddy." He stops. Roderick's fingerprints need to be on the blasting machine.

His heart is a jackhammer. He moves Roderick to his side on the floor. He wipes the machine and manipulates Roderick, putting the fingers of both hands in likely places. One more try. He struggles to lift the dead weight and bends forward dropping Roderick on the plunger.

Nothing. What went wrong? "Christ!"

A roar knocks him down onto Roderick. Following is a rain of debris, shards bouncing inside the open door. He gets to his feet. Curtains of smoke shroud everything outside. A tremor races under him. He flings himself out to the patio, grabs a chair not to fall. He runs.

On the beach, he hears the start of an avalanche. He pivots. The east wing leans sideways toward the breezeway and the dining room he just left. The bridging above buckles, pulling the wings together, and the west wing topples partly onto the east wing. Heavy timbers bounce left and right.

He watches as the upper floors crumble, burying the kitchen in a whoosh of smoke and grit, tumbling toward him. He steps backwards into the edge of the surf. A dead rooster rolls between his feet.

There's a deeper explosion. Fire shoots from the rubble and lights up the wreckage. The patio is sinking into some underground vault he's never explored. Another feat of miraculous man-made architecture. A wave laps over the swimming pool.

How can this be? Boom made a huge mistake. Or did he? He trudges through knee-high surf to the end of the man-made beach, and cuts toward the street. Neighbors will gather fast. Somebody will call the fire department and police.

At the end of the block, he cuts over to Duval and takes the side street that runs parallel toward his office. He feels his cell phone in his jeans' pocket. Everything else is gone. Gone for good. His lover and friend are dead, and he's leaving the scene of a crime, his crime. He checks his cell. Twelve-forty. Not even an hour has passed since he announced to Roderick that he'd survived Christmas Eve.

Chapter 37

Guilt

The downtown sidewalk is crowded with people celebrating, carrying their drinks in plastic cups. The sparkle of earrings and flash of a red satin gown pass at a fast clip. Somebody yells a remark. He hopes his wet clothes won't make him memorable. He tries to walk at a slow pace, act like a normal Key West drunk. He's crossing the side street to his office when sirens blast. He steps to the curb. Three fire engines, going as fast as they dare, on a street populated by staggering tourists.

He opens his office door and goes inside without turning on the lights. He wants to wake up on the futon in the morning with only one lie to remember: that he left just after midnight, and everything was fine, Roderick asleep in his bedroom... Madeline still dead.

Sleeping in his office isn't unusual. He sits on his chair at the table in front of the model. A streetlight through the glass cubes makes its wall material glow. Not something Roderick would approve, but lovely. Tremendous. Never to be built. All for the best. He takes a bottle of Pellegrino out of the mini-fridge. He's shaky, probably dehydrated, having drunk scotch for dinner. He doesn't think any of the neighbors on South Street are aware of his existence, but it's possible someone knows about him and saw him run. He wouldn't be aware of the explosion unless somebody tells him. Would it have woken him several blocks away? Maybe. He'll say something woke him, but he went back to sleep. He'd better say he heard sirens.

He can't remember if he told Ian he was leaving on Christmas Day. Roderick might have told him. That would be good, not like he was fleeing. God, he doesn't want to be detained and miss that flight. He remembers the call on his cell and reaches for it. His hand comes back with the phone and a folded piece of paper. Madeline's final request. He closes his eyes and lays his head on the table. He sits up. He'll mail it from home. Madeline was already dead for two days, according to the death certificate — if the sleazy doctor actually filed one.

Her second death should be around 12:30 a.m., if she's found in the rubble and someone checks. Not his problem to interpret that event. Roderick's death would be at least fifteen minutes later. August would have been gone, according to his lie. Risky in many ways, but there's no choice. Ian will know he wouldn't have left Roderick alone before midnight.

Boom will say that August was there earlier that night, trying to stop the demolition, which will prove that August knew it was going to happen. If they find Boom — but they won't find Boom. As long as Roderick's money to Boom's account doesn't lead them somewhere. He takes out his cell and deletes *Boom* from his contacts. He soaks his copy of the contract in the sink and mushes it into pulp. He divides it into two handfuls and flushes them separately to be sure there's no clog.

How will he explain the posthumous note when he gives it to Lenore? He promised. He has no choice. The abortion is urgent. He'll have to lie and say he found it somewhere.

He looks at his cell. Garo, the voicemail from over two hours ago. He starts to calculate Paris time and remembers that Gars is back home. It's after 2:00 a.m.

"August, Sweetheart, I can't wait to see you. I was in the air when you called. Now I'm home and ravenous for you."

He laughs out loud and his finger moves toward the call button. Stop. They'll check his cell phone records. They always do in films. He can't create evidence that he's awake. He deletes all his calls, so there's no record of his talking to Boom, then realizes he shouldn't have done it. His paranoia is causing him to act guilty. Now he needs to lose the phone. It will have to wait till he gets home to Gars.

He takes off his jeans and shirt and lies down, covering with the light blanket he keeps for this kind of occasion — as if there's ever been one like this. If he gets to Lenore's early, he can go straight on to the airport. Try to get on standby for the morning flight to Miami. It's a perfect excuse for not having heard about the explosion.

He'll never sleep. Concentrate on breathing slowly. Everything is normal. Everything is fine now. Except... no luggage. How will he explain not going back to pack or get his coat in the morning? His laptop and briefcase are here. He wouldn't bring Hawaiian shirts up North. But his coat... He remembers a clothing store a block away. Or the sporting goods store. Maybe a ski jacket, anything to make it seem like he's prepared for the trip. Damn! It's Christmas. He rolls onto his side, facing the wall, and settles for a few hours of rest.

He wakes to diffused light through the glass cubes. It's lovely. The weight of the Ushers is gone, and he'll soon see Garo. Nothing can dull his expectations. Only seven o'clock, way early in Key West time.

A shower, a shave... he can do this. The sooner he delivers the note and gets to the airport, the less time he'll have to learn about the explosion. If Roderick actually had permits in the works, it might all be settled without him.

What are the chances of that? He steps into the shower and breaks into a wild laugh, too loud and too long.

He's never been to Lenore's. He Googles a walking map and heads out. The address Madeline gave him is on a small street near Old Town. Not the kind of neighborhood he would have expected. Two-story wood-frame, pastel green shutters and door, matching gingerbread on the porch railing. Lush magenta bougainvillea draped over a trellis, and a banyan drooling roots to the ground. The foliage creates a dim, cool den halfway across the front of the house. He would have guessed her as an aluminum and slate girl, clean and sharp, a box filled with sunshine in a multi-story condo, overlooking the Gulf.

He calls a taxi before he rings the bell. He hears her moving around, and she comes to the door and peeks through a frilly curtain. She's wearing a terrycloth robe, hair pulled flat into a ponytail, her tan already faded. Eyes bleary, puffy. She unlocks and motions for him to come in. There's minimal space to stand among the nursery furniture in the living room. She must have had everything moved immediately. The crib is made up with a sheet and blanket, a stuffed black cat with a winking eye at the foot.

August follows her on the narrow path toward the sofa. "I can't stay. Taxi's on the way." He holds out the note.

She takes it and reads, backs into the sofa and sits, holding the paper up to him. "No. No! It's not true. Maddy had it fixed!" She drops her arm and clutches her thin stomach.

"What?"

"The baby. Her genes. She paid a ton of money. I'm not going to abort our baby. It's all I have." She wipes her eyes, naked and moist, and clamps her lips for several seconds. "It's half Maddy."

"Lenore, it was incest. You need to get the abortion as soon as possible. It was her dying wish. To end the sin."

She stares at him. "It wasn't incest." She shakes her head. "You believe that crap? Roderick is insane. There's no sin."

He wonders. Does *in vitro* fertilization count as sin? Her look almost convinces him that everything is fine. He still doesn't know what's real.

"You know, Bub, I was with Maddy when she died. There was no note. You're the father. She set it all up." She flings the paper to the floor. "It's not her handwriting. You wrote this lie to get off the hook. I thought you were a nice guy, but now I see."

"That's crazy! Roderick is the father. He admitted it."

Tears are leaking down her cheeks. She crosses her arms and puts a bunny-slippered foot on the note. "I don't believe you. I'll ask Roderick about this."

He sits beside her. He wants to give her a hug. "You can't. He's... not talking —"

"Yeah? He would lie anyway." She looks away. "I can tell you're lying, too. You're no fucking good at it."

He stands and heads for the door. "My taxi's here. I have a flight. I'll be back, and we can talk more." He waits till she looks at him, trying to penetrate her shield. "I'm not lying, Lenore. You know you need to do it."

"I'll call the clinic. Or, I'll get a test. There must be a test. I'm not having an abortion because you tell me to. Fuck you."

He nods. He kept his promise. He steps outside. Not a pink taxi in sight.

Chapter 38

The Getaway

News of the explosion is on the screen in the airport lobby. Reporters are using their excited voices, mourning the loss of the "authentic Victorian mansion," speculating natural gas as the cause. There's footage from last night, firemen in tall boots, hosing the blaze. Fire all the way across the house. Why? It doesn't matter now. Unless the police drag him to jail, he's on the first flight to Miami.

He goes to the counter and shows his I.D. and ticket. He's told he can get a flight in forty minutes, then wait in Miami for a seat to La Guardia. He'd do anything to get out of Key West right now.

His gate is just past security, within sight, the luxury of a small airport. He spots quilted jackets on a rack and walks into a shop. Burnt orange or dark maroon? No time to care. He sets his briefcase between his legs and slips on the maroon. Not bad.

He calls Garo and leaves a message that he's desperately trying to get there soon.

The wait seems forever, but everything is normal. Exhaustion settles over him when he takes his seat. The worst is over. He still can't reach Gars, so he texts that he's leaving for Miami and will text his arrival time when he knows it.

It's nearly nine when the taxi drops him at the apartment building. They haven't connected in person, but Gars has guaranteed a lavish late dinner. He steps over a crust of ice in the gutter and dodges patches on the sidewalk. A Christmas tree blinks in a first-floor window. As he opens the door, he notices the year of the building engraved on the brick wall. A nice old custom. He's looked at it before, but had forgotten the year was 1832. The year when the original Usher foundation was set, the same for St. Paul's Episcopal...

Garo flings open the door. Garlic perfumes the air. He's wearing his thick white robe, smelling of soap from the shower, his perfect cheeks recently shaved, and damp hair draped over his shoulders. His gorgeous smile. "Snazzy jacket. Can I take it off you."

August hears an uncomfortable tinge of Roderick in the phrasing. Emotion surprises him. He drops his briefcase and nuzzles into Garo's neck. Everything else flies away.

As Gars moves onto the bed, August climbs atop his flanks, without thinking, like his most memorable sex with Roderick. It's a first with Gars, but August has gone too far to change positions. Nothing is said. Garo's smell, his skin, his hair, his sweat, they are the universe.

He awakens alone in the dark, a moment of confusion, thinking he's in Roderick's bed. He turns over... the sparkle of Manhattan through the curtains. He stretches and wallows in the cool sheets. Soon the clink of dishes leads him into the dining room.

"Ah, my sleeping beauty." Gars glows with bliss. "I couldn't decide whether to wake you. Sit and sip."

More notes of Roderick. Must be imagining it. He raises his glass. He sees the wall clock above it. Nearly midnight. A full day gone. "The first good sleep I've had in the last two months."

Over dinner, he tells his story, every detail about the Ushers, *him*, the plaster chunk, and Roderick's predictions, the best he can remember. He can't read Gars' expressions, or tell whether he believes any of it.

He admits he knew better than to hire mafia or let Roderick involve him in illegal activity. He plans to tell the rest, but when he gets to the last night, blowing up the Victorian classic isn't something he can admit. It wasn't him. It couldn't have been. And how can he expect Garo to believe Madeline's resurrection, or what he went through with them?

"Roderick was sleeping when I left. The explosion woke me up in my office, but I didn't know what happened till I saw the newsflash."

There's an uncomfortable silence and he wonders if Garo is fastening on some careless detail to question. He tries to relax his face.

He gets out his cell. "Let me show you the house." He finds some early shots, exterior and interior, but the magnificence is lost. The images are flat and muted, like amateur shots of the Grand Canyon. He thought he took more. He comes to a picture of his driver's license. He doesn't remember taking that one.

He keeps scrolling, back to shots of Madeline and Maddy J. at the Dog Parade. One of Ian with his horns. He gets to a photo of Roderick on stage the first night that he doesn't remember. "This is Roderick." He searches for words to explain their relationship.

Gars takes the phone to get a closer look. "Augie, you don't have to tell me anything more. Let's forget about everything that happened during our separation."

"I don't know how I got drawn into accepting that demolition contract. I believed Roderick. I thought I was saving his life." He clenches his teeth. "I could be prosecuted. I deserve it."

"August, no. You were caught up in Roderick's psychosis and schemes. He was a genius. They gaslighted you. You're innocent and sympathetic."

"No. It was real." He sees there's no way to make Roderick sound genuine, or the evil power of the house believable.

He gives up. "You mean gullible. But I didn't imagine any of it." He pulls back his lip, showing the gap. "I lost this tooth, suddenly, for no reason — the same tooth that Roderick and Madeline lost years ago — the same kind of crack as in the wall!"

"Let it go, Augie. My god." Garo reaches across the table to take his hand.

He wipes his eyes. Garo believes his innocence and that's all that matters now. He gestures to include the ceiling and the walls, noticing a tremor in his hand.

His voice wavers. "Being here with you — in our home — is more wonderful than I remembered." The year of its construction drops into his head. He sweeps it away.

Garo gives him a look. "Augie, are you sure you don't have PTSD? I guess you wouldn't know it."

"I'm good." He steadies the hand holding the wine glass. "I should contact the police tomorrow and tell them what I know about the explosion. It's better if I don't wait for them to find me. They might need me to go down there."

"I don't leave until after New Year's. I can go with you. We'll have a mini-vacation. Rekindle our love..."

At first, it's a dream come true, but thinking of possible complications with the police, talking to Ian about Roderick, convincing Lenore to... "Let's wait till we can concentrate on vacationing."

Gars looks worried. "I'm available if you change your mind."

August asks about the Paris hotel, food, cafés, sightseeing, avoiding questions that might require lies.

Garo answers with little enthusiasm. "Paris was empty without you. I'd rather take you there than talk about it. We'll make our Paris from scratch."

"Yes — soon."

"I didn't enjoy myself. I didn't want to." He tugs at the taut skin of his stomach. "At first, I compensated with croissants. I had to run those off. There were torso shots in half the scenes."

August doubles over, chuckling. "I can't even guess how many croissants I ate." He opens his robe to check. "Probably worked mine off with stress."

Garo lifts his eyebrows. "You look fantastic. I love the tan."

August visualizes Happy Hour at the pool, amusing moments at breakfast with the Ushers... Maddy J.

Garo is complaining about long nights of memorizing. "I think they decided I can act, rather than just parade my abs. Which is great — but the speaking parts got longer and my abs got flabbier."

August groans. "You're obsessed." Having time left over for a love affair seems unlikely, or that's what Garo is trying to convey.

Gars comes over to his side of the table and massages his neck. August cringes, catches himself. Roderick is still in his system. "Sorry, I wasn't expecting it."

"Augie, I'm concerned. You're... distant, stressed. We can't ever go through two months like that again. It's time we put some strings on this relationship. Some rings! How's that sound?" Gars looks down to take August's hand, dark eyelashes grazing his cheeks.

"Garo, I want to marry you more than anything, but I can't talk about it now. There's too much to settle in Key West."

"I understand." His eyes are wet. "I'm not going to lose you, am I?"

August shakes his head.

Epilogue

The Key West police wake him the next morning, requesting him to come down to answer a few questions in person as soon as convenient. He books a flight for the twenty-seventh.

He takes a taxi directly to the police station and is escorted to the office of Detective Frances Osgood. She's writing in her notebook and doesn't look at him until he pulls out the chair in front of her desk. A down-to-business woman, short hair and large frame glasses. He tells her he hopes he can be of assistance.

She nods and asks him to recount the events on the night of Christmas Eve. He outlines the evening, leaving out Boom, concentrating on Roderick's grief and mental breakdown. "I stayed with him till he fell asleep because I was afraid he might do something to harm himself." He tells her he didn't know about the explosion till he was waiting for his flight on Christmas morning. "I hadn't seen my partner for two months, and I just wanted to get home. I was horrified, but I didn't know how I could help by staying."

She gives him a disapproving look and asks about the state of the house.

He explains that the east wing was ready for demolition, and Roderick was angry because the permit hadn't arrived. "He started drinking scotch in the early evening. I had plenty myself, but I stayed awake till he fell asleep. Then I walked over to my office so I could get some rest and leave in the morning." He mentions Roderick's habit of playing his electric base in the middle of the night.

"What time was that?"

"A little after midnight."

She points her pen at him. "So, in the morning, you left town, without knowing if he was alive?"

He swallows hard and covers his mouth with his hand. "I know — it was terrible, but he had to be dead. Viewing the aftermath on the news — I just wanted to get far away from all of it."

She's slumped, an elbow on the metal desk to prop up her chin, her mouth showing she doesn't like his answer. "You were lovers."

She must have talked to Ian. "I was his architect. We had sex a few times, but he knew I was going back home to Garo."

She squints and makes a note, then asks about the state of the property when he left. He tells her it was fine.

"Did you look inside the east wing?"

"No."

"Not at all curious? She motions as if to cover her eyes. "See no evil, huh?"

The word makes him pause. How much does she know? He says that he suspected the demolition was set up to be done, with or without a permit. His knee is jiggling and he tucks it behind the chair leg. "I knew work was progressing. I tried to stop Roderick, but couldn't bring myself to call the police on him."

"You knew about the explosives."

He startles. "I figured they were delivered at some point. Roderick wouldn't say anything to me. I threatened to report them."

"*Them*? Who else, besides Roderick Usher?"

Heat crawls up his neck. "The demolition engineer."

Osgood pulls out her notes. "Luca Montresori. He had a bank account here. Now closed. Not a surprise, right? Where can we find this Montresor —?"

He throws up his hands, maybe a little too dramatic. "No idea. He was one of Roderick's contacts." He's come to believe that's true.

"The debris is covered by sand and, at high tide, the gulf, so the investigation will be ongoing. There was an unprecedented King Tide that night with the full moon. Very unusual that late in the year." She pauses, watching his face.

He hopes she sees nothing besides his bewilderment. Was gravity really the power behind that tide? Roderick would have a theory. Osgood writes a few lines and closes her notebook. He stands and hands her his card, repeating that he would like to help. It all feels too easy, way too easy, not over. With the evidence under a few feet of water twice every twenty-four hours, he can hope. Since nothing was said about Madeline, he assumes her death was lawfully recorded.

"You'll be asked to come back for questioning when we know more. Possibly next week. It's not over — not by a longshot."

He makes a fast exit, wanting to turn back to ask what's in question, but he's seen the guilty party do that too many times in *Columbo* reruns. He steps out onto the sidewalk, trying to put it all out of his head. He calls Ian to say a quick goodbye.

Ian insists on a late lunch. "I need to talk to you."

More stress, not sure why Ian "needs" to talk. He waits in the shade by the door of the Half Shell, hoping he won't have to lie.

Ian strides up with his arms open wide and gives him a bear hug. His horns are replaced with gauze bandages. August hugs back with warmth.

He sees August looking at the patches. "My year's up. I'm transithining back to a normal person. Betht — best — I can. Not used to my tongue yet." He sticks it out.

"That was fast." August focuses on the black stitching. He blinks. "Looks good."

"I got anthy — antsy. Friend of the family did it yesterday. I have to remember to talk slow." He wipes away a tear. "I'm sorry, Augie. I know you must be feeling worse than I do."

He lowers his eyes. "Yeah." He motions Ian to go ahead inside. They sit at one of the rough picnic tables near the bar and order beers and burgers.

Ian looks around, as if someone might want to listen. "I wasn't expecting this. I thought Roderick was halluth... having a breakdown."

August nods. "I don't know what to make of it either."

"I'd hoped you did, so you could lay it out for me."

Frosty glass steins are set in front of them. They drink. August looks at Ian over the mug. Before he knows what's happening, he's on the verge of telling him about Madeline's reappearance... the dying embrace. It was an embrace. That's all he can call it. He gulps his beer.

Ian slaps the wooden table and swipes at his eyes. August has nothing to offer.

"I know Roderick must have set off the explosives, or had Boom do it, but I'm wondering about your theory. Exactly what happened and why the west wing fell, too. There's a lot of talk around town. And Boom? What company was he with? Didn't you check on him? I saw him hanging out at Sloppy Joe's later that night. Now he's gone into thin air, apparently. The police can't locate him."

"Not sure I ever had his real name. Mafia, probably. Roderick found him and insisted we go ahead. I was a little surprised you went along with it."

"I didn't." He nods. "Roderick knew how to work us."

"Exactly. I couldn't stop him."

"Boom must have rigged it wrong to take down both wings. Didn't he know what he was doing?"

"He seemed to. It looked fine to me, what I saw. My theory is a chemical, Betonamit. Boom must have injected the foundation and gone too heavy on one side. The west side of the east wing might have crumbled faster, out of sync, and dipped toward the west wing. Maybe it toppled, one wing over the other." August shrugs his shoulders. "I wasn't there, you know. Or there might have been a softer grade of sandstone on that side. *Pouf*, it's called. I assumed it was all the same stuff, coming from the same place, but that wall was stuccoed, being in the breezeway. I didn't look under the surface. I should have checked it in the cellar. Should have done a lot of things."

"All water under the bridge — literally. I heard that everything above the foundation was swept out to sea. Debris headed North in the Gulf Stream."

"Huh. I would think most of it's buried. But who knows?" August shrugs. "There's the power of the house..." He takes a long drink of beer. "*His* power. You know about *him*."

Ian pretends a shiver. "Yeah, *him*. I'd rather not talk about *him* anymore."

"You and me both." August holds out his stein for a clink. "That's the silver lining. To the end of... it."

Ian scratches his ear. "On a less depressing note — did you know that Roderick left me the property? Security on the loan, along with the other properties, in case their value fell short. He insisted I take it." He wipes his eyes with his wrist.

"What can you do with it? I mean..."

"No, it's fantastic! The waterfront property is worth a few million. It's cleared and nearly ready for building. Except for needing some beach replacement. I just have to wait for the investigation to end. Could be months, I guess."

"I haven't gone back there."

"They'll probably dig everything up, searching for Roderick, but I bet he's out to sea."

"Seems unlikely they'll find him at this point."

"Everybody who knew the Ushers has a theory. It's disgusting! All the so-called friends who enjoyed their hospitality, now saying how they knew there was something wrong with them, all along — something illegal going on. All kinds of griping about lead poisoning, saying guests always made sure not to drink the water — I never heard that. You?"

August shakes his head. "Most people drink bottled anyway."

"Saying the Ushers contaminated the ocean... as if they blew their whole house into the water on purpose. Athholes — assholes! Key West hypocritical assholes."

Ian looks hard at August. "I bet you drank plenty of water there, and you're fine."

He knocks on the wood table. "Every day." He desperately wants to get out his cell and Google "lead poisoning."

"So, the big question. How would you like to be the architect for my new project on the property? Roderick said that would make him happy. Maybe we can do something with your original design."

"Are you serious?"

"The east wing would need to be less extreme, with plumbing and air conditioning, but I love that Victorian and retro-glass combination. I'd turn it into a hotel. It's zoned for it."

"Wow." Does he dare? He hadn't known if Ian was serious about most of his projects, believing they might be part of Roderick's con job. He hadn't considered spending more time in Key West without Gars, but to build his own creation... Maybe Gars would move down. "I would love to, Ian. I don't even need to think about it."

"I'm thrilled! I was afraid you might be traumatized and never want to step foot onto that property again."

He swallows. "I'll have to suck it up."

"One more thing. Roderick asked me to give you this." He unzips a leather attaché and hands the Swedenborg book across the table.

August puts out a stiff hand. The volume opens to the page with Roderick's note, and the index card drops into August's fries. He picks it up and reads aloud: "Evil sentience caused by collocation and arrangement of stones. Aspects multiplied and strengthened by reflection…"

"I don't think he meant the note for you. He just wanted you to keep the book... I took it to humor him, not that I believed..."

"I guess the stones have been permanently disarranged."

August asks the taxi driver to stop by the Usher property on the way to the airport. He's hoping some deep psychological fear won't paralyze him. Best to find out now if he's going to be capable of handling Ian's project.

The taxi pulls to a stop at the curb. He starts to say it's the wrong place — the wrought iron gate and fence, festooned with yellow police tape, and waves lapping beyond them. There's a lone wreath hanging on the gate and a basket of red roses toppled next to it, stems bent over and mostly without petals.

What did he expect? He tells the driver to wait and pretends to fumble with something in his overnight bag till his heart stops pounding and his legs regain use. After several seconds, when it becomes ridiculous, he hoists himself out.

The gate is unlocked. Instead of going around, he rips the

police tape and walks through on the sand. Only sand remains, not a single paver or chunk of Chattahoochee, no palms, no pool, no ridge of sandstone foundation. As if a tsunami rolled through and dragged everything clean. A freak King Tide. An effect of global warming?

He walks out the footage as he heads toward the ocean. Must be close to low tide. He turns at the weed line before a steep drop-off, and parallels the water to the end of the property. There the fence runs perpendicular to meet the public sidewalk. He follows it, testing the integrity of the wrought iron every few feet. Almost laughable, three sections of iron fence enclosing nothing. Just a swath of clean sand, except for a bit of seaweed, and a scattering of mangrove pods and tiny shells.

Farther down, a black cloth is caught up in a curlicue near the base of the fence. He's almost on it when he realizes it's a cat. One of the cats, flattened and stiff, hanging like a Christmas stocking. The innards have been eaten out, and the sun baked and nearly dried her. It has to be Maddy J. Not a trace of white on the chest fur. She must have stayed with Madeline through the explosions and the rain of debris, even the fire. His eyes well up. Brave little girl. He touches her tail with the toe of his shoe. He can't leave her hanging here, like an old, stiff rag. He checks his cell. There's time to go to Lenore's, although he'd rather not.

When the taxi arrives, he asks the driver to open the trunk, and he dumps his dirty shirt and underwear loose in his luggage to take the plastic bag for the cat. He's able to pluck her off the wood gently through the plastic without touching her directly. Yes, female. She's not smelly at all, amazingly preserved by salt and sun. A work of nature, nature's art. The driver gives him a look as he sets the bag on the floor between his feet.

Soft jazz seeps through the door at Lenore's, and she opens it with a wide smile across her face. "August. Nice to see you." He knows it's an act, her face a shining, innocent signboard, saying there's nothing to talk about, no thoughts of an abortion.

"I'm not here about that." It will wait. He lifts the plastic bag at his side. "I found little Maddy. She must have drowned. I couldn't leave her on the beach." He grits his teeth and holds the bag out to Lenore, expecting a recoil or a scream.

She snatches it and hugs it to her midriff. "I'll lay her to rest under the banyan tree. She was the only loyal friend Maddy had — besides me. I see that now. Her nasty brother was just the tip of the iceberg."

He starts to object, but has nothing convincing to say. He can't tell her that he was loyal to the end. He can't tell her about the end. If the bodies are found and autopsied... maybe.

In his seat on the plane, finally, he Googles lead poisoning. Nausea, anemia, constipation. Clicks on another article. Aggressive behavior and headache.... His head is pounding. The way he's been acting, his brain does seem affected. He's been nauseous and blamed it on nerves. But it takes months or years to absorb enough lead to be poisoned... unless the concentration is high. "Lead is an EDC... Endocrine Disrupting Chemical... can cause hormone disruption alternating sexual identity in animals." He hunches over his screen. Weird. Glances at the person next to him — asleep. He clicks on another article. "Mood disorders. Early aging... anxiety..." There's much more. "Periodontal bone loss and tooth loss in men." Interesting. Only in men? Bluish-gray nail beds. Cyanosis. A lot to process and sort through for the truth. More research needed.

He asks Google if mice have clitorises. "U-shaped." He shuts down.

His flight is late, and he waits until morning to tell Gars about Ian's offer. At the kitchen table, having garlic bagels with their coffee, the world is bliss. Gars has bought a new espresso machine and the aroma alone brings on a caffeine high. It's a cold morning, but sun streams between them, dust motes dancing.

August tells Garo the news about Ian's project. Gars jumps out of his chair. "I knew it!" he says. "Didn't I tell you?"

"You did!" They high-five, and hug, and dance a few steps across the kitchen.

August motions Garo to sit down. He spreads the top half of his bagel with cream cheese. "I'll book a flight back to Key West after New Year's. I need to check in with the police again, and I'll talk to Ian about the project." He looks into Garo's eyes. "My big Paris vacation should wait till spring, when both of us can relax. Don't you think?"

Gars nods and chews, resigned.

"But if the investigation drags on, I might be able to do Paris sooner. Otherwise, I can visit you, at least once a month. Or maybe, you can come to me." He looks up at Garo's face. "No more blackout months. I can't take that again."

"Neither can I. Seriously, never more —"

"Never." August recalls the first time he left for Key West. His fears and jealousies. Trial by fire. Literally.

A thin crack running a third of the way up the pale-yellow wall catches his eye. He follows it to the corner of the ceiling. He points. "How long has that been there?"

"Dunno. Might be new. I'll have it spackled and painted."

August stiffens. He's reminded of the lies underlying his life now, the crack in his moral base. New secrets to live with. But he's not evil. Neither was Roderick — he wishes he would have told him, consoled him. He runs his tongue over his molars to the gap. He'll schedule an implant and get a blood test for lead. He can afford to do whatever is necessary.

A cockroach watches him from the floor near the wall. A stowaway looking for breakfast? His foot moves fast to stomp it. He lifts his slipper and inspects the damage. Nope. Not over — not by a longshot.

About the author

Vicki Hendricks is the author of noir novels *Miami Purity*, *Iguana Love, Voluntary Madness*, *Sky Blues*, and Edgar Award Finalist *Cruel Poetry*. Her novel *Fur People* falls into the little-known category of animal-hoarder noir. Her most outrageous and unnatural short stories are collected in *Florida Gothic Stories*.

Retired from teaching, she now lives in the boonies of central Florida. After years of scuba, sailing, skydiving, and other research, she gets her adrenaline rushes mostly by trapping cats for TNR.

Acknowledgements

My heartfelt thanks to Fahrenheit Press, especially Chris McVeigh, for believing in this bizarre creation on the first go, despite a missing chapter. We are obviously of weird minds. Thank you, Max Grey, for dealing with my zillion emails.

I'm in debt always to A. Neil Smith, an old friend and reader, as well as mind-reader, who championed the novel. Without his help, I bet it would still be a docx.

Many thanks to my early, loyal readers. First, my husband Brian Sullivan, who was alarmed, as usual, to see what came out of my brain, but offered helpful advice, nonetheless; then Dave and Dawn Ash, who slogged through sections of pages printed out of order and made sense of them, enough to give wonderful comments. And once again, thanks to my friend Mary Anne Bennett with her keen eye for continuity errors.

Much thanks to Mike Dennis for encouragement all the way from Panama, and to Mitzi Szereto and Mark Safranko for offering many suggestions for publishers and keeping up my spirits.

Thanks to Ray Johnson for expertise in the area of architectural business and some basics in my early process of writing.

I am grateful to SJ Rosan for architectural usage correction, knowledge of New York law, and the relief of knowing I haven't said anything too ridiculous about real architectural elements.

More books from Fahrenheit Press

Pure by Jo Perry

Caught in a pincer movement between the sudden death of Evelyn (her favourite aunt) and the Corona virus, Ascher Lieb finds herself unexpectedly locked down in her aunt's retirement community with only Evelyn's grief-stricken dog Freddie for company.

As the world tumbles down into a pandemic shaped rabbit-hole Ascher is wracked with guilt that her aunt was buried without the Jewish burial rights of purification. In order to atone for this dereliction of familial duty, Ascher – in her own words 'a profane, unobservant, atheist Jew, frequent liar and grieving loser' –volunteers to become the newest member of Valley Haverim Chevra Kadisha, a Jewish burial society on-call twenty-four-seven during lockdown and performing Mitzvot at no cost to the bereaved.

What follows is a journey through the insanity of lockdown in Los Angeles as Ascher attempts to bring peace to a troubled soul, and perhaps in the end redemption for herself.

"The mystery will get under your skin, for sure, but the humanity of this novel will resonate far beyond the page."

Red Honey by Saira Viola

Red Honey is the much-anticipated new book from the hugely critically acclaimed Saira Viola.

With an introduction from Todd Robins, editor of Vautrin Magazine, *Red Honey* is a collection of never before published short stories & flash fiction from a recognised giant of the genre - to say people are excited about this book is the biggest understatement of the year.

"A great amount has been done in literature over the years but every now and then someone comes along and shows us a completely different approach

to the ancient art of the scribe. So hail Saira Viola and discover her twisted and beautiful imagination. Literature needs Saira Viola. Her writing is sharp direct and gripping." - Benjamin Zephaniah

According To Mark by H.B. O'Neill

Robert is unravelling.

Following a devastating break up he finds himself distraught, desperate, and increasingly confused.

When his literary hero, Mark Twain begins to communicate with him, Robert initially takes solace in Twain's innate wisdom. Quite quickly though warning bells start to sound, and it becomes clear that Mark's whispered, often cryptic advice, could prove dangerous.

As Robert's mental health continues to deteriorate, he embarks on a quest around London using Twain's words as his guide and inspiration.

Will listening to his hero lead to solace and recovery, or is it an undertaking that can only end in tragedy?

"According To Mark entertained me. It horrified me. It moved me. It disturbed me. It rattled me. It broke my heart. It gave me some odd hope."
– H.C. Newton

The Beloved Children by Tina Jackson

Three young women; Chrysanthemum, Rose & Orage are thrown together performing as The Three Graces on the stage of Fankes' Theatre during the closing days of the Second World War.

It's there they come under the spell of wardrobe mistresses Dolores and Janna – a chance encounter that will guide and change all of their fates forever.

Set in the dying days of vaudeville theatre and laced with mysticism, fortune tellers, ghosts, and evocative descriptions of the closing days of the War – *The Beloved Children* will literally make you laugh out loud and perhaps even shed the odd tear.

The Beloved Children is wise, funny, heart–breaking, joyous, poignant, and entirely entirely enthralling.

Tina Jackson has conjured characters that you will fall unapologetically in love with and placed them in a world that you won't want to leave.

"This gloriously offbeat tale has shades of Angela Carter, with its beguiling characters weaving a magical spell." – Kitty Marlow, The Mail On Sunday

The Perception of Dolls by Anthony Croix

The triple murder and failed suicide that took place at 37 Fantoccini Street in 2001, raised little media interest at the time. In a week heavy with global news, a 'domestic tragedy' warranted few column inches. The case was open and shut, the inquest was brief and the 'Doll Murders' – little more than a footnote in the ledgers of Britain's true crime enthusiasts – were largely forgotten.

Nevertheless, investigations were made, police files generated, testimonies recorded, and conclusions reached. The reports are there, a matter of public record, for those with a mind to look.

The details of what took place in Fantoccini Street in the years that followed are less accessible. The people involved in the field trips to number 37 are often unwilling, or unable, to talk about what they witnessed. The hours of audio recordings, video tapes, written accounts, photographs, drawings, and even online postings are elusive, almost furtive.

In fact, were it not for a chance encounter between the late Anthony Croix and an obsessive collector of Gothic dolls, the Fantoccini Street Reports might well have been lost forever.

"It's almost as if history is trying to erase the whole affair." – Anthony Croix